Will wasn't prepared for the little tingle of awareness that sizzled through him at the feel of her small, warm hand in his.

Their gazes clung. "One more thing," he told Blythe, without releasing his hold.

"Yes?"

"Regardless of what we've done or been or what's happened in the past to bring us to this point, I've always believed that marriage is forever. Once we say 'I do,' there's no going back. Whatever happens, we talk it out, work through it."

Even as he said the words he heartily believed, he wondered if he could stick to them. What if she was another Martha, a snooty, snotty, spoiled rich girl who expected him to wait on her hand and foot and give her whatever her heart desired? He suppressed a shudder. Well, whatever the future held, he'd just have to keep his end of the deal. They'd already shaken hands.

Penny Richards has been publishing since 1983, writing mostly contemporary romances. She now happily pens inspirational historical romance and loves spending her days in the "past" when things were simpler and times were more innocent. She enjoys research, yard sales, flea markets, revamping old stuff and working in her flower gardens. A mother, grandmother and great-grandmother, she tries to spend as much time as possible with her family.

Books by Penny Richards

Love Inspired Historical

Wolf Creek Wedding
Wolf Creek Homecoming
Wolf Creek Father
Wolf Creek Widow
Wolf Creek Wife

Love Inspired

Unanswered Prayers

Visit the Author Profile page at Harlequin.com for more titles.

PENNY RICHARDS

Wolf Creek Wife

HHARLEQUIN® LOVE INSPIRED® HISTORICAL

Recycling programs
for this product may
not exist in your area.

LOVE INSPIRED BOOKS

ISBN-13: 978-0-373-28371-2

Wolf Creek Wife

www.Harlequin.com

Printed in U.S.A.

"I know the plans I have for you," declares the Lord. "Plans to prosper you and not to harm you, plans to give you hope and a future."
—*Jeremiah* 29:11

This book is for my good friend and favorite librarian, Ginny Evans. I can't thank you enough for your support and all the hard work you do to "get out the word" about my books.

Chapter One

Wolf Creek, Arkansas, Early March 1887

Blythe Granville vaulted into the saddle and settled herself astride the horse, even though the action hiked up her skirts to show a shameful portion of ankle. Without so much as a glance at the scandalized young man who'd saddled the rented mare, she kicked the animal into a trot and headed out of town.

The Arkansas winter had been long, cold, wet and filled with shame, anger and melancholy. Today, Saturday, was the first day to hint at the promise of spring, the first to offer an escape from the strictures of her new life.

The feelings of unrest were new and totally unlike her. She'd always been the shy, quiet sister to her two brothers, Philip and Win Granville, and her half brothers, Caleb and Gabe Gentry—all self-assured, confident individuals who were successful in a variety of ways. She was the embarrassment of the family. The failure.

Even her mother, Libby Granville, was following

her dream of opening a library. And to cap the climax, she'd recently accepted retired doctor Edward Stone's marriage proposal. Her mother was marrying a man who adored her, while Blythe's fledgling dreams of finding love were reduced to ashes and she was teaching school in a little town in Arkansas.

Her mother, who had been living in Wolf Creek for a while, and Win, who had moved there permanently near the end of December, had settled into their new lives just fine, but the slow pace of Wolf Creek was smothering what little spirit was left in Blythe after the recent debacle that destroyed her life and any future she'd hoped to have. Wolf Creek was a nice, quiet place to live and raise a family if you liked small, leisurely paced places, but she'd grown up in Boston and loved the hustle and bustle of the big city.

Nevertheless, here she was and here she'd stay, thanks to Devon Carmichael, with whom she'd eloped just after Thanksgiving, finally giving in to his constant pleas to marry him. Three days later, on the afternoon after they'd returned from their wedding, Philip, who'd hired a Pinkerton detective to look into Devon's background, had confronted her with the news that her new husband was not Devon Carmichael, but one Wilbur Delaney. Not only had he lied about his background, he already had a legal wife hidden away somewhere. Devon, the man who had promised to be faithful to her for the rest of his life, was a bigamist, not to mention a liar and a thief.

Blythe was beyond mortified by the scandal that ensued, and worse, she was horrified that she had consummated her marriage to a man who was not actually her husband. The ever-practical Philip was more concerned that the wedding had given Devon control of the inheritance she'd received from her father on her twenty-first birthday. Hoping it was not too late, she and her brother had gone immediately to the bank, only to find that the money was gone, moved to heaven only knew where, and so was Devon, alias Wilbur.

As news of the scandal spread throughout Boston society, her friends had turned their backs on her one by one, and Philip had suggested—no, insisted—that she move to Arkansas with Win, who would be making his permanent home in Wolf Creek. Philip told her that it would be a good place to let her heart and emotions heal and to make a new life for herself.

The problem was that Blythe did not want a new life. She liked her old one just fine, thank you very much! And even if she did want to start over, she wasn't sure how to go about it. Though her two Granville brothers were scandalized that she wanted to go into trade, she'd always dreamed of owning her own boutique where she would style and sew gowns for the socially elite.

Part of her wondered how she could have been so naïve as to fall for Devon's lies. The realistic part of her knew it was in part because she was inexperienced and innocent and also because, at twenty-three, she was on the shelf and overly anxious to find a husband and be married. Simply put, she'd been in love with the notion of being in love rather than the man himself, and that made her easily swayed.

Devon's betrayal had dashed that dream and crushed her girlish fantasies. According to her brothers, her chances of ever finding a husband who would overlook her lack of common sense was almost nonexistent, so, at Philip's insistence, she'd come to Wolf Creek with no plans beyond lying low and licking her wounds.

She'd been surprised when, within days after her arrival, Mayor Homer Talbot had come to plead with her to take the job as schoolteacher for the remainder of the year, since he would be losing his prize instructor, Allison Grainger, when she married Sheriff Garrett on New Year's Eve.

Blythe realized teaching was a noble calling, but it wasn't hers. Her mind wasn't filled with letters and numbers and geography lessons. It was overflowing with images of bolts of fabric in every color and texture, delicate laces and satin ribbons, pearl buttons and faux flowers. Even so, she'd agreed to finish out the year. As her mother said, at least it would help pass the time.

Feeling the tension on the reins, the mare tossed her head, bringing Blythe back into the dreary present. She slowed the horse to a walk. At least the wild ride had soothed her smarting pride. She turned the mare down a narrow lane and rode for several minutes, praying as she went, asking God's forgiveness for being so headstrong, asking Him to help her settle into her new life, to find happiness in Wolf Creek, and if not happiness, something worthwhile and satisfying to fill the emptiness she saw stretching out forever.

Stopping to get her bearings, she spied a pretty white house in the distance. As she sat wondering who lived there, she became aware of the chuckling of a nearby creek and the barking of a dog. Deciding to investigate, she dismounted and headed toward the sounds. She'd no more than reached the edge of the creek bank when the dog—very huge and very black—approached and began barking at her.

Blythe stood stock-still, her hand clenched around the horse's reins. She hadn't been around dogs much and had never seen one the size of this creature. It was big and raw-boned and as black as night. As she stood there, uncertain what to do, the hound came closer, barked and then turned and started back the way it had come. When she only stood there, he repeated the gesture twice more. Realizing that he didn't intend to tear her limb from limb, she began to understand that he was trying to get her to follow him.

After tying the reins to a bush, she trailed after the dog to a spot about twenty yards farther down the creek, where she found him licking the face of a man lying on the damp ground.

Blythe's heart began to race. Who was it? What had happened? Should she go for help? Even as the questions raced through her mind, she was running to his side, taking in impressions as she went. Whoever he was, he was a big, burly man. Young.

Kneeling beside him, she realized that despite his size, he was very fit and clearly no stranger to hard work. She couldn't tell the color of his eyes, but his just-a-bit-too-long hair was a rich chocolate brown, a little curly and a lot unruly…as the man himself looked. His nose was bold, straight and well-formed. Several days' growth of beard covered his lean cheeks.

Sudden recognition caused her to draw in a shocked breath.

Will Slade.

And she knew exactly what color his eyes were. Black. As black as sin.

Will, the owner of a small sawmill, had been one of the favored subjects of town prattle, all because his pretty wife had run away with a bigwig from Springfield and divorced him. After that, he was rumored to hit the corn pretty regularly. Those same gossips claimed that he'd sobered up and was once again walking the straight and narrow, though he'd grown bad-tempered and moody. She'd also heard that his wife wanted him back.

All Blythe really knew about him was that he'd intervened on her behalf when a pushy reporter who'd followed her from Boston had made a scene at the train station the day she and Win arrived in town.

She stared down at Will, wondering what she should do. His breathing was heavy, labored. Had he fallen off the wagon, got drunk and passed out? She was almost afraid to try to wake him, since she'd heard that some people got mean when they were liquored up. She leaned down to see if she could smell alcohol on his breath.

Nothing she could discern. She did notice, though, that there was a rattling in his chest. Alarmed, she pressed a palm to his forehead. He was burning up with fever. He wasn't drunk; he was sick. What should she do? she wondered as she chewed on her lower lip. The testy Mr. Slade was not her favorite person, even though he had come to her rescue, but it would be criminal to leave him here to develop pneumonia—if he didn't already have it.

She glanced up through the still-bare trees. The day and the temperature were falling fast, and the clouds moving in looked swollen and rain-filled. The sunny springlike afternoon was fast reverting to winter, and the man lying on the cold, wet ground needed to be in a warm bed being spoon-fed chicken broth with Doctor Rachel Gentry attending him.

Genuinely worried, Blythe grabbed his shoulder and gave it a rough shake. The dog barked. "Mr. Slade, wake up!"

Nothing. She tried several more times with the same results while the dog stared at her, drool collecting at the corners of his drooping lower lip. Uncertain what else to do, she lightly slapped Will Slade's whiskery cheeks. Before she had any inkling of what he was about, his eyelids flew upward, his heavy brows drew together and one hand had grabbed her wrist in a hard clasp.

The dog growled and the man on the ground barked a hoarse, "Stop it!"

Blythe gave a little yelp of her own and stared from her captured wrist to the dog and then to Slade's face. The expression in his eyes was murderous, but she had enough wits about her to realize that fever dictated his actions.

"I was only trying to wake you. You need to be inside, out of the damp air," she explained, trying to pull free. "If I help you, can you stand?"

"Stand? Of course I can stand," he snapped.

Then he looked around and frowned when he realized he was lying on the ground. If Blythe didn't know better, she'd think she saw a hint of panic in his eyes.

"What happened?"

"I haven't a clue," she told him. "I was out for a ride

when your dog—" she glanced at the beast sitting near
his master's shoulder "—led me to you. All I know is
that you're sick, and I need to get you to the house and
go for the doctor."

She might as well have been talking to the dog.
Will Slade's eyes were closed and the tenor of his
breathing told her he was unconscious again.

Blythe pushed to her feet and stared down at him.
She had no idea why he was out in the middle of the
woods when he was so ill, but common sense told her
that the house she'd seen must be his. How could she
get him from here to there? She certainly couldn't
carry him! The sensible thing to do was to ride into
town and bring back someone with a wagon, but a
foggy mist was settling in and she feared that if she
left him and the rain started in earnest, his condition
would worsen.

Think, Blythe.

She recalled a piece she'd read in the newspaper
a few months earlier about how the Plains Indians
moved the sick, wounded and elderly on a contrap-
tion made with two long poles and pulled by an animal. She didn't have any poles, but maybe she could
fashion something comparable. She had designed an
intricate and detailed wedding gown, for heaven's
sake. How hard could it be to take a quilt and make
something to drag an unconscious man through the
woods?

Telling Will Slade that she would be back as fast
as possible, knowing he didn't hear her, she gathered
her woolen skirt in her fists and ran back to the lane
toward the house and barn in the distance. She heard
the dog barking at her and, when she turned, she saw

that he was still sitting beside his owner. The canine's devotion was admirable; she'd give him that.

Twenty minutes later she'd assembled a makeshift travois from a quilt she'd dragged from one of the beds and a couple of long pieces of rope she'd found in the barn. She tied the riggings to the saddle horn and let them trail along the horse's sides, then attached the other ends to the corners of the quilt. The dog barked at her at regular intervals, and she was struck by the uncanny notion that he was urging her to hurry.

"I'm going as fast as I can," she grumbled. By the time she finished, her fingers were numb with cold.

Back down on her hands and knees, she shoved with all her might until she'd rolled the sick man onto the quilt. With a little prayer that he wouldn't fall off or the knots give way, she led the mare out of the clearing while the dog trotted along beside his master. Thank goodness the rain had held off.

Her good fortune was short-lived. By the time the little caravan reached the front porch and she'd tied the horse to the hitching post, it had begun to drizzle. She was chilled to the bone and wanted nothing more than to be out of the weather in front of a fire.

The problem was how to get the unconscious man inside.

Unable to come up with another idea, she undid the ropes from the saddle horn and tied them around her waist. Using the muscles of her legs and arms and every bit of strength she could muster, she inched her way up the porch steps and shuffled across the painted porch boards and through the doorway that led to a combined kitchen and sitting area.

Once they were inside, she closed the door and

untied the ropes from around her middle. Rain fell in sheets. A crack of lightning rent the sky, followed by a boom of thunder. Blythe cringed. She hated storms, and this one was gaining strength by the minute.

The dog barked from the other side of the door. Did he want in? She gnawed on her lower lip in indecision. Would Will be furious at her if she let the creature inside? And did she want the huge animal in the same room with her, when she wasn't sure he liked her much?

When he began barking again, she grabbed a flour-sack towel from the tabletop and jerked open the door simultaneously as another boom of thunder hit. The mutt almost knocked her over in his haste to get inside. Despite the situation, she almost laughed. The big baby was as frightened of the storm as she was. So much for his bad-dog act.

"Wait!" she cried, throwing herself across his back to keep him from going any farther into the room. To her surprise, he stopped and stood while she rubbed the rain from his glossy fur and dried his feet. Satisfied for the moment, he settled his lanky body down next to the fireplace, never taking his eyes from her.

What now? she wondered, looking at the sick man once more. She'd planned to get him settled and ride to town for help, but it was storming, and the day was all but gone. Not only did she dislike dogs and storms, she was also no fan of the dark. There were streetlights to illuminate the gloom in Boston, but out here, surrounded by woods, it would be pitch-black when night fell. If she left the safety of the house, she would be terrified. She might even get lost in the unfamiliar area. Perhaps the storm would pass in the night and she could ride for help at first light.

The sick man sat up suddenly, once again taking Blythe by surprise. His wild-eyed gaze roamed the room. "Lie down, Mr. Slade."

He frowned at her. "Martha? What are you doing here? I told you not to come back here."

Martha? For just a second Blythe had no idea who he was talking about and then she remembered that was his former wife's name. Good grief! The fever was making him delirious.

"I'm Blythe, not Martha, Mr. Slade," she said, kneeling beside him and pressing against his wide shoulders.

"Blythe?" he asked with another frown. "Do I know you?"

"We've met. Lie down, please." She felt the tension in him relax and, with only a minimum of resistance, he did as she asked.

"Close your eyes and rest."

Surprisingly, he did. Blythe sighed and got to her feet. Like him or not, he was a sick man who needed her help. Should she stay and help him however she could or take a chance and try to make it to town?

It crossed her mind that if word got out that she'd stayed overnight in the home of a single man, she would once again be the talk of the town, but she pushed the thought aside. Under the circumstances, she had little choice. It was almost dark. It was storming. A very sick man who needed tending lay on a quilt in front of the fire. She knew it was her Christian duty to do what she could for him, no matter what the outcome might be.

Everyone would understand. If not, then her reputation would suffer again. It was already in tatters. What else could be done to her? Would she be tarred and feathered? Her only regret was that her mother would be beside herself with worry if she wasn't home by suppertime.

Hands on her hips, Blythe regarded her patient. First things first. Heat. She fed kindling to the glowing coals in the fireplace and added a couple more split logs. A blaze soon crackled and warmth began to spread throughout the room.

Grateful for the much-needed heat, she took off her scarf and coat and hung them on the back of a chair near the fire. Then she unpinned her hair and finger-combed it so it would dry faster. She didn't need to get sick, too. Without considering the inappropriateness of it, she unfastened her muddy skirt and stripped down to her petticoats, hanging the skirt, as well. It should be dry by morning and she could brush off the worst of the dirt.

The next thing was to get the sick lumberman into bed. She looked at him lying on the floor, all six-foot-plus of him, and knew that was an impossibility. She'd gotten him inside, but there was no way she could get him into bed. The next best option was to make him a pallet near the fire.

After locating a quilt box, she spread a couple of blankets onto the floor next to the hearth and once again rolled him onto the pallet. It was a struggle, but she managed to tug and pull until she got his wet coat off. Thankfully, his lightweight jacket had kept his shirt more or less dry. His denim pants were damp, but she'd managed to get him home and inside before they'd gotten too wet.

Sick or not, she drew the line at removing them. Her inexperience might have led her into the trap Devon had set for her, but she didn't intend to deliberately put herself in a pickle again. She pulled off Will's boots and piled several quilts on top of him, tucking them beneath his sock-clad feet.

"Who are you?"

Once again the sound of his raspy voice caught her off guard. She met his questioning, fever-bright gaze. He had no remembrance of her telling him her name just moments before.

"Blythe Granville."

"What are you doing here?"

"I found you unconscious in the woods and brought you back here out of the weather."

He managed a hoarse laugh and turned his head aside when it turned into a fit of coughing. When the spell passed, he gave her a look of disdain. "I don't feel so good, but I've never passed out in my life, lady."

"Well," she told him with a hint of asperity, "you did today." Typical man. Unwilling to admit to the least sign of weakness.

"I'm thirsty."

The fever. "I'll get you some water." She got to her feet and went to a long, tall table situated beneath a window to dip him a cup of water from the bucket. She carried it back to him, once more dropping to her knees.

"Do you need help sitting up?"

He looked at her as if she had lost her mind and snapped a surly, "Of course not."

He did manage to push himself upright, but it looked as if it took every ounce of strength in him. He drank down all the water and handed her the cup. "I remember you."

"Do you?"

"You're that banker's sister who fell for some man who lied about giving you a better life."

Though Blythe had played the fool, she didn't like the fact that Will Slade had reminded her of it, or that his opinion no doubt echoed that of most of the people in Wolf Creek. Why was it that everyone wanted to paint her as a bad person because she thought she'd fallen in love?

She held her tongue. "You need to rest, Mr. Slade. Do you have any sort of medicine that might help your cough and fever?"

He lowered himself back onto the feather pillow. "Ma brought me some willow bark…on the shelf."

The words seemed forced from him, as if their short conversation and the mere drinking of a cup of water had worn him out. "Willow bark?"

"For tea." He scraped a hand down his face and closed his eyes. "Brings down a fever. Whiskey and honey for the cough."

Blythe had never heard of using willow bark tea for a fever, but he seemed familiar with it, so she'd give it a try. As for giving him whiskey…she was less sure about that. Wouldn't it be risky to give anyone who'd once had a problem with alcohol any sort of liquor? Still, she supposed she'd have to take a chance on it. He certainly needed something.

She was about to ask where she could find the spirits, but when she glanced over at him, she saw that he was out again. She rummaged around until she found a jar of dark amber honey, complete with a hunk of honeycomb, a bottle of whiskey and two plain white mugs. The teakettle on the back of the stove was about half full and piping hot. Blythe poured the water over some willow bark to steep and more into a second thick mug. She stirred in a generous measure of whiskey and honey, added a bit of water from the bucket to cool it and carried both remedies to her patient.

He drank it down faster than she felt he should have, and by the time he finished it and the willow bark tea, she realized she was feeling a bit hungry, even though she'd had little appetite since leaving Boston. She'd find something in a bit. It was more important to finish doing what she could for the man resting on the floor.

She found a cloth, poured a basin of water and carried them to his side. For several moments she bathed his face and hands, hoping that the combination of the cool water and the tea would bring down his fever. He sighed in his sleep, as if to let her know her ministrations were nice.

Working over him gave Blythe ample opportunity to study his face from a woman's point of view. Everything about him was uncompromisingly masculine and, from what little she'd observed, he did and said whatever he pleased, the opinions of others be hanged. Win claimed Will was a man's man. Was that why Martha had left him for someone else? Had she found someone who would treat her more gently or perhaps cater to her every desire?

Blythe passed the cloth over his forehead and noticed the lines between his heavy eyebrows. Worry? Frowning into the sun? There were grooves in both cheeks that might be dimples when he smiled—*if* he ever smiled. She'd never seen him with anything but a scowl. What would a smile do to his somber, attractive features? Would his eyes crinkle at the corners? Was that why those little lines were there?

Though it was doubtful that she would ever allow herself to be tempted by a man again, there was no denying that he was quite nice-looking—if one liked their men big and burly and surly. She didn't. She liked slender men with grace and elegance and charm.

An errant memory of Devon's face filled her mind. When they'd first met, she believed she'd found everything she'd been longing for in a man. Not only was he handsome and fascinating, everything about him had given the impression of sophistication and refinement—from the immaculate cut of his clothing to his knowledge of how the elite world of society worked. Most important, he'd claimed to love her. She'd learned the hard way that his outward façade was as false as his declarations of love.

As usual, the mere thought of his lies and betrayal brought back the anger that had simmered just below the surface since she'd learned the truth about him. She removed the cloth from her patient's forehead and tossed it into the wash basin, where it landed with a little splash.

Troubled without really understanding why, she pulled the quilts up to Will's chin and went to find something to eat. She discovered a chunk of cheese and some slightly stale bread wrapped in a towel that would do nicely with a cup of tea. The dog stared at her with disapproval in his eyes and saliva dripping from the corners of his mouth until she'd offered him a portion of her meal.

Her hunger sated, she stood in the center of the large kitchen area, her hands pressed against her aching back. She'd done all she could for her patient at the moment. Weary beyond words, she carried a footstool from the parlor and set it next to the large rocking chair near both the fire and her patient. She found another woolen blanket in a small bedroom, wrapped herself in it and settled into the chair.

She was asleep in minutes.

Will woke at some time during the night. He felt some better. He turned onto his side and realized that he was on the floor. What on earth was he doing on the floor? In a bit of a panic, he raised himself to one elbow and looked around the room. The first thing to snag his attention was a drift of white eyelet trim that was attached to… Was that a woman's petticoat?

His gaze moved upward. An unfamiliar woman was sleeping in the rocking chair. Why was he on the floor and why was an unknown woman in his chair…in his house? What was going on? He thought about waking her to ask, but with his head pounding and his breathing rattling around in his chest, the last thing he wanted was any kind of confrontation or conversation. All he wanted to do was sleep. He didn't recall ever being so sick, and he didn't like the helpless feeling that made it hard to even move.

He lay back down and continued staring at her. Even that was a strain.

On closer examination, she looked familiar, but he couldn't put a name to the face. She looked young and innocent sitting there with her head lolled over to the side. Even as sick as he was, it was obvious that she was really pretty with her slightly curly brown hair tumbling over her shoulders and her eyelashes casting shadows onto her face. Despite the fact that she wasn't wearing a skirt and her feet were bare except for her white stockings, she sure didn't look like the kind of woman who would stay over with a man any more than he was the kind of man who would let a woman stay over. A sudden, vague memory of her giving him medicine for his cough surfaced through the murky fever fog of his mind. Maybe she was a nurse, he thought, yawning and closing his eyes. They flew open immediately. There were no nurses in Wolf Creek. He shivered and pulled the covers closer around his neck, feeling the weariness pulling at him once more. He'd ask her who she was tomorrow. It was nothing that couldn't wait until morning.

The barking of the dog woke Blythe from a deep sleep. Someone was outside. She could hear the sounds of men's voices and the scrape and stomp of boots on the porch. Sleepy and confused, she bolted upright, her gaze automatically seeking her patient. His eyes were open, and though he looked a bit puzzled, he seemed much more alert than he had the previous evening.

When someone began to pound on the door, she realized with a bit of dread that a search party had arrived. While she was deciding what to do, Will pushed himself to his elbows. Simultaneously, the door burst open, revealing a group of men, among them Sheriff Garrett, his deputy, Big Dan Mercer, the preacher and her brother. All wore looks of shock on their faces.

"Blythe Granville!" Win cried. "What on earth is going on? Are you determined to ruin yourself?"

"It's pretty obvious what's going on, if you ask me," the preacher said.

Blythe closed her eyes against a sudden feeling of light-headedness and nausea as a feeling of déjà vu swept through her. She started to get to her feet to explain and realized she was wearing only her blouse and petticoats. While she sat wondering how to approach the mess she found herself in, Preacher McAdams turned to Will, who was wearing his familiar frown.

McAdams pointed an accusatory finger at him. "You will do the right thing by this young woman, William Slade. I expect you to marry her as soon as possible."

Blythe gasped and glanced at her brother. "I can't marry him," she cried at the same instant Will shouted, "Are you out of your mind? I'm not marrying anyone. Especially not her."

Blythe had seldom seen her easygoing brother so furious. "Oh, but you can," he said to her in the tone she knew brooked no arguing. He shifted his furious gaze to Will. "And you are. Marrying her."

Though it hardly seemed possible, Will's anger topped Win's. "Over my dead body," he growled.

"That can be arranged," Win snapped. Then he turned to her.

She didn't know what hurt the most: the heartbreak or the disappointment in his eyes.

"Get dressed."

She reached out toward him. "Win, you're jumping to conclusions. I can explain."

Instead of answering, he turned and left the room. The others followed.

Chapter Two

For several seconds after the door closed behind her brother, Blythe sat wide-eyed and still. She was afraid to move, afraid to even breathe, lest Will, who lay with his eyes shut, his fists clenched at his sides and his jaw rigid with anger, light into her the way he had Win. Knowing she had no choice, she stood, reached for her skirt and pulled it on, not bothering to brush the dirt from the hem or go to another room to dress. It was a little late for misplaced modesty. Besides, his eyes were still closed.

"I can't believe the mess you've made of things."

Her? She was being blamed once again? Blythe looked up from settling the waistband of her skirt and saw that Will's eyes were open and he was glowering at her.

She was usually hard to rile, but after everyone in the rescue party jumping to conclusions and Will's lack of gratitude, her usual self-control was nowhere to be found. She finished buttoning her skirt, then glared back at him.

"Why, thank you, Miss Granville, for finding me

and doing your best to take care of me while I had a raging fever and a hacking cough." Her voice reeked with disdain.

His gaze shifted from hers. She hoped he felt guilty for his attitude.

"I *am* grateful for that," he said, though he sounded anything but.

"Please, Mr. Slade," she said, looking down her straight nose at him. "Don't insult my intelligence by spouting platitudes you don't really mean."

"Fine," he snapped. "Why didn't you take me to town instead of staying here with me overnight? Then none of this would have happened."

Blythe stared down at him, her eyes wide with disbelief. Was he serious? "How much do you weigh, Mr. Slade?"

Dull color crept into his whisker-stubbled cheeks. He knew where this was going. "Somewhere between one eighty and two hundred pounds would be my guess."

He started to say something more, but she stopped him with an upraised hand. "I suppose I should have just left you in the woods while I hitched the wagon, then picked you up, tossed you over my shoulder, dumped you into the wagon bed and let you get even wetter while I drove you into town in the middle of a storm." She didn't tell him that she had no idea how to hitch the horse to the wagon, much less drive it.

He threw a forearm over his face and drew in a deep sigh that set off a fit of coughing. When he finished, he looked at her with another daunting frown; Blythe took her coat from the back of the chair where she'd left it to dry and shrugged into it.

"I would fetch you some of your cough remedy, but I'm having second thoughts about coming to your aid, since it's clear you don't appreciate anything I've done," she quipped. "My mother has a saying that I didn't really understand until a few minutes ago."

"Oh?" he challenged with an uplifted eyebrow.

"'No good deed goes unpunished.'" Then, because she was so miserable that he felt no gratitude for the sacrifice she'd made for him, and because she still had to deal with Win, she added, "It's plain to see why your wife ran off with another man."

The shock and anger in Will's eyes were impossible to ignore. Blythe longed to call back the spiteful words, but that was the thing about things spoken rashly and in anger. There was no taking them back. Even if one apologized, the words were out there, ready to be called up at a moment's notice. Instead of even trying, she lifted her chin and turned to let herself out the door. Let him stew in his own juices and fetch his own medicine! She was finished with the dreadful man.

Will lay in the back of the bouncing wagon, his head aching, his chest tight and fury simmering through his veins. It wasn't enough that he was so sick he'd have to get better to die; he also had to deal with the blasted Granvilles. Again. More specifically, Win Granville, who'd been trying to buy the mill from him for more than a year. Even though things at the mill had started going wrong before Martha walked out more than two years ago, Will had no intention of selling as long as he could scrape together enough cash to keep the saw blades turning.

As if he didn't have enough on his mind, he'd received a letter from Martha a couple of weeks ago, saying that she'd made a terrible mistake, that she'd found out the man she'd left him for was a liar, and she wanted to come and see him and talk things through. The long and short of it was that she wanted him to give her a second chance.

For the space of a few heartbeats he'd considered it, but then reality settled over him. He knew her well. Martha didn't play fair. She would come fully equipped with a plan that involved using every strategy in her womanly bag of tricks, including regrets, tears and apologies, and vows of lifelong devotion. If all else failed, she would park herself on his doorstep until she got what she wanted.

With that sobering thought, the moment of insanity had passed and he'd promptly sent her a letter telling her not to waste her money on a train ticket and saying that after her betrayal he had no intention of marrying her again. In fact, he added, her behavior had soured him on the entire female species. He might never wed again.

Looking back, he wondered why he'd ever married her in the first place. She'd been far too flighty and flirty, too superficial by far, but she was a beauty who knew how to use her feminine attributes. He'd been taken in, and once she got what she wanted—marriage to a successful businessman—the real Martha had emerged and he'd known without a doubt he'd made a mistake. Still, his mama had told him that marriage vows were sacred and not to be broken, and he'd have stayed married to her until the Second Coming if she hadn't walked out on him.

For months after her departure, the embarrassment of what she'd done had driven him to drink, and he'd spent far too many hours looking for answers to his misery in the bottom of a glass. When the pain eased and he sobered up, he'd realized, through talks with his friends, that even though nothing was ever the fault of one person, Martha would never have been satisfied with him or a life in Wolf Creek.

Martha liked men, especially men with money who could grant her heart's desires, which were many and varied. For two years he'd done his best to give her everything she'd wanted, but when someone had come along who could give her more, she'd wasted no time in flying the proverbial coop, telling him that he spent far too much time working.

Trying to explain that if he didn't cut trees into boards he'd have no money to buy her the fripperies she was so fond of had made no impact on her. All that counted was what she wanted. It didn't help matters that it was about that time that equipment at the mill started breaking down and he didn't have enough cash flow to keep both the business running and his wife happy.

So, here he was, two years later, Martha hounding him to come back and the mill still barely scraping by. He felt as if he'd been treading water. Now there was this newest…situation.

Had he really passed out in the woods? His jaw tightened. Not exactly a manly act. If he lived to be a hundred, he'd never hear the end of it. And why, out of all of the women in Wolf Creek who might have stumbled onto him, did the one who found him have to be Win Granville's sister?

Rumor had it that she'd been through a situation somewhat similar to his back in Boston. She'd thought she was marrying a rich guy, but the joke was on her when he'd cleaned out her bank account and she'd found out the marriage wasn't even legal. That didn't say much for her intelligence, did it? Like most pampered, rich women, she probably wasn't good for much besides playing hostess at parties or showing off her jewels at the theater.

She was smart enough to figure out how to get you back to the house and inside when she saw you were sick.

Well, he'd give her that, and despite his anger over everything that had happened this morning, he was grateful for what she'd done for him. If she hadn't come across him by chance, there was no telling how long he might have lain on the wet ground with the cold rain pouring down on him before he came to and made his way back to the house. *If* he'd been able to make it to the house.

Blythe Granville was no bigger than a minute. Will tried to imagine her getting him onto the travois and then up the porch steps and inside. The fact that she'd figured out a way to do that proved that she wasn't just another pretty face, that she was, in fact, intelligent. The truth was that Martha's behavior had left him suspicious of all women, and to add fuel to the fire, Blythe was a sister to Win Granville, who refused to take no for an answer when it came to Will selling the mill. Beyond that, Will had no particular dislike of the woman.

He broke into a fit of coughing that had Dan Mercer looking over his shoulder.

"You all right, bud?" Dan asked.

"I'll live," he grumbled.

"Hope so."

Will tried to smile but didn't think he managed more than a grimace. He didn't remember ever being this sick in his life. In fact, he could count on one hand the times he'd suffered from any kind of ailment. He closed his eyes, hoping to sleep, even though the wagon was wallowing in the rough ruts in the road and seemed to hit every hole. Despite the jarring ride, the sickness that left him weak and feverish finally allowed him to drift in and out of a light sleep.

Blythe sat silently in the buggy next to Win. She hadn't spoken a word since she'd stepped out onto the porch and watched while Big Dan Mercer hitched up Will's horse and wagon. No one had spoken to her, either; no one so much as looked at her. It hurt, but she'd refused to let any of the search party know just how much it hurt. She'd stood there with her arms folded across her chest, her chin high, refusing to let the tears that threatened slip down her cheeks. She'd never shed so many tears in her life as she had since late November, and she was sick of crying.

After tying her horse to the rear of his buggy and giving her a look of patent disapproval, Win had held out his elbow and she'd taken it, though she'd rather have grabbed a rattlesnake. Without saying a word, his every movement stiff with censure, he helped her into his buggy. Everyone else was on horseback. She should have known her stylish brother would not sit astride a horse; it might wrinkle his trousers, she thought unkindly.

The men had helped get Will loaded into the back of the wagon, making sure he was well protected against the cold morning air, and the silent group had started back to Wolf Creek.

And here they were, she thought with a heavy sigh. And here she was, smack-dab in the middle of another scandal.

"What on earth were you thinking, Blythe?" Win asked, glowering at her.

She clenched her hands in her lap and stared straight ahead, counting to ten in hopes it would prevent her from yelling at him when she answered.

"Oh!" she said, her voice dripping with contrived drama as she placed a hand over her heart. "Silly me! I was thinking that Mr. Slade was a very sick man I found passed out in the woods and that perhaps he should be inside, since a storm was brewing."

"There was no way to get him to town?"

"Well," she said in a lighthearted tone. "I suppose I could have dragged him back to town behind my horse."

For the first time Win looked at her with curiosity instead of condemnation. "Drag him? What are you talking about?"

When she explained that she'd had no way to get him into the back of the wagon—if she'd known how to hitch it up—she elaborated on how she'd made the travois and added, "None of it was easy, believe me. Especially getting him up the steps."

"Do you mean to say that you dragged him up the steps on a quilt?"

A feeling of frustration nudged aside her irritation. "I did. By the time I got him inside, the storm was in full force and it was getting dark. I thought about trying to ride to town for help, but he was burning up with fever and coughing his head off. I did what I thought was best at the time. And believe me, brother," she added in a voice laced with sarcasm, "I did think about the consequences of my actions, but I figured there wasn't much else that could be done to me."

"That's an abysmal attitude," he said, shooting another disapproving glance at her.

Blythe lifted her chin and returned the look with scorn. "I prefer to think of it as a practical attitude. It isn't as if my staying overnight will ruin my reputation or my chances of finding a husband."

A muscle in Win's jaw tightened. "Oh, you'll have a husband within the week, if I have anything to say about it."

So much for soothing the troubled beast, she thought, the annoyance draining from her. She was so tired of worrying about every move she took, every word she uttered. Part of her wanted to give up, give in and just go along with whatever Win told her to do, but the part of her that was tired of doing what her brothers thought was right asserted itself. She was an adult. A modern woman. She may have made a mistake, but she had learned from it, and that one transgression was no reason to treat her as if she had no more sense than God gave a goose! Her anger made a comeback.

"Are you insane, Winston Granville? This is the nineteenth century. You cannot force two perfect strangers to marry."

"Of course I can."

"Ooh!" she said. "Men!" She turned on him angrily. "Do you know what the incident with Devon taught me? That if men aren't using women, they're manipulating them or treating them like imbeciles."

"That isn't fair, and it isn't true."

"Isn't it?" she challenged.

"Be reasonable, Blythe. Think about your future. This is your chance to pull yourself up and regain the respect you lost with the Devon fiasco."

She looked at her brother as if he had lost his mind. Perhaps he had. *Fiasco?* She had fallen in love with a man who'd appeared to be everything she'd wanted in a husband; he'd taken her virtue, her money and her self-respect, and Win considered it a *fiasco*? Why was it no one understood that she'd gone into that marriage with trust and love? Why couldn't they see how hurt and miserable Devon's betrayal had left her? She sighed. She didn't much like the problems that came with becoming an adult and living with the choices she made.

"So you think that if I marry a man whose wife left him, one who is rumored to have a fondness for whiskey, a man who has no desire to be married to anyone—*especially me*—" she added, recalling Will Slade's hurtful words "—that all my troubles will miraculously be over. What kind of future would that be? Certainly not a happy one."

"People marry for lots of reasons," Win argued. "Happiness is often the least of it. At least you'd be settled."

Ah. Settled. Translated, that meant that she would be out of his hair, no longer his and Philip's responsibility. Oh, she knew quite well how the minds of her brothers worked. Both were geniuses when it came to solving problems. And if one solution took care of *two* dilemmas, so much the better. She also knew that if Win's mind was set on this marriage, neither she nor Will stood a chance. She almost felt sorry for him.

Well, she hadn't been a Granville all these years without picking up a few tricks along the way. Perhaps she could shame her brother into forgetting the whole preposterous notion.

"And you wouldn't have to worry about what to do with me anymore, would you, Win? You could go on with your life with me stuck out in the country and there would be no constant reminders of my *fiasco*."

"That isn't fair, Blythe!" Win said, darting a shocked look her way. "That isn't it at all. You know we all love you. It's just that you sometimes make poor decisions."

More of those dratted tears stung her eyes. "Well, *that* certainly isn't fair!" she said in a low, intense voice. "When have I ever not been the soul of propriety? The epitome of good sense? Besides that one mistake with Devon," she added.

"Don't forget last night. The people who found you certainly won't. It'll be all over town before breakfast that you spent the night at Slade's place."

"To *help* him," she emphasized and followed the statement with a lusty sigh of frustration.

"You know as well as I do that the *why* doesn't matter. People will talk. They especially like gossiping about the missteps of others. Those who were willing to give you the benefit of the doubt will start wondering, and those who already condemned you for your mistake will rub their hands with glee, delighted to see one of the high-and-mighty Granvilles brought low. No matter the situation, everyone will expect Slade to do the right thing by you."

"That's just despicable of them, and it certainly won't be the right thing for me."

"Maybe not, but it's the way things are. And you know how Brother McAdams is about even a breath of a scandal touching one of his flock."

"It wouldn't have to be a scandal if everyone would just listen to the truth and stop being so judgmental!" she cried. "Besides, Mr. Slade has been divorced. Do you want your sister marrying someone like that?"

"I admit it isn't the perfect situation," Win said. "But by all accounts the fault lies with his former wife. She left him, and she's the one who filed for the divorce. Everyone says he was devastated."

"See!" she said, throwing her hands into the air. "Even more reason not to do this. If he's devastated, he must still love her. It's ridiculous to push two people into a marriage neither one wants just to satisfy some silly convention of society."

He shrugged. "He'll get over her, sooner or later. Maybe you can help him."

Blythe lifted her face to the heavens and threw her hands up into the air. "Lord, can you believe what I'm hearing?"

Once again she sought to strike a blow to her brother's supreme confidence. "Forgetting someone isn't something you do willy-nilly," she said. "You, of all people, should know that."

More than ten years earlier Win had lost his fiancée, Felicia, in a carriage accident while she was on the way to the church. Some drunk had not stopped at an intersection and tried to turn his horse at the last minute when he saw her carriage. His landau had spun around and plowed into Felicia's, causing hers to roll over.

The gaze Win turned to Blythe was as bleak and cold as a winter's day. His pain made her feel small and mean for daring to pick at his sorest spot. The feeling lasted until he spoke his next sentence.

"You have until Slade recovers to accustom yourself to the idea that you are marrying him."

"I will not accustom myself to the idea. We would both be miserable. I'm twenty-three years old, Win. Perfectly capable of taking care of myself."

He cut another sideways look her direction. "And you're certainly doing a fine job of it, aren't you?"

"You are a horrible, dreadful man!" she huffed, folding her arms across her chest and tapping her foot against the floor of the buggy. She turned toward him. "And let me tell you something. You may be able to force me to do what you want, but you may have a hard time convincing my potential bridegroom. He doesn't look like the kind of man to be coerced into doing anything he doesn't want to do. He could make mincemeat of you."

"Don't forget I was boxing champ at Harvard," Win reminded. "Stop worrying and leave Slade to me."

Blythe knew there was no use arguing any further. "Gladly."

Neither sibling spoke another word during the remainder of the trip to Wolf Creek, which suited Blythe just fine.

By the time they reached the big, white, two-story house where her mother lived, Blythe wanted nothing more than to escape to her room and never come out. It was a feeling she'd experienced a lot the past few months. Somehow she managed to hold back the tears while Win helped her down from the buggy.

Without bothering to thank him, she raced up the front steps and pushed through the door, rushing up the wide staircase. She barely heard her mother call her name. Secure for the moment in the sanctity of her bedroom, she slammed the door and threw herself face-first onto the bed, where she promptly lost her tenuous grip on her control and burst into tears.

How could one person possibly be so miserable? And how and why did she keep getting into these life-altering situations? Even more disturbing, it didn't look as if things were going to get better anytime soon, if ever. Sobbing so hard she barely heard the knock at the door, she rolled onto her back and flung an arm over her eyes.

"Come in."

"Sweetheart?"

Libby Granville's voice held the soothing tone Blythe remembered from her childhood. Her mother's embrace and that soft, calming tone had always brought comfort, whatever was ailing Blythe. As usual, the tenderness she heard in her mother's voice caused her to cry even harder. For long moments Libby just lay beside her, letting her get out all the hopelessness.

When her weeping subsided to an occasional hiccup, Libby handed Blythe a clean handkerchief and brushed back the tendrils of hair clinging to her wet cheeks.

"I'm sorry, Mama," she said at last. "I never meant to cause another big to-do. I'd never deliberately hurt you or bring shame to our family. I thought that if I left Boston, I'd leave all the ugliness behind."

"You will, sweetie," Libby told her, giving her cheek a pat. "I've been the subject of gossip and so have a lot of others here in town. People tend to forget in time." She smiled at Blythe. "Why don't you tell me what happened?"

Blythe outlined every detail of the previous afternoon, starting with the reason for her ride. Libby listened without comment, and Blythe finished by saying, "And now Brother McAdams told Will that he absolutely would do the right thing by me, and Win is backing him up."

She looked into her mother's eyes. "I think Win is just tired of dealing with me and the Boston situation. He wants me out of his hair."

Libby chuckled. "Well, that did knock the props out from under your brothers. They're accustomed to fixing things, and they didn't have a clue how to make that right. I really think that's why Win is pushing so hard on this."

"So marrying me off to a man we hardly know will fix all my woes and stop the gossip?"

"I believe he thinks so."

"But he doesn't even like Will."

"He doesn't like that Will won't sell to him," Libby clarified. "I know your brother, and I suspect that he admires Mr. Slade's tenacity."

"What do you think, Mama?" Blythe asked.

Libby hugged her tighter. "I know from personal experience that there will be more talk about you and Mr. Slade. Some will say that you should have come for help no matter what, and some will think you did the best you could do. Of course there will be a huge hue and cry for Will to marry you to make an honest woman of you."

"Nothing happened!"

"I know that. You know that, and so does Mr. Slade. But the old ways of looking at things are pretty much set in stone. It would take a strong person to flaunt those customs. Are you that person?"

Blythe sighed. She knew she wasn't. She hated strife and turmoil and being the topic of conversation. And she hated the notion of being forced into a marriage with a man she didn't even know. "You did."

"I didn't have much choice after Lucas kicked me out and took my boys from me." She smoothed the hair away from Blythe's face. "I think we should take a wait-and-see attitude. A lot will depend on how much pressure Win puts on Mr. Slade, and a lot will depend on Mr. Slade's character."

Libby rose from the bed. "You sleep for a while. Things may look different after a few hours."

Chapter Three

"She talks like she isn't going to do it," Libby told her son as he ate the breakfast she'd fixed for him while he returned to his house to get ready for Sunday services.

"She'll marry him," he said, pinning his mother with a determined look. "We have to do something to stop this insane course she's on."

Libby sat down across from him and rested her forearms on the table. "What insane course is that, Win?" she asked with a lift of her shapely eyebrows.

Win frowned. "She's obviously not very good at making the right choices. She needs a strong man to keep her in line."

"Oh, good grief!" Libby cried, losing all patience with her stepson. Having borne the brunt of a man's controlling nature herself during her first marriage, she had little tolerance for some of the ridiculous moral codes one was expected to live by. "She helped a sick man, Win! She didn't run off with him."

"Not this time," he reminded.

"That isn't fair. You know as well as I do that she

had no idea who Devon Carmichael was or what he was up to, just as I had no clue about the kind of man Lucas Gentry was when I married him. Any young woman might have done the same."

"Maybe," Win acknowledged.

"There's no maybe to it. You know I'm right. Your poor sister was almost destroyed when she found out the truth about Devon, and she's a long way from being over it. I know time can change things, but I fear she may never trust another man with her heart."

Win's mouth twisted into a wry smile. "She'll be the better for it, believe me."

Libby looked aghast at the comment. "I cannot believe you've become so cynical. Please tell me you don't mean that, that you haven't given up on finding love again."

Seeing the concern in her eyes, he sighed. "To tell you the truth, Mother, I don't know if I have or not. Love can be extremely painful. I'm starting to think that marriages of convenience are the best way to go."

"I'm sure there are advantages, but there is nothing like the love of a devoted spouse and a good marriage to bring you happiness."

"Like Blythe found?" he quipped with a mocking lift of his eyebrow.

"Are we back to that?" When Win didn't answer, Libby said, "I guess her choice does play a huge part of her future, doesn't it? I just thank the Good Lord that we found out the truth about Devon before she had a baby or two."

"That is a blessing," Win said. "And you're right. Her past does have a direct bearing on her future. You know as well as I do that finding a decent husband in

Boston was out of the question, and the selection of suitable men around here is slim at best. If you factor in what happened last night—which will be all over town by noon—I think you'll agree that an arranged marriage is an ideal solution. There are no expectations beyond the basic, no broken hearts."

Libby's narrowed eyes told him that she did not agree with his assessment at all. "Sometimes I wonder if you even have a heart. You flirt with every female who crosses your path and flit from woman to woman, but all you're doing is toying with them. It's almost like you buried your heart when we buried Felicia."

"Maybe I did," he told her. "She may have been the love of my life."

Libby saw the sorrow in his eyes. "Even so, it's been a long time, Win. There are different kinds of love, and it's time you started thinking about a wife and a family."

He didn't reply.

"What about Ellie Carpenter? I know you feel something for her."

"She's a very special woman," he said, nodding in agreement. "And she won't give me the time of day."

"Well, her situation is complicated."

"Her situation could be fixed with a visit to a lawyer's office. A notice in some major newspapers and a couple of legal papers filed at the courthouse and she could have the scoundrel who abandoned her declared legally dead. She hasn't. Why do you think that is?"

"I have no idea."

"Neither do I, but the most logical thing is that she still cares for him, lowlife though he certainly is."

"Or," Libby offered, "maybe she's afraid there's no one out there who's willing to take on a woman with a background like hers and a child like Bethany. It's something few men would assume willingly. On the other hand, maybe she uses her husband as a way to keep from getting too close to anyone for fear she'll be let down again, the same way you use your flirting."

"I hadn't thought of that," Win confessed. "Which is all the more reason that love should be left out of the equation. It simplifies everything if you go into a marriage as a business arrangement."

"You're impossible," she said with a shake of her head.

"I'm serious. Everyone says Slade was devastated when his wife walked out, so it would be a perfect arrangement for him and Blythe. Two brokenhearted people bound only by a marriage license."

The expression on Libby's face was almost comical. "Win, this isn't some struggling business that you think you can fix. We're talking about two people's lives here. You can't treat this like a merger."

"I don't see why not."

Seeing that she was getting nowhere with him, Libby asked, "When do you plan to pursue this ridiculous course of action?

"As soon as Slade is well enough to be reasoned with."

Libby stood and reached for his empty plate. She'd done all she could do for the moment. "If he's as hardheaded as you say he is, this could get interesting."

After his mother left him, Win recalled the things Blythe had said during their conversation on the way home. She'd asked if he really wanted her to marry someone like Will Slade, and Win admitted it was a valid question. He didn't want his sister legally bound to just anyone, especially someone who had a problem with alcohol. He'd see the results of that mistake too often.

As for Slade being divorced, unlike most people, Win had no problem with that; after all, Martha was the one who had cheated and done the divorcing. Libby was a divorcée and there was not a better person alive. She'd been a great mother to him and Philip, and a wonderful, caring wife to their father, who'd been left paralyzed after her first husband, Lucas Gentry, had given him a severe beating.

Win hadn't gone through life without realizing that things often happened that no one could control, but he was a man who liked fixing things. He picked up his coffee cup and stared at a hazy-looking landscape across the room. He really did want Blythe to be happy. He didn't want to force her into a disastrous marriage. On the other hand, she just kept getting into scrapes that caused her to look foolish. Of course, there was no sin in that. Almost everyone fell into that category at one time or another.

When her mother left her, Blythe undressed, leaving her dirty clothes in a pile next to the bed. It was Sunday and she knew she should have a bath and get ready for church services, but under the circumstances, she thought she would stay at home. She wasn't ready to face the town gossips or the condemnation she knew she would see in Brother McAdams's eyes.

She slipped between the muslin sheets and wished she never had to leave the comfort and anonymity of the bed. She heard the occasional clatter of silver against a plate and the muted sounds of her mother's and brother's voices. Rolling to her side, she curled into a ball of misery.

There was little doubt that they were talking about her and what to do about her latest *fiasco*. Her brother would push for marriage, believing that it would solve everything, when all it would really do is tie two already-unhappy people together for a lifetime. Her mother would be her advocate, but Blythe wasn't sure how long Libby could hold out against Win's incredible ability to sway others to his way of thinking. It was, after all, what made him such a success in the business world.

Despite the dozens of emotions that raced through her mind one after the other, Blythe finally escaped her newest predicament by drifting off into a sound sleep. Her last coherent thought was that maybe she could be like Rip Van Winkle and sleep for years and years and years and wake up to find this all behind her.

Blythe woke sometime in the afternoon. She pulled on a flannel robe and went down to find something to eat, her footsteps dragging. Her mother had returned from church and was probably in her room taking her Sunday-afternoon nap.

She took the platter of ham Libby had baked from the pie safe and placed a generous helping on a pretty floral plate, adding some potatoes and green beans. She was starving. Other than the small chunk of cheese and piece of stale bread she'd shared with the dog the evening before, she hadn't eaten in more than twenty-four hours.

She tucked into her cold meal and let her thoughts wander over the events of the morning. Recalling the shock on everyone's face when they'd walked into the house and seen her in her petticoats almost robbed her of her appetite. Other than making a mistake in judging Devon's true character, she'd had no excuse when it came to the *fiasco*, but this situation was far different. Even now, she didn't know how else she could have handled things.

Her thoughts drifted to Will Slade. Will. Somehow, even though some might condemn her for being so familiar, it seemed fitting that she should think of him by his given name. In for a penny, in for a pound, she thought in defiance. She wondered how he was doing and if he was as sick as she'd thought he was. Would he be all right? In spite of everything, she prayed he would be.

She was cleaning up the kitchen when she remembered Will's dog. Like her, he hadn't had much to eat, and with Will gone, there was no one to feed him. She didn't fool herself into thinking Win would ride out there and feed the beast. Gabe or Caleb might if she asked them, but it was Sunday and they always had visitors over.

She sighed. There was nothing to do but to take care of the animal herself, though the very thought of facing the drooling creature sent a shiver down her spine. She looked at the ham and reached again for the butcher knife. Working carefully, she cut all the fat and meat from the bone. When she was finished, she had a nice bone and lots of scraps that she knew the dog would enjoy. She wrapped it in waxed paper and tied it up in a dish towel.

After dressing in a much-worn skirt and shirtwaist, she donned a coat and headed for the carriage house, telling Joel, her mother's stable hand, to hitch up the covered buggy. He complied, though he didn't seem happy about it. She told him where she was going, so he could report to her mother, and said she would be back before suppertime.

The ride to Will's place was a chilly, muddy trek. The afternoon sunshine gave no hint of the torrential rains of the evening before. Blythe found peace in the knowledge that there was no one out here to stare or point accusing fingers at her. No one to whisper speculations about what had happened between her and Will Slade.

As soon as the house came into view, the dog sensed her approach. Leaping up from his place on the porch, he ran to the bottom of the steps, lifted his head skyward and began to bark and growl. When his racket failed to make her stop or go away, he broke into a loping run toward the buggy. Trembling, but determined not to let him intimidate her, Blythe kept going.

When she reached the hitching post, she pulled the mare to a stop. Immediately the dog put his massive paws on the floorboard of the buggy and barked once, almost as if he were trying to tell her something, the way he had the previous day.

Though her hand shook, Blythe held it out toward him and crooned in a trembling voice, "It's okay, boy.

It's okay. Are you hungry? Hmm? I've brought you something to eat."

He barked again, as if to say yes.

She leaned over, untied the dish towel with the ham leavings and turned back toward him. "If you want to eat, you'll have to move," she said. As if he understood, he backed up a couple of steps. Thank the Good Lord, he wasn't barking anymore!

Taking her courage in hand, she climbed down from the buggy. The brute began to jump up and down in excitement. Fearful that he'd snatch the food from her hands and rip off an arm in the process, she took another few cautious steps.

Not two yards from the carriage, the dog, impatient for her to deliver the food he smelled, reared up on his hind legs and placed his massive paws on her shoulders. Not expecting such a thing, Blythe staggered backward beneath his weight. Before she knew it, she was on the soggy ground, flat on her back.

It happened so fast that she didn't see it coming. Even if she had, there was nothing she could have done about it. The dog outweighed her by several pounds. She was lying there with her eyes closed, trying to catch her breath, when she felt hot, doggy panting on her cheek and a rough tongue make a long swipe from her chin to her ear. She opened her eyes and saw brown eyes gazing down at her. A wet nose was pressed against her ear.

The hound licked her face again.

"Aarrgh!" she said, suppressing a shudder. Without a thought as to how he might react, she shoved his head aside with one hand while using the other to push herself into a sitting position. Undeterred, the hound gave her another swipe across the cheek.

At least he wasn't attacking her! Determined to do what decency and compassion dictated she should for Will's mutt, she pushed to her feet and scrubbed at her slobbery cheek with her skirt tail, shuddering at the memory.

Anxious to be done and be gone, she unwrapped the leftovers, picked up a juicy hunk of fat with her fingertips and tossed it to him. It vanished in a single gulp. She shook her head in amazement. The rest followed in short order. Last, she threw the ham bone in his direction.

She was wiping her fingers on the clean edges of the messy towel when an image of how she must have looked lying on the ground flashed into her mind. She started to laugh. What would her snobbish friends in Boston think if they knew that the woman who had such high hopes of owning her own boutique and could have had any number of wealthy young men for a husband was instead teaching children in a one-room country schoolhouse, driving around in the country alone…dressed like a cleaning woman and carrying on a conversation—of sorts—with a dog?

Without warning the laughter turned to a sob. She dropped the dish towel to the ground, leaned against the hitching post and covered her face with her cold hands. She cried for the trouble she'd caused her family and for her ridiculous longing for a husband and her silly naïveté. For loneliness and lost dreams and the loss of her identity. For love and those crazy, pulse-pounding moments she'd experienced with Devon…something she was certain she would never again experience.

After a moment a whining sound drew her attention from her misery. She lifted her head, wiped at her wet eyes and opened them. Through the haze of her tears, she saw that Will's dog stood in front of her, his head cocked to one side, looking at her with those sad brown eyes that seemed to say, "What's the matter?"

Good grief! Was she so desperate for compassion she thought she could see it in the eyes of a massive dog? Knowing that her tears were in vain and would solve nothing, she drew herself up straight, sniffed and wiped her eyes and nose on the hem of her skirt. *Take that, Bostonians!* she thought, glancing back at the hound, who was demolishing the waxed paper she'd wrapped the scraps in.

"Stop that!" she cried.

He looked up at her, a piece of paper hanging from the corner of his mouth. Blythe watched in amazement as, with an unconcerned flick of his tongue, he slurped it into that massive cavern. He chewed a couple of times and swallowed. Licking his chops one final time, he gazed at her, obviously wanting more.

"That's all," she told him, grateful that he no longer looked as if he'd like to have her for dinner. There was plenty of water in the creek, so she'd done all she could for the moment. With a sigh, she gathered the dish towel from the ground and headed back to the buggy. The dog watched as she untied the rig, climbed in and backed it up. Then he picked up the bone in his mouth and began to trot alongside.

She halted the horse. "Git!" she yelled, waving her hand at the dog. "Go on! Go back!"

He just stared at her. She clucked to the horse and off she went. The mutt followed. She increased her speed. He stayed beside her, loping along as if the pace were nothing. Surely he'd get tired and turn back, she thought.

She stopped and tried again to make him go away, but he only dropped the bone, sat down and looked at her with his tongue hanging out, panting. Blythe took off at an even faster clip, bouncing over ruts and holes, certain that the next time she looked the big black hound would be nowhere in sight.

She was wrong. Every time. Since she had no idea how to make him go home, he was still behind her when she rolled into the carriage house. He followed her through the wide doors, dropped his bone and sat down on a pile of straw, watching her warily.

"What's that?" Joel asked, casting a wary glance at the dog as he helped Blythe down.

"The biggest dog *I've* ever seen," she told him.

"Me, too. Where'd it come from?"

"It's Mr. Slade's dog. I took some scraps out to him, and he followed me home. I didn't know how to get rid of him." Wearily, she turned and started toward the house.

"What am I supposed to do with him?" Joel asked.

She faced the hired hand and held out her hands, palms up. "I'm open to suggestions."

Joel shrugged and shook his head.

Blythe mimicked the gesture. "I guess he's here until his owner gets better or I figure out something else. Let him sleep out here. I'll see to it he has something to eat every day. He's huge, but he seems harmless. If he gives you any trouble, I'll have Colt or

Dan come over and see if they can do something with him."

"Okay," Joel said, but he didn't sound happy.

Neither was Blythe.

Chapter Four

When Will opened his eyes, he felt much better, but when he lifted his hand to rub a palm over his whiskery cheek, he was as weak as a newborn kitten. He raised his head and looked around, then realized that he wasn't in his own bed. A rush of panic swept through him and then bits and pieces of hazy memories started popping into his head.

He'd been sick, sicker than he recalled being in a coon's age. He had a vague recollection of going outside sometime around daylight, hoping the cold morning air would help cool the fever raging inside him. After that, everything was pretty much blank.

There was a slight memory of having talked to Martha, but that was impossible. Martha was in St. Louis, living the good life with her new husband. Will glanced toward the window. It looked like the sun was almost overhead, so he'd guess it was somewhere around noon.

"Will? Are you awake?"

The soft, feminine voice came from the doorway. Dr. Rachel Gentry stood there. She was so close to delivering her baby that she looked ready to pop. Always a pretty woman, the pregnancy gave her a plump and healthy glow that seemed to radiate from within her.

"More or less," he told her in a raspy voice.

"I thought I'd see if you were awake yet and if you feel up to eating something."

Just then his stomach rumbled and she smiled. "Maybe so."

"Good. Let me check you out first." She crossed the room and picked up the stethoscope from atop the dresser. "How do you feel?"

"Like I've been run over by a train," he told her, pushing himself up on his elbows. The room took a little dip. He groaned and closed his eyes at the unaccustomed weakness. Good grief! He wasn't going to pass out again, was he?

Rachel had turned at the sound. "Don't move too quickly," she advised. "You've been very sick since you've been here. Your temperature has been up and down." She took a thermometer out of a solution, shook it and held it out. He looked at her as if she were crazy. "Open. Under your tongue."

Reluctantly he did as she said. While they waited for his temperature to register, she listened to his chest, front and back. "You sound much clearer." She let the stethoscope dangle around her neck, removed the thermometer and looked at it intently. Smiled. "Your temperature is almost normal, thank goodness."

After shaking the thermometer once more, she returned it to its solution. "It's a good thing Blythe found you when she did or you might have died out there. As it is, you had a touch of pneumonia. It's a good thing you're so healthy normally."

Blythe. Granville. Will clenched his jaw. He supposed he should be grateful, and he supposed he was, but of all the people who might have stumbled across him, why did it have to be the rich city girl? Except for the time he'd come to her rescue at the train station, she'd always been cool and uppity whenever their paths crossed. Of course, if the gossip around town was true, she had a right to be skittish around men. More than most, he knew that being used by the opposite sex could leave a person a little wary.

Something Rachel had said suddenly struck him. "What do you mean, 'since I've been here'? Didn't they bring me to town this morning?"

Rachel laughed. "Hardly. That was day before yesterday. You've been out of your head with fever. I was pretty worried about you for a while, but it looks like you're on the mend now. What sounds good to eat?"

"What time is it?"

She looked at the watch pinned to the front of the apron she wore. "Almost noon."

"How about a big hunk of beef?"

Rachel laughed again. "How about some oatmeal and toast with lots of butter and brown sugar?"

Will made a face of disgust. "How about we compromise? I'll take the oatmeal if you add a couple of eggs on the side."

"Done. I'll have it ready in a jiffy," she told him, heading toward the door.

When she was gone, he thought about what she'd told him. He'd been here two and a half days! Unbelievable! He could count on one hand how many times he'd been sick in his whole lifetime, and he'd never been so bad that he was out like a light for this long.

As silly as he knew it was, knowing that he'd succumbed to that kind of helplessness made him feel less a man. A woman had had to help him to the house, for goodness' sake. How had Blythe Granville managed that? She was a little, bitty woman.

To make matters worse, she was big-shot Winston Granville's sister. The Boston businessman-turned-banker had been a thorn in Will's side for a long while now. He had to admit that he was tempted from time to time to take Granville up on his offer, but stubborn pride wouldn't allow him to give up. Slades had never been quitters. Besides, all he knew was lumbering, and he had no idea what he'd do with himself if he sold out. So he hung on, sometimes by the skin of his teeth.

With his thoughts all a-muddle, he must have slipped into a light sleep. The next thing he knew, Rachel was back with his food. Her father, Edward Stone, was with her. He must be having a good day, Will thought, since Stone was using only his canes. A victim of a stroke several years before, he was left with some weakness in his legs and was sometimes forced to use a wheelchair.

"How are you feeling, young man?" he asked now as he followed his daughter into the room.

"I think I'm going to make it," Will said in a hoarse voice.

"Well, I'm glad to hear it."

Rachel set the tray on the dresser and she and her father helped Will into a sitting position. Once he was settled with the tray across his lap, he reached for the mug of coffee and took a big swallow, disregarding its hotness. "That's the best thing I've had in ages."

"You're just hungry," Rachel said. "Dig in."

Will did just that, giving equal time to the sweet oatmeal and the savory eggs while carrying on a conversation with the two doctors about what had been done for him while he was sick.

"What about Banjo?" Will asked, worried about his dog. "Has anyone been taking care of him?"

"I understand Blythe went out to feed him Sunday afternoon and he followed her back to town," Rachel told him.

Will's fork clattered to his stoneware plate. Not only had she helped him, she'd taken it upon herself to see that his dog was cared for.

"He followed her to town?" he asked. "That's not like him. He doesn't care much for strangers." The big, black hound wasn't mean, but he was protective, and most people were more than a little frightened of him.

"Well, it seems he took to Blythe. Maybe he just wanted some companionship," Edward suggested.

"Where's he staying? Is he just roaming around town?"

"Simmer down, Will," Rachel said. "He's fine. He's staying in the Granvilles' carriage house, and I'm sure Blythe is seeing that he's well fed."

Miss Granville didn't seem like the kind of woman who would take to any kind of dog, unless it was some yapping little mutt with a finicky appetite that wanted to do nothing but sleep in its mistress's lap. Pound for pound, Banjo was as big as she was—maybe bigger. It looked like he owed her for more than rescuing him from possible death.

"All in all, I'd say you owe that little lady a big 'thank you,' especially under the circumstances," Edward said, echoing Will's thoughts.

Will frowned at the older man. "What circumstances?"

"Why, all the gossip that's been flying around town about the two of you spending the night alone together at your place."

The sudden wave of nausea that washed over him had nothing to do with his food or his illness. It had everything to do with the memory of a group of men bursting into his house, finding him and Blythe together, and the preacher saying that Will should make an honest woman of her. As if there was anything on earth that could persuade him to do that. He'd had enough of women and their demands to last him a lifetime.

"Except for going to school to teach, she's just about become a recluse, and she was pretty close to that already, thanks to that mess in Boston."

"I heard she ran off with some fellow who took all her money."

"Actually, they eloped," Rachel said, a hint of steel in her usually soft voice at the implication that Will was making light of her sister-in-law's difficulties. "And it isn't as if she just met someone on the street and ran off. Devon Carmichael had insinuated himself into Boston society quite nicely. Everyone took him at face value and assumed he was everything he represented himself to be."

Will felt properly chastised. From his own experience with Martha, he knew that some people were good at pretending to be something they weren't. In fairness, he couldn't fault Miss Granville for believing some man's lies.

"I'm sorry if my choice of words implied otherwise," Will told her. "That's just what I'd heard."

"Well, the truth is that she loved him enough to elope. Then, as if she wouldn't have had a hard enough time with that scandal, he cleaned out her bank account and left town within a day of their return to Boston."

"And if that weren't bad enough, she discovered he was already married," Edward added.

Though the Wolf Creek grapevine was pretty accurate, that detail had escaped Will's ears.

"I'm thankful she found and helped you, Will, but the poor thing is paying the price for her good deed."

Though he'd weathered his own scandal and personal humiliation when Martha ran off with the big shot from Springfield, Will found it hard to believe that things were as bad for Blythe as Rachel and her father were painting them to be. Martha had left him for another man; Blythe Granville had helped someone in need, a sick man. There was no comparison in their actions.

"I'll be sure and thank her properly when I'm up and about," he told them, trying his best to think of some way to make things right.

"That's all well and good, Will," Rachel said, "but I don't think an apology is what the town has in mind for fixing things."

"C'mon, Rachel. There shouldn't even be anything to 'fix.' I was unconscious. I didn't even know she was there until the rescue party barged through the front door."

"I don't know what to tell you," she said with a sigh of frustration. "All I know is that I hate to see history repeat itself here."

"This, too, will pass," Will said, quoting one of his mother's favorite sayings.

The corners of Rachel's lips lifted in a sad smile. "I suppose you're right, but what kind of damage will be left behind when it does?"

Chapter Five

Blythe bade the last of her students goodbye and went to the desk to gather her lunch pail and shawl, thankful that the day was over and she wouldn't have to face the never-ending string of mothers who came to chastise and condemn her. The past two days had been interminable. She wasn't sure how she could make it through the rest of the week, much less the remainder of the school year.

The mother who'd shown up during the lunch recess had been particularly hostile as she'd read Blythe the riot act for behaving in a manner unfit for someone whose job it was to shape young minds and lives. Blythe had listened to the tirade in stony silence. In fact, she feared she'd blanked out during most of the bitter lecture. After two days of it, she could almost recite the familiar refrains by rote.

When the mother had finished her ranting, Blythe had assured the woman that nothing untoward had happened between her and William Slade, but the harpy had not been impressed with the explanation and stormed away, saying that she intended to talk to the mayor about finding a replacement.

As Blythe watched the portly matron stomp across the greening grass in front of the schoolhouse, she was thinking that the woman would have to stand in line. No doubt Homer was inundated with mothers with similar requests.

Once she got home, she shared a cup of coffee and a slice of pound cake with her mother and then went to change into her everyday clothes. As had become routine, she made her way outside to feed the dog that had taken up residence in the carriage house.

If his tail wagging was any indication, he was always happy to see her. She had no idea what Will Slade would say about the dog following her home. Truth to tell, she hadn't been too happy at first, but she had to admit that it was nice not having to make the trip to the country every day to tend to his mutt.

When the dog was fed and watered, she decided to walk to Rachel's and check on the patient, even though she was feeling a bit headachy and dizzy herself. She prayed she wasn't taking whatever it was that the cantankerous Mr. Slade had.

According to the Wolf Creek grapevine, he was better. Or worse. She'd even heard that he had pneumonia. She didn't want to start any new conversations about him with her family, so she'd refrained from asking her mother or brother if they'd heard how he was faring. Checking on his progress seemed the decent thing to do, so here she was.

The door to the surgery opened to reveal Danny, her half brother Gabe and Rachel's son. His freckled face broke into a smile when he saw her standing there. "Hello, Aunt Blythe. What are you doing here?"

She leaned down and kissed him on the cheek. "Hello, Danny. I came to see how Mr. Slade is doing."

"Mama says he's a lot better," Danny told her. "You can go in and see him if you want."

Go in and see him? Though she might have decided to see if he was feeling better, that did not include facing Will and his blatant animosity face-to-face. "Oh, no! I don't want to intrude. I'd just like to speak to your mother."

"Sure thing. I'll go fetch her."

Danny took off down the hall in a dead run, leaving Blythe standing by the door, twisting her gloves in her hands.

"How's Banjo?"

The sound of the deep, raspy voice startled her so badly she gave a little gasp. Obviously, Will was awake and had heard her talking to Danny. Despite telling herself she shouldn't, Blythe found her footsteps headed toward the room where the question originated.

Almost fearfully, she peeked around the corner.

"For cryin' out loud," he said in a grumpy voice. "Come on in. I don't bite."

Could have fooled me, Blythe thought, taking slow, tentative steps and stopping a few feet inside the doorway. Will lay propped up on some pillows, wearing his usual scowl and several days' growth of beard. If she thought his appearance disreputable before, he looked ten times worse now. Scruffy. Tough. Dangerous. And, she thought grudgingly and not for the first time, he was also very handsome, despite his unkempt appearance.

His dark gaze was locked on her face, making her squirm. Searching her mind for some safe topic, she said the first words that came to mind, "I'm sorry. I have no idea how your banjo is."

"What?" Will frowned and the expression in his eyes said without words he thought she had a few loose marbles rolling around inside her noggin.

She gave a slight shrug. "You asked how your banjo was. I'm afraid I have no idea how I'm supposed to know that."

For a few seconds Will sat very still. Then he covered his mouth and coughed a few times. When he looked at her again, Blythe imagined she saw a glint of humor in his eyes. Silly notion! He wouldn't know humor if it walked up and slapped him in the face.

"Uh… Banjo is my dog," he explained. "Rachel told me you went to the farm to feed him and he followed you home."

Blythe felt her face flame and resisted the impulse to place her hands against her hot cheeks. How embarrassing! He must think she was a fool. Most people did, it seemed. "Yes, he did. I'm sorry. I tried and tried to make him go back, and he just wouldn't go."

"He can be a bit hardheaded," Will admitted. "Is he okay?"

"Oh, yes. He seems fine, and he eats well." She gave a little shrug. "I'm not familiar with dogs, so I can't say for sure. He's staying in the carriage house."

Silence reigned in the room for a few seconds. "Thank you for checking on him."

"You're welcome."

There was another lull in the stilted conversation while Will stared at Blythe and she stared at the floor and chewed on her lower lip.

"What did he do when you first went out?" he said at last.

Blythe recalled the sheer terror and determination she'd felt the afternoon she'd gone out to his place and climbed down from the buggy.

"Well, I was afraid he'd tear me limb from limb," she told him. "But when I got out of the carriage and tossed him some ham fat, he was fine."

"That's probably the best thing you could have done. He's not really a mean dog, just very protective of his territory. His size alone keeps most people at a distance," Will said.

Indeed. An unexpected image of herself as she must have looked, flat on her back, being held down by the huge animal, flashed through her mind. She clamped her lips together to suppress a smile, wondering what his owner would have said had he been there. She imagined it would have been amusing to anyone watching.

"Is something funny?"

"Not really," she said. "At least not when it happened. I was furious, actually!"

"What did happen?"

"He knocked me down. Banjo."

"He did what? When?"

"That first day. I guess he got impatient for his supper, and as soon as I got down from the buggy, he jumped up and put his paws on my shoulders. The next thing I knew, I was on my back and he was licking me in the face."

Recalling the disgusting slobber and his dreadful breath, she gave a little shudder. There was nothing funny about that. "It was really, really horrible."

Will looked appalled. "Blast that miserable mutt," he said and then mumbled something beneath his breath. "Look, Miss Granville, I can't tell you how sorry I am for causing you so much trouble."

"Please don't concern yourself about it. I think he may be getting fond of me."

"He must be if he followed you home. He doesn't take to many people so fast."

The topic of the dog talked out, silence ruled again. Blythe knew he was staring at her, but she kept her gaze fixed anywhere but on him. It was time to go, she thought. She'd done what she'd come to do, so there was no reason to prolong the agony for either of them.

Surprising herself, she dared to glance at him and heard herself say, "You must be feeling much improved. You're more alert and you look much…better."

He gave a disgruntled snort and scrubbed a palm over his hairy cheek and chin. The utterly masculine gesture caused a little hitch in her breathing.

"I imagine I look like a hobo off the train. But I am feeling better," he said.

"Someone said you had pneumonia."

"The old Wolf Creek grapevine, huh?"

"Well, yes."

At the conversation's casual turn to the two of them being the prime topic of the talk around town, they both grew very still.

"Yes," he said, breaking the awkward silence. "Rachel says that if you hadn't happened by, I might not have made it. Thank you."

The two simple words sounded genuine and he looked sincere.

"Then I'm glad I came along when I did," she told him, a little surprised to realize that despite her present circumstances, she meant it. How could she be sorry for playing the Good Samaritan and doing what the Lord expected of her, what she expected of herself? She clasped her hands together.

"Well, I should be going. I just wanted to check on you and let you know your dog is fine."

"I'm sorry for causing you so much trouble," he said again, repeating his previous words almost verbatim.

"Oh, Banjo isn't really a problem," she assured him.

"I'm not just talking about Banjo, Miss Granville. I'm talking about *all* the trouble."

Will saw all the color drain from her face. She seemed to actually *wilt*. Her brown eyes drifted closed and she pressed her lips together in a prim line. Which was a crying shame, Will thought. Lips as pretty as hers should never do anything but smile. Berating himself for thinking of her in such a personal way and for finding anything about her attractive, he watched as she straightened her small frame and lifted her round chin, changing from a shy woman to one of confidence and dignity. Unlike Martha's quick change in attitude from anger to victim, the transformation in Blythe's demeanor was impressive, something no doubt passed on from generation to generation of well-heeled young ladies.

"There's no need to trouble yourself, Mr. Slade," she assured him in a clipped, no-nonsense tone as she raked an errant strand of brown hair behind her ear. "I've become accustomed to dealing with things of this nature. The people who know me will accept the truth, and those who don't…well, some people refuse to let the facts of a situation alter their viewpoint. I'm sure it will all go away eventually."

Become accustomed? Will thought, once more admiring her poise. No one should have to *become accustomed* to being the subject of everyone's dinnertime conversation. She was right about the rest, though. Why was it that most people seemed to want to believe the worst?

"The preacher and your brother think that I should—"

"I've heard what they think," she interrupted. "And I well remember your answer."

Will had no memory of anything he'd said at his place, but knowing it must not have been good, he felt the heat of embarrassment rising in his face. "It's nothing against you, Miss Granville," he told her. "It's just that my first marriage wasn't a very good one, and at this point in my life I don't think it's anything I'm ready to try again, which I'm sure you of all people can understand."

The barest hint of a cynical smile lifted one corner of her mouth, but there was no denying the mortification in her eyes. "Indeed I do."

"So you understand my position," he stated.

If possible, she grew even paler. "Yes."

Will hated that the situation was making her life

more difficult, but, short of marriage, he had no idea how to fix things.

"Please don't worry about me, Mr. Slade," she told him. "I know my brother and half the town expects you to marry me to save my reputation, but I see no reason why you should pay the piper for a choice I made. I'm a grown woman, and I weighed the pros and cons before I made my decision."

That revelation was a surprise and more than a little humbling. "You decided to stay, knowing there was the possibility it would put you in a bad light again?"

She nodded. "It seemed to me that it was the Christian thing to do," she told him. "And, besides, I really didn't have much choice. It was clear that you needed help, and just as clear that I couldn't get back to town." She gave a slight lift of her narrow shoulders. "Word gets out and people talk. It's the way things are."

"I guess I'm wondering why you made that choice, especially since you came here trying to escape similar circumstances."

"That's why."

"I'm sorry," he said, frowning. "I'm afraid I'm confused."

The jaded smile on her lips was out of place on her innocent-looking face. "Since I was already the talk of the town, I didn't see how things could get any worse. Besides," she added, "I hate storms and the dark. I couldn't imagine riding to town for help in the middle of a thunderstorm in the dead of night. I'm not familiar with the area and I was afraid I'd get lost. And there was the small problem of you being far too ill for me to leave, even for a couple of hours."

Maybe because he wanted so badly to receive absolution, Will thought her rationale made a certain kind of sense. The sort of "what have I got to lose?" mind-set. Blythe Granville was nothing like he expected her to be, and she was far different from the picture she presented to the world.

She was, in fact, a study in contradictions. She'd dealt with a dog that was known to chase away strangers. That in itself was beyond belief. Banjo and Martha had tolerated each other at best. By all appearances, Blythe was a spoiled, rich girl who'd somehow managed to get a man twice her size out of the woods and into a safe, dry place and in doing so had not only put her reputation in jeopardy but poured fuel onto the fire of the scandal she'd left Boston to escape.

He'd have expected the debacle with the bigamist husband would have embittered her, but that didn't seem the case. Either she'd been brought up to be an independent thinker, which was unusual for young women—especially wealthy young women—or the incident had forced her to view the world from a different perspective.

"Except it has, hasn't it?" he asked.

"I beg your pardon."

"Made things worse," he said, spreading his hands wide. "This thing with us."

Her chin lifted a fraction. "A bit."

"Hello, there!" Rachel's cheerful voice preceded her into the room. "Danny said you were here, Blythe. I was finishing up in the kitchen." She went to Blythe and gave her a warm hug.

"That's all right. I just stopped by to check on Mr. Slade and let him know his dog is doing fine."

"Oh, good," Rachel said. "Our patient is coming along nicely as well, thanks to you. It's a wonder that you happened along when you did."

"Just a fortunate coincidence," Blythe said, embarrassed by Rachel's mention of it.

"Very fortunate for Will." Rachel smiled. "I just wanted to say hello. I'll let the two of you get back to your conversation." She smiled that sweet smile at Will, who ground his teeth.

He knew exactly what she was doing. Why couldn't people just mind their own business and let him tend to his? He hated that he was the cause for more scandal, but he definitely didn't want a wife, and he certainly didn't want one he hadn't handpicked—not that he'd done such a good job of it himself. Dr. Gentry could just keep her wishing and hoping to herself.

"I should be going, too," Blythe said, once more the somewhat gauche woman he'd seen when she'd first arrived.

Will nodded. "Thanks for stopping by, and I really appreciate you taking care of Banjo. I hadn't expected that."

"It's nothing. It's just what—"

"Anyone would have done," he interrupted.

She ducked her head in embarrassment. "I'm glad you're doing better."

"Do you think you could bring him by to see me?"

"Who? Banjo?"

"Yes."

"If it's all right with Rachel, I'd be glad to. I could bring him tomorrow if you think she'd let you sit outside on the back porch for a while. I don't think she'd much like having a dog in her surgery."

"That sounds like the best idea I've heard all week." He'd always worked outside, and this lying around doing nothing was about to send him 'round the bend.

"I'll check with her and see if tomorrow after school is okay."

"That sounds great."

They said their awkward goodbyes and Will sank back against the pillows. He was a long way from feeling one hundred percent, but he was on the mend, and at least with Banjo coming for a visit, he had something to look forward to.

Rachel had come to pick up Will's supper dishes when Edward poked his head around the door frame and announced, "Win Granville is here to see Will."

Will's heart took a sickening nosedive. He wasn't sure he was ready to go head-to-head with Granville just yet.

"Absolutely not!" Rachel said, coming to Will's rescue with a shake of her head. "Go tell him that Will is still far too sick to deal with any confrontation."

"It doesn't have to be confrontational," a voice said from the hall. A familiar figure moved into view behind Edward, who looked apologetic. Rachel gave a sigh of resignation.

"Hello, Win," she said to her brother-in-law.

He responded with a brief nod. "Rachel." He smiled the charming smile that sent the ladies of Wolf Creek into a near swoon and bent to kiss her cheek.

Will had to admit Granville cut a fine citified

picture in his stylish Boston duds. He fairly oozed money and style. Was it that same polished sophistication that first caught Martha's attention when she'd fallen for the Springfield dandy? It was certainly a far different look from the denim and flannel that Will himself wore.

"You're looking extremely lovely today," Win told Rachel.

She gave him a withering look, but she was smiling. "You should know by now that flattery doesn't work with me," she reminded him. "This isn't a good time, Win. Really. Will has been very ill and he just regained consciousness this afternoon. I'd prefer he didn't have any company for another day or so."

Will noticed that the doctor made no mention of Blythe's earlier visit.

"He certainly doesn't need any unnecessary stress on his system while his body is trying to heal," Rachel stated in a firm voice.

"I just need a few minutes, and I promise not to upset your patient."

Rachel looked skeptical but gave a brief nod. "I'm holding you to that," she told him, pointing at him with a slender finger. "Dad and I will leave the two of you alone," she said as she picked up Will's tray and followed her father from the room.

"I suppose you know why I'm here, Slade," Win Granville said, moving closer to the bed.

"I suppose I do."

"And?"

Will met Granville's sharp gaze head-on. "And I think that forcing two innocent people into marriage for the rest of their lives is a terrible price for them to pay just to keep folks from talking."

"It's the way civilized society works," Granville said in a smooth tone.

"Then someone needs to change things."

A muscle in Granville's jaw tightened and his hands curled into fists. Despite his promise to Rachel, Will knew the other man was holding his temper in check—barely. "Well, so far they haven't, so here we are."

Weariness pulled at Will. He wanted nothing more than to lie back on his pillows and go to sleep. Instead, hoping to get rid of his unwanted visitor, he decided to try a change in tactics. "Look, I have nothing against your sister. I'm sure she's a fine woman, but I don't want to ever get married again."

"You're missing the point, Slade. This isn't about you and how a marriage will affect your life. It's about a blameless young woman who loved someone who took away her reputation, as well as her inheritance, and then walked away. Surely you of all people can identify with how she feels."

Of course he could. He knew exactly how she felt.

"Boston society isn't very forgiving," Granville continued. "Everyone in our circle of so-called friends was whispering about her behind her back. The young men who'd once competed for her attention were making crude jokes. She had to get away from it or lose her mind."

The woman who'd slipped quietly through the back door paused midstep at the sound of male voices. She'd hoped to sneak in to see Will without anyone being the wiser. Now she eased the door shut and stood with her hand on the knob listening…

Will knew Martha's leaving had caused quite a stir in Wolf Creek, and everyone had done their fair share of talking about it. That was just how things were. Anyone and everything was fair game. He knew his former wife had gotten the worst end of it, but he'd also been the butt of a few critical comments back in the days when he was hitting the corn.

"Are you listening to me, Slade?" The harsh question brought Will's attention back to the conversation.

"Yes."

Pinning him with a hard look, Granville continued with the tale of his sister's woes. "My brother and I thought Wolf Creek would be more forgiving of a simple error in judgment and that maybe she'd find a man to love her the way she deserves to be loved."

"And I'm sure she will," Will said.

Granville gave a short laugh. "Because she helped you, that chance is gone. Her life is ruined for the second time. Don't you think that marrying her is the right thing to do?"

Personally, Will thought that pushing her off on a virtual stranger was absolutely the worst thing for her.

"After what I went through, I don't think there's a woman on earth I'd trust with my heart," Will said, hoping to make Granville understand. If either he or Blythe ever did entertain the notion of love and marriage again, it would happen after they'd both had time to heal, to learn to open up and trust again.

"I'm not asking you to give her your heart. I'm

asking you to give her your name, so she can hold up her head in the community."

Will did feel sorry for Blythe, and he understood Granville's thinking. The man just wanted his sister to be cared for and accepted, and felt this newest smear on her reputation would dash all hope of that. Will understood perfectly, but forcing them into marriage was a crazy proposition at best. "And you believe a few words in front of a preacher will do that?"

"I'm thinking that it would be a good way for both of you to start fresh. Think about it. You'd share the same space in a peaceful coexistence. No pressure. No expectations." He shrugged. "It could even be a good move for your business."

Will frowned. Good move for his business? What did that mean?

The woman standing at the door heard footsteps approaching from the living area of the house. Cautiously, she turned the knob and eased through the narrow aperture onto the small back porch, managing to close the door just in time to avoid discovery.

Evidently the people of Wolf Creek were still exerting social pressure to satisfy their peculiar mode of right and wrong. As usual, Will was being his stubborn self, which worked to her advantage. And she had heard one other interesting tidbit. She tucked it away, certain it would be of use at some time in the future...

"Time's up."

The abrupt interruption came from Rachel, who stepped through the doorway wearing her doctor face.

She walked past Win and headed straight to the bed, where she picked up Will's wrist to check his pulse. He could have kissed her for her perfect timing. Granville's heart might be in the right place, but he was absolutely off his rocker if he expected William Slade to jump just because he said frog!

No expectations. Peaceful coexistence. Make it worth his while...

"Your heart is beating way too fast, Will, and you look terrible. You have to get some rest," Rachel said, pulling one of the pillows out from behind him and pushing on his shoulder, indicating that he should lie down.

"I was just leaving," Win said, heading toward the door. He stepped into the hallway and turned. "Just think about it," he said and disappeared from view.

"Did he get out of hand?" Rachel demanded once he was gone.

"Not at all," Will told her, a little surprised their talk hadn't turned into a shouting match.

"What are you supposed to think about?" she asked.

Will cocked a dark eyebrow in mocking question. "What do you think?"

"He wants you to do the right thing by Blythe."

Will's brief laughter was raspy-sounding. "For the last time, I have no intention of marrying a woman I barely know just to satisfy the conventions of society."

"It's hard, Will. I know what she's going through," she said, referencing the well-known but mostly forgotten fact that she had borne Gabe Gentry's son, Danny, out of wedlock years before Gabe, much like the prodigal son, had come back to town and the two finally reconnected and married.

"It'll all blow over when something juicier comes along."

Chapter Six

Win had been gone no more than a few minutes when Edward spoke from the bedroom doorway. "I hate to interrupt again, but Will has another visitor."

"Tell them he isn't up for any more visits today," Rachel said, giving the cover a final tug.

She might as well have been speaking to the wall. Behind Edward, an ostrich plume came into view and a stunning brunette stepped around the doctor. For the second time in the past hour, Will felt his stomach take a sickening lurch.

Edward turned to the woman, his usual pleasant features rigid with displeasure. "I asked you to wait in the parlor, Miss, uh…"

"Rafferty," Will's former wife supplied, ignoring both him and Rachel, who looked as if she could bite nails. All Martha's attention was focused on Will. "Hello, Will," she crooned in a familiar throaty voice.

"What on earth are you doing here, Martha?"

She gave a short laugh and sashayed toward the bed. "Well, that isn't much of a welcome for someone who's traveled so far to see you. As soon as I got the news about you being so sick, I hopped on the first train to come and see how I could help during your recuperation."

She turned to Rachel with pleading in her eyes. "Please don't make me leave after I've had such a lengthy trip. I won't stay long."

Rachel glanced at Will to confirm that she should let the woman who'd ruined his life stay.

"It's fine, Rachel," he told her. "She's right. She won't be here long." His voice held a bit of steel.

Martha had the audacity to look affronted, a technique she'd perfected through the years. Though it was hard to see from the bed, Will thought he saw the sheen of tears in her eyes. Good grief! She was really pulling out all the stops. She should give up men and take up acting for an occupation.

Both the look and the tears were typical Martha ploys. No matter what the problem might be, she thought if she just acted innocent and confused, everything would go her way. It had worked well for her until things had fallen apart, but Will had gotten a lot smarter in the two years she'd been out of his life, and he'd grown a tougher skin, one that was immune to pitiful looks and pouting red lips.

"Don't be angry, Will. Just because things didn't… work out for us doesn't mean I don't care about your well-being," she told him in a faltering voice.

Will closed his eyes for a few seconds, reaching up and massaging his suddenly pounding temples. "What does your current husband have to say about this little spur-of-the-moment trip to visit your former husband?"

Martha frowned and darted a pointed look from

Edward to Rachel, saying without words that she wished they would go away and give her and Will a little privacy.

With a final look at Will, Rachel and her father left the room. Martha turned to shut the door, but Will stopped her. "Don't close it."

She whirled around with a practiced grace he remembered well. "Why ever not?" she asked, her eyes wide and blameless.

"Rachel and Edward might get the wrong idea."

"Funny man." She sauntered back to the bed and placed her palm against his cheek, smiling at him like an indulgent mother. "We were married, for goodness' sake."

Will reached up and manacled her wrist with his fingers. "But we aren't anymore," he reminded, moving her hand.

Martha snatched her hand free and clutched her reticule.

"You didn't answer my question," Will prompted. "What did your husband have to say about you coming to see me?"

For the first time since she'd pushed her way into the room and back into his life, she looked uncomfortable. Feigning nonchalance, she sat down in the wooden rocker that sat next to the bed and glared at him. "If you must know, I never married Scott."

That was a surprise. Will wondered why he hadn't heard that bit of gossip bandied about town. Probably because she hadn't kept in contact with any of the friends from her "old" life. "Really? Why not?"

"It turns out he was already engaged to some silly little debutante with scads of money."

Served her right for cheating on him, Will thought uncharitably. "When did you find that out?"

"A couple of months after I arrived in Springfield," she told him, tapping her fingernails on the wooden arms of the rocker.

"Did you stay with him after you found out?"

"Why do you care?" she snapped, barely holding on to her good manners.

"Care?" He shook his head. "I don't," he told her with blunt honesty. "I'm just curious. Trying to put all the pieces together."

Her gaze didn't quite meet his. "If you must know, yes, I stayed with him for a few months until I could figure out something. And then…then I realized that I wanted more and I ended it."

Will knew that the "more" she wanted was a wedding ring on her finger. He actually smiled at "figure out something." When that was translated, it meant she had to have time to find another chump.

"And then what? What have you been doing since then?"

Her angry gaze met his. "What do you mean?"

"It's been nearly two years, Martha, and you filed for and got a divorce. What did you do when you left Scott? Find another protector?"

He could almost see the cogs turning behind her troubled violet eyes, could almost hear the angry words that trembled on those perfect lips, but Martha had had something in mind when she'd come here and, despite her irritation, she was clever enough to know that she couldn't ruin things by spouting off. Instead she produced a solitary tear that slid down her pale cheek.

"What's happened to you, Will?" she asked in a husky voice. "You were never so cruel before."

"Before? Oh, yes. Before my wife left me for another man and ripped out my heart. You're right. I was too naïve back then, so smitten with you that I fell for every lie you told me."

In typical Martha fashion, she ignored her own accountability and latched on to the part of his statement she could use to further her purpose. "Oh!" she cried, clasping her hands to her chest. "I didn't realize my leaving would hurt you so. You must have loved me very much."

Will met her gaze head-on. "I suppose I did. Or at least I thought it was love," he admitted. "But whatever it was, it's gone."

"Don't say that!" she cried, leaping to her feet and leaning over him on the bed. "I made a terrible mistake. I admit it. It was wrong, and it was sinful, and I know it will be hard for you to forgive me, but I came the minute I heard how sick you were, because hearing that…that something might…happen to you—" her chin trembled and another tear leaked from the corner of her eye "—just broke my heart, and I realized what a fool I was to throw away what we had."

"What are you saying, Martha?" he asked, though he knew exactly what was coming.

"That I'm sorry for all the pain I've caused you, Will, and I'll spend the rest of my life making it up to you, if you'll just give me another chance."

After that, Will got rid of his ex-wife as quickly as possible. He'd had to resort to pretty blunt speech before she could be persuaded to leave, but leave she finally did. She'd left in tears, slamming both doors behind her as she went. Will knew the emotion behind her tears was more likely fury that things hadn't gone her way than from a contrite and broken heart. Her parting gibe had been that she wasn't done, not by a long shot.

Will would have worried about it if he hadn't been so tired from all the company. Instead of replaying the scene over and over as he usually would have done, he closed his eyes, rolled to his side and fell into a deep and dreamless sleep.

On Saturday morning, Blythe woke late. The familiar feeling of dread hung over her. She couldn't recall the last time she'd felt happy and eager to start the day. She was exhausted—mentally and physically. Despite her determination not to cry another tear, she felt the scalding moisture fill her eyes and slip down her temples into her hair. What a gigantic, colossal, stupid mess she'd made of her life! As if that weren't bad enough, she must have indeed picked up a milder version of whatever it was that had afflicted Will Slade.

Ever since her conversation with Will on Tuesday, she'd been plagued with a dull headache, sniffling, coughing and light-headedness. At her mother's insistence, Homer had allowed her to stay home from her teaching position, which, even though she was sick, at least prevented her from having to deal with any more irate mothers.

All her life she'd tried to be a dutiful and loving daughter, aunt and sibling. She was honest, trustworthy, hardworking, and tried to be the best Christian she could. What had she done to displease God? Why was He punishing her?

A feeling of guilt swept through her. She had done her best to be all the things she should, and even though she knew she often fell short, in both cases she'd made choices based on the information she'd had. God had nothing to do with it.

For the first time in a long time—maybe since the day she'd discovered Devon's perfidy—she prayed. She prayed for forgiveness of her uncharitable thoughts, her anger and her sometimes immature behavior, for guidance and the wisdom to make better choices in the future. She prayed that she could rid herself of the resentment that seemed to consume her and that she could balance her old self with the new, more authoritative Blythe Granville in a way that would make her better and stronger, not bitter. When she whispered, "Amen," she felt more calm and at peace than she had in ages.

There was no changing the past. All she could do was learn from her mistakes and make the best of her future, whatever that entailed. She pushed herself into a sitting position and looked out the lace-draped window. The Saturday morning looked sunny, springlike. What could she do with it?

After dressing, she went downstairs, where she found her mother about to start breakfast.

"Put that skillet away."

Libby turned to look at her daughter in surprise. "What?"

"Don't cook. Let's go to Ellie's for breakfast. My treat. I got paid last Friday."

"Oh, that would be nice. Should we stop by and see if Win wants to join us?"

That was all she needed to make her day go downhill in a hurry! "He's a grown man perfectly able to find food when he wants it. Besides, I'm in the mood for a mother and daughter chat." Despite her prayer, Blythe was still a bit perturbed at her brother.

Libby frowned. "Are you all right?"

"Of course," Blythe assured her with a smile. "What makes you think something's wrong?"

"Well, for starters, I can't remember the last time I saw you smile, and you've almost been a hermit since you got here. What's changed?"

"My attitude, maybe. Oh, Mama, I've been wallowing in my misery, blaming God, blaming Devon and wondering *why* it happened to me…" She shook her head. "I finally realized that the why doesn't matter. I made a bad choice. Whining and placing blame doesn't matter. What does matter is what I do next, how I handle things from here on out.

"I can't let the past make me miserable. I can take this new life that I didn't want one day at a time, and I can choose to make it pleasant or miserable. I guess it all comes down to choices. I *choose* to be happy today."

Without a word, Libby crossed the room and pulled her youngest child into her arms for a big hug. Then she cradled Blythe's face in her hands. "That's a good philosophy, sweetheart. Mature thinking."

"Thanks, Mama." Blythe's smile was a little wobbly. "Now let's go and have one of Ellie's fabulous breakfasts and see what the townsfolk say about me daring to show my face in public."

Libby laughed. "That's my girl."

As usual, Ellie's Café was filled with the clatter of silverware, the homey aromas of fresh coffee and frying meat and the hum of dozens of conversations.

When Blythe and her mother walked through the doors, no one paid much attention. So far, so good, she thought. Spying an empty table in the back near the kitchen, she wove her way through the maze of tables and chairs.

Ellie, who was just passing through the swinging doors from the kitchen, carrying two plates piled high with food, spied Blythe and offered her a smile of welcome. The simple gesture lifted her spirits. No wonder Win liked the pretty, auburn-haired café owner.

They were barely seated when the conversations began to dwindle away, one by one, as Ellie's regulars began to notice Blythe and Libby's arrival.

The semi-silence was broken when two youthful voices chorused, "Good morning, Miss Granville."

Cilla Garrett and her brother, Brady, were sitting at a nearby table having breakfast with their father, Wolf Creek's sheriff, and his new bride, Allison. Blythe wasn't sure when she'd been so happy to see her students.

She and her mother murmured hellos to the children and then Blythe dared to look at Colt and Allison to gauge their reaction. Colt had been with her brother and the others when they'd burst into Will's cabin last Sunday morning, but she didn't recall him commenting on the situation one way or the other.

There was no censure in the eyes of the newlyweds, who were both smiling. A relieved breath trickled from Blythe. She watched as Allison excused herself and made her way toward their table.

"Hello, Allison," Blythe said. "Please. Sit for a minute if you've finished your meal."

"Thank you." The former schoolteacher pulled out an extra chair and got right to the point. "How are you holding up?"

"I'm fine."

Allison nodded, accepting Blythe's answer, but the expression in her eyes said she didn't believe a word of it. "How are things going at school? More to the point, how are *my* two doing?"

Blythe thought it was wonderful that Allison now considered Colt's two children her own. She tried to smile. "Cilla and Brady are good students, but to say things have been rough is putting it mildly. At least four mothers came Monday and Tuesday and told me they're planning to talk to Homer about replacing me. I've been at home sick the latter part of the week, so I was at least spared the agony of hearing what a horrid person I am for the past few days."

Allison winked at her. "Don't worry about it. There isn't much anyone can do right now but complain. You were the answer to Homer's prayers when you came to town, and there's no one else to step in if he lets you go. He'll use Lydia to fill in, but she doesn't have the credentials she needs to teach fulltime. Colt knows Homer pretty well, and he says he'll use the 'don't judge' tactic along with the 'Will was sick, it was storming' approach." She reached out and covered Blythe's hand with hers. "I've been where you are."

"What?" Blythe cast a surprised glance at her mother, unable to believe what she was hearing.

"The night the posse brought in Meg Allen's first husband, Elton Thomerson, and his cohort, Joseph Jones, for breaking out of jail, I was taking care of Cilla and Brady. We were all sleeping when Colt came by very late to check on them. He didn't wake us, but he was so tired that he sat down on the sofa and fell asleep. When he woke up around daylight the next morning, a couple of people saw him leaving the house, started talking, and here I am. Happily married to the man."

"But you loved each other and you'd have married him anyway," Blythe pointed out.

"Well, yes, but it might have been a while down the road, and I'd have missed all this extra time with him. After my first love treated me so shabbily, I was so fed up with men, I was afraid to take a chance. That sort of forced our hand."

"Are you trying to draw some comparison between your situation and mine?" Blythe asked.

"I don't know," Allison said, shrugging. "Maybe."

"Let me assure you that William Slade is not Colt Garrett."

"Oh, I know that!" Allison said with a wink and a cheeky smile. "Colt is much handsomer."

Though they were both good-looking men, Blythe felt Allison's statement was debatable.

"I guess I'm just saying you should be open to whatever God has in store for you. Who knows? Maybe the situation with Devon brought you here for some wonderful plan you don't know about."

"I can't imagine what it might be," Blythe said, "but the sentiment is nice."

Allison laughed. "I would never have imagined that plain little me would be married to the handsome sheriff and mother to his two rotten kids."

Before Blythe could reply to that, Ellie came to the table with a blue-and-white-speckled coffeepot and two mugs. She poured coffee for the two newcomers and kissed her sister's cheek.

"It's good to see you out and about," she said to Blythe.

"Thank you."

She smiled at the Granvilles. "What will you ladies have this fine spring day?" Blythe and Libby placed their orders. "Will Win be joining you?" Ellie asked oh-so-casually.

"We didn't ask him," Libby told her with a laugh. "He'll probably be in later."

Blythe didn't imagine the soft color that stole into Ellie's cheeks. When she left to put the order in, Allison shook her head and looked from one of her table companions to the other. "My sister is absolutely crazy about Win."

"Well, from what I've observed, the feeling is mutual," Libby said drily. "The question is, what happens now?"

"I have no idea. We've all been telling her that she needs to hire a lawyer and do something about Jake so she can move on with her life. It's been more than twelve years since he skipped out on her and Bethany."

Blythe knew enough of Ellie's past to know that her husband had taken one look at their newborn daughter, seen that she was mentally disabled, and taken off. According to everyone who knew her, Ellie had never shown any interest beyond friendship toward any man until Win came to town.

"It's been almost that long since Win's fiancée was killed," Libby told Allison.

"Isn't it amazing how mixed up things can get?" she asked.

"It certainly is."

"Hello, ladies," Colt said, approaching the table.

"Hello, Sheriff."

Allison turned to smile up at him. He stopped behind her and placed his big hands on her shoulders, almost, Blythe thought, as if he couldn't bear to be near her without touching her. Colt had never cared much for society's conventions, either. If he wanted to touch his wife in public, he would.

Blythe couldn't help noticing that Allison tilted her head for just a second so that her cheek could brush his hand. A little pain of longing pierced her heart.

"I hate to disturb you, sweet thing, but the kids are getting a little restless."

"Oh, of course!" Allison said, standing as he pulled out her chair and then draped her cloak over her shoulders. She rounded the table and kissed both Libby and Blythe on the cheek. "Stop by and see me someday. I hardly know what to do with myself now that I'm not teaching."

"You're certainly not idle, sister dear," Ellie said as she approached the table carrying Blythe's and Libby's breakfasts. "She helps here almost every day in some capacity or another."

"I'm glad to do it."

When all the goodbyes were said, Blythe and her mother settled down with their meals. Gradually the conversation around them returned to normal. Somewhat surprisingly, it wasn't as bad as she'd expected it to be.

After breakfast, she and Libby walked home, where she donned an everyday skirt and shirtwaist.

"I'm going to take Banjo to see Will," she told her mother. "Rachel gave me permission to take him Wednesday afternoon, but since I was sick, it didn't happen."

"Are you sure he's still there? He might be back home by now."

Blythe smiled. "If he'd gone home, do you think he'd have left the mutt behind?"

"Good point."

Ten minutes later she was knocking on the Gentry house's front door. She was nervous about facing Will again, even though they had settled things the last time she'd seen him. Though she'd been shaking inside, she'd felt very adult telling him that she'd considered the repercussions of her actions before deciding to stay with him overnight, but deep inside, she'd feared her reputation would not recover anytime soon.

Anyway, it was settled. He'd declined to marry her; and since she had no desire to marry him, she'd told him not to worry about it. As anxious as she was about seeing him again, it felt good to know they had not let Win coerce them into doing something neither wanted. More important, she had handled the situation on her own.

It wasn't long before Rachel answered the summons

and gave her sister-in-law a hug. "Come on in," she said. "How are you feeling?"

"I still have a cough, but I'm much better."

"Good. Will was disappointed that you couldn't come on Wednesday, and then he felt guilty for passing on his sickness."

"At least I didn't have it as bad as he did," Blythe said.

"That is a blessing," Rachel agreed. "If you'll go on around back, I'll make sure he's dressed and send him out. He's really had cabin fever the past couple of days."

Blythe hardly heard. She was still trying to grasp the fact that Will had been concerned about her health.

"I knew if I let him go home, he'd go right back to work, and he doesn't need to do anything strenuous for at least another week."

Blythe couldn't imagine trying to keep the big, outdoors-loving man entertained. "I can only imagine."

Rachel looked at her with raised eyebrows. "Can you?"

Blythe laughed. "Okay, then," she said. "Let's get him outside. Banjo and I are headed to the back porch."

She stood on the edge of the porch, her arms wrapped around one of the square posts, looking out over the houses down the way, and Banjo was dozing in a patch of sunlight when Will stepped out, clad in his usual Levi's and plaid shirt.

When the dog heard him, he jumped up and fairly leaped through the air to get to his master. The dog's tail wagged so fast and furiously that his whole body shook. Will squatted down next to the big canine and began to shower him with hugs and rough petting.

The happiness Blythe saw in both Will's and the dog's demeanors made her heart glad.

Will looked up at her, the first genuine smile on his face she'd ever seen. The difference it made to his stern features was breathtaking.

"He looks great. Thank you for taking such good care of him."

"It was no trouble. I just wasn't sure you'd be happy about him following me home."

"There isn't much you could have done about it. He minds me really well, but you were just a stranger. A stranger who'd fed him." He grinned again.

Blythe felt her heart skip a little beat and gave herself a mental set-down. "He's really smart."

"He is," Will agreed.

"If he hadn't kept after me to come follow him, I probably wouldn't have found you that day in the woods."

"Then it seems I owe you both a debt of gratitude," Will said, getting to his feet. As soon as he did, Banjo trotted over to Blythe, gave her hand a lick and sat down beside her.

"It looks like I'll have to fight you for his affection."

With a grimace, Blythe wiped her hand down the side of her skirt. "I doubt that. Once the two of you are back home, everything will be just like it was before you took sick."

"Maybe. Look, Miss Granville," he said, his scowl now full-blown. "Will you take a seat, please? I'm feeling much better, but I'm still as weak as a kitten, and it would be ungentlemanly of me to sit before you do, and if that doesn't happen soon, I'm liable to fall down."

Blythe felt hot color rush to her hairline. "Oh! I'm sorry. I wasn't thinking." She dropped down into one of the rocking chairs with a decided lack of grace.

Will followed suit and heaved a sigh of relief. "Thank you again for everything you've done."

Before Blythe could think of a suitable reply, a lilting feminine voice said, "Will Slade! Just look at you!"

Both Will and Blythe looked toward the woman rounding the corner of the house. Blythe's heart sank. She knew without a doubt that the gorgeous stranger could be none other than Will's former wife.

Blythe's panicked gaze found Will's. He looked as shocked as she felt, which told her that her guess about the identity of the newcomer was right.

Martha was turned out as if she'd just stepped from a bandbox, perfection from her leather shoes to the feather concoction atop her stylishly coiffed head. She was a slender brunette clad in a fashionable blue walking dress that had not been purchased from Gentry Mercantile. Blythe watched as Martha sauntered toward the porch, an enticing smile on her shapely lips. Martha Slade, or whatever her name was now, was, in a word, stunning.

Considering that she considered style her bailiwick, Blythe was beyond mortified. She had no interest in competing with the older woman, and she certainly wasn't trying to impress anyone, but no female liked to be one-upped by another, especially when it came to fashion.

Blythe wished she'd worn something besides her simple white shirtwaist and slightly faded skirt that was also now adorned with a smear of dog slobber.

Her brown hair, which she'd twisted into a loose knot at the nape of her neck, was windblown, and she tucked a straggling strand behind her ear. She felt like bursting into tears. Again. Next to her, Banjo fixed his gaze on the newcomer and growled low in his throat. The hair down his back bristled.

Martha shot the dog a hate-filled look.

"What are you doing here?" Will asked, not bothering to hide his irritation. "I thought we'd finally settled everything yesterday."

"Now, is that any way to speak to someone who has your best interests at heart?" Martha chided, coming around the porch and spying Blythe for the first time. Martha's all-encompassing, condescending glance raked Blythe from head to toe and immediately dismissed her as no one of consequence. "And this is…?"

Blythe was about to say that she was just leaving when Will spoke up.

"This is Blythe Granville, Martha, the woman who pretty much saved my life. Miss Granville, this is my former wife, Martha Rafferty."

Blythe nodded but didn't speak.

Hearing the name Granville took the edge from Martha's overly confident smile. For once, Blythe was tickled pink to bear her family name.

"Miss Granville."

"Blythe came to let me visit with Banjo." He pinned

the other woman with a challenging look. "Since you're here, you can be the first to congratulate us. Blythe and I are getting married as soon as possible."

Chapter Seven

Blythe's shocked gaze darted to Will's. Were her ears deceiving her, or had he just announced that he was marrying the woman he'd just days ago said he wasn't? She felt as if she should say something, but nothing came to mind except the thought that she wished a hole would open up and swallow her.

"We did just agree that it would be the best thing to do, didn't we, Blythe?"

The expression on his face was neutral, but his eyes seemed to plead with her to agree. Why? What was behind this sudden change of mind and heart? Understanding dawned in a flash. Will felt it was worth marrying a stranger to be free of Martha's clutches!

Blythe thought she'd convinced herself that she didn't want to marry him, that one more scandal didn't matter, so why did meeting his former wife—his arrogant and condescending former wife—tempt her to say otherwise? Nothing had really changed except that now she'd seen firsthand just how determined and manipulative Martha Rafferty was.

The pseudo marriage proposal had come out of the blue, prompted, Blythe was certain, by Will looking for an easy way out. She wasn't sure how she felt about being used as a means to an end, but she admitted to feeling a rush of relief. It had taken every ounce of calmness and control in her being to remain steadfast in her earlier pronouncements of being fine with his refusal to marry her. A woman had her pride, after all, and she would die before resorting to begging a man to marry her. Yet now that he had made the offer, she was sorely tempted to take him up on it and solve her problems once and for all.

The thought of getting out from under Win's control held a certain appeal as well, but even though marriage would put her in good standing with the community, did she really want to marry the dour Will Slade? Would she be exchanging one bossy male for another? Was marrying a stranger to "fix" her problems—and his—worth sacrificing possible future happiness, or was there a possibility that they could grow to care for each other the way Caleb and Abby Gentry had done? Was she crazy for even considering his ridiculous proposal, if that's what it was?

What about love? What about children?

Children. She drew a shallow, shuddering breath. She might be inexperienced, but she was not so innocent that she believed a man and woman could live together for the rest of their lives without intimacy at some point. Imagining that was both frightening and a little heady. She glanced at Will and saw him regarding her with a disturbing intensity.

Then, without meaning to, she heard herself saying, "Yes, we did."

* * *

The three words were spoken so softly Will wasn't sure he'd heard it. The expression of bewilderment on her face was both comical and somehow heartbreaking.

"You can't be serious about marrying her, Will."

Martha's scathing comment forced Will's attention back to her. The look on her face wasn't pretty.

"Why not?"

"I would think that would be obvious. She's already been involved in one scandal. How can you be certain she didn't plan this…this incident with you just to snag a husband?"

Will heard Blythe suck in a sharp breath. It wasn't the first time Martha had said something inappropriate or just downright mean about someone. He'd have thought he'd have stopped being surprised long ago. He shot Blythe a quick glance and saw her lower lip tremble. Blythe Granville might be a rich, maybe even spoiled, debutante, but everything in him told him that she was not a schemer. He clenched his hands into fists.

"That's enough, Martha. I'd appreciate it if you didn't speak of my future wife in such a derogatory way, especially when you're hardly in a position to point fingers at anyone."

The sound that escaped Martha was very close to a hiss. The look in her eyes told him that if she had something she could use to inflict pain, she'd use it on him. She turned and glared at Blythe.

"Forgive me, Miss Granville," she said, though they all three knew she was nowhere near sorry. "Congratulations."

With a final furious look at Will, she pivoted on the toe of her fancy boot and flounced back the way she'd come.

For long seconds the only sounds Will heard were those of singing birds and Banjo's soft breathing. At last he dared to glance at Blythe, who looked as dazed as if she'd awakened to a new world.

"Don't pay any attention to her." The gruffness of his tone came from concern, not irritation.

Blythe turned toward him and blinked but never spoke a word. Will began to grow a bit uneasy.

"Blythe."

"Yes?" she asked, her gaze meeting his.

"You don't have to stick by it."

"What?"

"Agreeing to marry me."

She nodded and drew in a breath that seemed to bring her back to near normalcy. At least her color was better and the dazed expression in her eyes wasn't nearly so pronounced.

"Oh, that," she said as if it were of no consequence.

"Yes. That. Why did you say yes?"

Her narrow shoulders lifted in a shrug and she gave a shake of her head. "I'm not really sure. Probably the same reason you asked. Why did you change your mind? I thought we agreed to let things play out."

"I thought so, too," he said. "And then, when she showed up so sure she could sway me, it just came out."

"I'd heard she was in town and I..." Her voice faltered. "I supposed she'd come to reconcile with you."

He nodded. "She's a very clever strategist. She plans her attack and pursues her prey relentlessly."

"It would have been easier all around if you'd just told her no."

"You don't know Martha. She never did take no for an answer if she thought she had any leverage at all. She let me know her first day back that she wanted me to give her a second chance, and she's been back every day this week pretending she's concerned about me, flirting, doing all the things I remember so well."

"So after you'd already brushed me off in the kindest way possible, you used the situation to get rid of her by making yourself unavailable." Her frowning gaze met his. "Don't you think marrying one woman just to rid yourself of another is a bit drastic?"

He blew out a deep breath. Put into actual words, his actions weren't pretty. Or admirable. Even worse, it was totally self-serving. "I guess I did," he said with a reluctant nod. "I hadn't planned it. Please don't feel you need to abide by what you said."

"Are you withdrawing your proposal, if that's what it was?"

Will cocked his head and looked at her. "You almost seem afraid I am."

She gave a slight shrug and scratched Banjo behind his ear. "I'm not sure what I'm feeling."

"Yet you said yes."

"I did," she said, unwilling to tell him that she was actually somewhat relieved. "My thoughts were all tangled, and then I just heard myself agreeing. I was as surprised as you." Her eyes narrowed in irritation. "There was just something about her attitude that put me off."

Well, that was interesting. He scraped a hand through his hair. "What an unholy mess!"

"I'm sure she'll waste no time spreading it all over town. What do you suggest we do now?"

Will gave in to the inevitable. "Look," he said. "Let's think about this. At this point in my life, I seriously doubt I'll trust any woman again, much less fall in love. I get the impression you pretty much feel the same about men."

Blythe looked uncertain. "Well, I had hoped to love again, but you're correct. I had serious doubts about finding the right person in Wolf Creek."

"All right," he said, leaning toward her and resting his forearms on his knees. "So let's don't think of this as a marriage. We can think of it as a sort of…business arrangement that benefits us both."

Blythe was regarding him thoughtfully, but he saw the spark of interest in her eyes. "A business arrangement?"

"Yes. I want Martha out of my life for good and you want to escape more gossip and restore your reputation. After we marry, she'll have no choice but to go back to St. Louis and the gossipmongers will have to find someone else to talk about. It makes sense, don't you think?"

"Well, actually, I guess it does in a perverse sort of way."

"So we both go into this marriage with no preconceived notions, no pressure to live up to anyone's expectations or hurting each other's feelings, no jealousy, nothing but a peaceful coexistence," he said, realizing he was spouting Win's earlier argument.

"That sounds like a…practical way to approach things," she agreed. "But…"

"But what?"

"What about…children?" she asked, glancing at him from beneath her lashes. "There can be no children if we have strictly a business arrangement. I would like them someday. Don't you?"

Will felt as if he'd been hit by a two-by-four. He hadn't expected this. What an idiot! He'd been so busy laying out his plan that he hadn't given a single thought to the most basic of human needs. He did now and knew without a doubt there was no way he could remain abstinent the rest of his life. Having children with Blythe Granville and everything it would entail took his breath.

"I would, yes," he said, aware that his voice was huskier than usual, even with his illness. When her gaze flew to his, he hurried to say, "Not anytime soon, of course."

"Oh, no! I agree. We'll need, um, time."

"Yes." Will thought he was bumbling around like a callow schoolboy, but despite her brief marriage, which he assumed had been real in every way but legally, Blythe was the picture of inexperience and innocence. He was eight years older than she. Innocence was something he'd left behind long ago.

She nodded and stared at the hands that were clasped in her lap.

"So are we agreed? We're doing this?"

"Yes," she said. "We're agreed."

To prove his intent, Will held out his hand to shake on the agreement, just as he would with any other business deal. After all, the handshake of honorable men was as binding as a legal document. To his surprise, Blythe stood, her own hand extended.

He wasn't prepared for the little tingle of awareness that sizzled through him at the feel of her small, warm hand in his. Their gazes clung. "One more thing," he told her without releasing his hold.

"Yes?"

"Regardless of what we've done or been or what's happened in the past to bring us to this point, I've always believed that marriage is forever. Once we say 'I do,' there's no going back. Whatever happens, we talk it out, work through it."

Even as he said the words he heartily believed, he wondered if he could stick to them. What if she was another Martha, a snooty, snotty, spoiled rich girl who expected him to wait on her hand and foot and give her whatever her heart desired? He suppressed a shudder. Well, whatever the future held, he'd just have to keep his end of the deal. They'd already shaken hands.

Seeing that Will was getting tired, Blythe and Banjo left Rachel's, crossing the railroad tracks at Third Street. Well, she'd solved the problem of regaining her respectability, but what had she gotten herself into? How was it possible that she and Will had entered into a business arrangement they'd both adamantly refused to consider less than a week ago?

Strangely, instead of trying to figure out why she'd agreed to the preposterous arrangement, her mind turned to memories of the day last December when she'd first returned to Wolf Creek with Win. A stranger had confronted her the instant she disembarked from the train, introducing himself as Turner

Davis, a reporter from Boston. She'd later learned that when the *Globe* had gotten wind that she would be going to Wolf Creek to start over, the newspaper had sent him ahead to make sure he didn't miss her when she arrived. Exhausted and embarrassed, she'd had no desire to talk to him or anyone else about the situation with Devon.

"Go back to Boston and leave me alone," she told him. When she turned to walk away, Davis's hand closed around her upper arm. Shocked by the action and more than a little uneasy, she tried to pull free, but his fingers dug into her flesh so cruelly that she had bruises the next day.

"Unhand me this minute, sir!" she commanded, adopting the tone her mother used when she was angry with someone. It was a tone that often made grown men tremble. Not this one.

"I just want to ask you a few questions," he wheedled, gripping her arm tighter.

"I have nothing to say to you."

"Aw, come on, sweetie. How about I buy you some lunch at that café down the street and we'll have a nice chat about your plans for the future?" The invitation was offered along with a fawning smile.

"I believe the lady asked you to let her go."

The statement, delivered in a tone that resembled a deep growl, gave the reporter pause.

Looking up, she saw that Will Slade had approached and was standing just behind her tormentor. His brows were drawn into a frown and his hands were curled into loose fists at his sides. Though she didn't actually know him, Ellie had pointed him out one morning when he and her brother were talking business at the café.

Like everyone else in town, she'd heard the rumors about him and had no feelings one way or the other about him or his situation. Being the subject on everyone's conversation herself lately, she imagined that he'd gone through much of what she had, since the loathsome correspondent in front of her appeared determined to make her life miserable. She was glad Will Slade had been close enough to overhear the whole confrontation and intervene.

"I believe this conversation is between me and the woman," the journalist said, flicking a dismissive glance over his shoulder at Will.

About the time Davis seemed to realize that the other man was big enough to break him in two, Will reached out, grabbed the reporter's hand and forcibly pried away the fingers wrapped around Blythe's arm.

"The *lady*," he said, emphasizing the term after hearing the disdain in the other man's voice, "asked you to leave her alone."

Blythe rubbed at her arm; Slade's fingers tightened around the other man's hand.

"I believe she also told you she had nothing to say to you."

"But she's news!" Davis cried, wincing and trying to wrench free. "I've come all the way from Boston to see what she does next."

"I don't care if she's good news, old news or bad news back in Boston, mister, or what she does next. She's in Wolf Creek now, and we don't hassle women here. If a lady tells you she doesn't want to talk to you, you go away. Got that?"

Blythe saw Slade's hand tighten a bit more before he released his hold on Davis. She almost smiled when she saw him massaging his bruised fingers.

"Now," Will said, giving a negligent flick of his fingers toward the hotel and boardinghouse, "I suggest you go check yourself into Hattie's and have a nice breakfast somewhere. If you're smart, and I really think that's debatable, you'll get on the first train headed back east and find yourself some other news."

"It's a free country," Davis snapped.

"It is that," Will agreed with a slight shrug. "And the choice is yours."

"And what do you plan to do if I don't do as you say?" Davis challenged.

A cold smile lifted one corner of Will Slade's mouth. "Like I said, it's your choice."

The newspaperman looked into Will's hard face for a moment longer. Then, straightening his tie and smoothing the front of his suit coat, Turner Davis threw back his shoulders and started down the street as if the whole incident had never happened.

"Thank you, Mr. Slade," Blythe said when the other man was out of earshot. "I appreciate your help."

Will Slade had turned toward her. There had not been one iota of emotion in his dark eyes; they'd looked as empty as her heart felt.

"It was nothing," he'd told her, and without a word, he'd turned and walked away.

Looking back at the brief exchange now, there was no way she could say he had treated her kindly, but he had not been harsh, either. He had at least championed her to the obnoxious reporter.

Recalling that day, she wondered if her memory

of that incident had somehow influenced her spur-of-the-moment decision to agree to marry him. All she knew was that she had to tell her family what was going on. It wasn't a conversation that she was eager to have.

Later that evening, Blythe waited until they were all seated at the supper table before she broke the news of her upcoming marriage. Win was passing her the peas when she pasted what she hoped was a reasonable replica of a smile on her face and said, "I spoke with Will Slade this afternoon and we've agreed to get married, after all."

"What?" Libby exclaimed. Under other circumstances the expression on her face would have been comical.

Win threw his hands into the air and said, "Hallelujah!"

Blythe wanted to reach over and give her brother a shake. She'd known he would be pleased, but she hadn't expected him to be quite so elated to be rid of her. She glanced at her mother, but Libby's surprised expression had become more thoughtful.

Win lifted his coffee cup. "How did you get him to change his mind?"

"More to the point, why did you change *your* mind?" Libby queried.

Blythe put a spoonful of the green peas on her plate, passed the china bowl to Libby and looked from her to Win. "Initially we'd decided against it, but I took Banjo to see him this afternoon, and his previous wife showed up. She said something rather unkind to me, and the next thing I knew, Will was telling her that she could be the first one to congratulate us, that we'd decided to marry, after all."

Her face wore a puzzled expression and she lifted her shoulders in a slight shrug. "I was so shocked I could barely think, much less speak, but the next thing I knew, I heard myself saying *yes*."

Her mother was momentarily speechless. Blythe was about to offer an explanation when Win intervened. "I'd heard the wife was back in town," he told them. "Colt says she got off the train the first of the week and set out to talk Slade into taking her back."

"It's true," Blythe said. "He told me she's been by every day trying to get him to change his mind. It seems she's tried everything from sweet talk to pleading and even seduction to convince him, but he's told her he isn't interested. She really is an odious woman."

"Oh, Blythe!" Libby lamented. "This is *not* a good situation."

"What's not a good situation?" Win asked, forking up a bite of potatoes.

"This marriage you insisted on!" Libby exclaimed, pointing an accusing finger at him. "You've succeeded in getting what you wanted, but your poor sister is condemning herself to life with a man who only wants to marry her to get rid of his previous spouse."

Her troubled gaze returned to Blythe. "You do understand that's why he suggested it, don't you?"

"Of course I do, Mother," she said a bit sharply, switching from the affectionate "Mama" to "Mother," something she did when she was upset with Libby. "I may be naïve, but I'm not stupid."

"Indeed," Libby said. "Personally I don't think it's

very smart for you to agree to marry a man because you find his first wife disagreeable. That's no way to start a lifelong relationship."

"I understand your concern, but Will and I had a long talk about it."

Libby leaned forward, resting her elbows on the edge of the table and her chin in her hands. "I can't wait to hear this."

"I haven't explained things very well, have I?" Blythe said. "In a nutshell, Will and I are looking at the whole thing as more of a business arrangement that has mutual benefits than a conventional marriage."

"Heaven help us! Why on earth would you agree to something like that?" Libby asked.

"It's pretty basic, really," Blythe said. "And in a strange way, it makes sense. We've both been hurt so badly we don't think we'll fall in love again. He wants Martha out of his life for good and I need to find some sort of respectability, some way to fix the hash I've made of my life."

"Those are dreadful reasons to go into a marriage," Libby said.

"It isn't," Blythe insisted, though in her heart she agreed. Still, she was about to convince herself that marriage to a stranger was far preferable to life as a social pariah. "It makes a lot of sense, really. And just to ease your mind, we've decided that the marriage will last no matter what comes along, and we'd both like to have a child someday." She drew in a deep breath and let it out. "I'm not sure when that might happen."

"Oh, Blythe! You're *settling*." There were tears in Libby's eyes.

Settling. It was something she and her mother had talked about often and was one reason Blythe had waited so long to marry. Libby had told her time and again not to agree to a lifetime with someone unless that man sent her heart to racing by just walking into a room. Not to say "I do" unless his smile made her toes curl.

"Perhaps I am, Mama, but I tried the love thing with Devon and that was a total travesty. I believed he was everything I'd waited for. I thought I loved him, even though there were things about him that troubled me from the beginning."

"Like what?" Libby asked.

"Like the fact that I knew he wasn't a Christian, something you told me to consider carefully before I decided on a husband. That should have been my first indication that he was wrong for me.

"The second hint that I should have sent him packing was when he told me he didn't want me to start my own business He thought I should stay at home and just be his wife. I wanted to please him, so I gave up on my dream of opening the boutique."

She gave a deep sigh. "I had such vivid images of us as the perfect couple. We would have a lovely home, beautiful children and live happily-ever-after, just like the princes and princesses in the fairy tales you used to read to me."

Libby smiled sorrowfully and gave a slight shake of her head. "Love can cause us all to make bad choices. You can't blame yourself for loving someone. If you made any mistake, it was rushing into the marriage. Then again, a lot of us fall for the idea of love. I suspect that's what happened with you and Devon."

Blythe knew her mother was referring to her first disastrous marriage to Lucas Gentry, Caleb and Gabe's father. "Maybe so, but I did fancy myself in love, and I was lonely and on the shelf and the last in my circle of friends to find a husband."

Her defeated look encompassed both her mother and brother. "I thought I was marrying Devon for all the right reasons, and look what happened."

She forced bravado into her voice. "This agreement between me and Will should be a much better situation. We neither have any expectations, so there shouldn't be any pressure. We'll just live together peaceably without all the ups and downs that come with loving someone, and everything should be just fine," she said.

Libby cast an exasperated look at her son, who had barely said a word since Blythe had launched into her tale. "Win, say something!"

Win actually looked a little pale. He speared a bite of the pork chop with his fork, dragged it through the gravy and finally looked up to meet his mother's gaze. "What can I say? It seems they've made their choice."

After dinner, Win lost no time excusing himself and heading to Rachel's. He felt like a miserable worm for pressuring his sister and Slade to marry. He wasn't God; he now realized how things worked out wasn't up to him. As he'd sat at the dinner table, listening to Blythe relate the pact she and Slade had made, Win had felt sick to his stomach.

She'd been so...*resigned.* As if her upcoming nuptials were the best she could ever expect from life. That was at least partly his fault. He should have been more compassionate, less judgmental, but he'd been so worried about what people were thinking and what they might be saying about the Granvilles that he'd pushed her too hard.

Now she was committed to a relationship that didn't look very promising, to say the least. As Big Dan Mercer, Colt's deputy, would say, Win felt lower than a snake's belly.

The simple truth was that things often happened that were beyond one's control. Blythe's situation was not her fault. Because she was the baby of the family everyone had shielded her to some extent, but both times she'd found herself in hot water it was because she'd followed her heart. Her very tender heart. Once for love, the second for decency and humanity.

It wasn't her fault Devon Carmichael was a schemer and a bigamist. It wasn't her fault a storm had come up while she was tending Will Slade, or that people were quick to judge without looking at all the circumstances, or that society had such rigid rules of conduct.

He let himself in the back door of Rachel's surgery and went directly to Will's room. The lumberman looked much better this evening and was actually sitting in a chair while he ate his supper from a small drop-leaf table.

Will looked up when Win entered, a wary expression in his eyes. "I assume Blythe told you our news."

"She did."

"So I guess you're happy now."

"I'll be happy if my sister is."

"Happy wasn't part of the deal," Slade said. "You wanted me to give her my name and make an honest woman of her. I'm doing that."

"Blast it all, Slade! She's my sister! Using her to get your ex-wife out of your life is pretty low." Win, who never lost control, was almost yelling. "She's a wonderful woman. She deserves happiness and love."

"You need to make up your mind what you want, Granville. Blythe knows what she's getting into. She's fine with it, and by the way, we're both using each other to get what we want. What we need."

Win stood in the doorway with his hands on his hips, breathing heavily. Slade was right. He did need to make up his mind what he wanted. About a lot of things.

He pinned Will with a hard look. "Be good to her."

"I'll take care of her. By the way, the wedding is tomorrow afternoon. Two o'clock. At Hattie's."

Win spun on his heel. "So soon?"

"There's no use waiting."

Slade was right. There was little more Win could say. With the results of his interference staring him in the face, he was reminded of something Libby always said: be careful what you wish for; you just might get it.

When Win left, Will threw his napkin on top of his plate of half-finished food. Once again he'd let his dislike for Win Granville color his exchange about the agreement with Blythe. Instead of trying to make peace, he'd been his usual pigheaded self. That needed to change, but he and Granville were both stubborn cusses, and that didn't bode well for the future.

He wondered what a future with Blythe would hold. He suspected she was nothing like Martha, thank goodness. What was she like? Was she the timid girl who refused to meet his eye and chewed on her lower lip when she was troubled, or was she the spunky woman who'd stood up for her actions and given him what for when he'd asked why she hadn't gone to town for help instead of staying with him at the house? Was she the fancy city girl who'd gotten off the train in December, or the woman who'd taken it upon herself to care for his dog while he was sick?

Most important, was there any chance for them to find happiness in a marriage starting with everything against it?

Time would tell.

And despite everything, his bruised heart leaped at the possibility.

Chapter Eight

Blythe's wedding morning dawned sunshiny and warm, something she'd always wanted for her special day, and from the look of things, the only one of her dreams that was ever likely to come true. Her marriage to Devon had not only been a hurried event but a secretive one. They had said their vows before a justice of the peace in a shabby office building, wearing their traveling clothes.

She'd had no music, no flowers, no reception where family and friends dined on fancy fare and wished the newlyweds a happy life. Instead they had gone straight to a hotel. He had taken her to dinner that night, but that was all the celebrating there'd been.

As she and her mother headed to Hattie's, Blythe couldn't rid herself of how beautiful Allison and Colt's wedding had been. The ceremony had taken place in the church and the reception had been held at Libby's. Allison had looked stunning in the creamy winter-white gown Blythe had designed for her. Everything had been perfect. The pair had held on to each other's hands, their love reflected in their eyes as their gazes clung throughout the ceremony.

Blythe would have none of that. Not even the special gown she'd been designing for the past year. She would wear the gray silk she'd worn to the Garrett wedding. She and Will would not look at each other the way Allison and Colt had. There would be nothing to remember this day by except that she'd made a bargain with a stranger in order to salvage what remained of her reputation.

When she and her mother walked into the parlor at Hattie's an hour before the ceremony was to begin, Blythe paused in the doorway, forced to rethink her feelings. Though there hadn't been much time to do anything fancy, what the ladies of Wolf Creek had managed to put together in such a short time was amazing.

She let her gaze drift around the room. Ferns, probably borrowed from every lady in town, stood on pedestals with marble tops. Tapers sat in silver, crystal and pressed-glass candleholders atop the piano and on the mantel. Chairs had been brought in from the dining room for extra seating, which was routinely done on the days Hattie's piano students held their recitals. Though it was too early for most flowers to bloom, someone had found some brave daffodils and mixed them with French mulberry and English ivy.

The dining room table was covered with an ecru crocheted cloth and held a delicious-looking array of cookies someone had baked. Slices of coconut pie with mile-high meringue, probably from Ellie, sat on floral china saucers. A magnificent silver coffee service that Blythe recognized as her mother's resided at one end of the table for easy access.

As she stood taking in all the details, she felt tears stinging her eyes. She glanced at her mother and saw that Libby's eyes were moist, too.

"This town has some wonderful people."

Blythe nodded, unable to speak.

"Oh! You're here!"

Hattie Carson, the owner of the boardinghouse, stepped through the swinging door that led to the kitchen, drying her hands on a dish towel.

"Everything looks wonderful, Hattie," Libby told her. "I can't thank you enough for letting us hold the ceremony here on such short notice."

"That's not a problem, Mrs. Granville," Hattie assured her, giving her a pat on the arm. "It is my business, after all." She turned and let her gaze roam the large parlor. "It does look nice, doesn't it? The ladies always manage to make even the smallest event special."

She turned to Blythe and gave her shoulder a pat. "You look a bit anxious, my dear, but you don't need to worry that pretty little head of yours. Everything's taken care of but a couple of small details."

Blythe sighed in relief knowing that she didn't have to worry about anything but showing up, but the truth was, it wasn't the wedding arrangements that had her a "bit anxious." It was the knowledge that in an hour's time she would be the wife of a man she barely knew, one she didn't think liked her very much. She would be expected to leave with him and, according to their pact, spend the rest of her life with him, no matter what. It was a terrifying notion.

She gave Hattie a weak smile. "Thank you, Mrs. Carson."

"The arrangements are very simple. I'll play the 'Wedding March' while you come down the stairs and Brother McAdams will do the ceremony. Colt will be Will's best man. He didn't know who would be giving you away. Do you have someone?"

"Yes," Blythe said. "Edward Stone."

"I couldn't have chosen better myself. Cilla Garrett has volunteered to play a few pieces while the guests are having their refreshments after the ceremony, if that's all right with you," Hattie said, directing the statement to Blythe.

"Oh, that's lovely," Blythe said, touched by Cilla's gesture. "It's sweet of her to offer."

"She said she wanted to pay you back for designing that pretty dress last summer."

"I was happy to do it."

"I know you were, dear, and let me tell you... that young lady has come a long way in a few short months. I've never seen such changes in a person before, and I've never had a student who took to the pianoforte the way she has."

Hattie tossed the towel over one shoulder. "Come with me," she said, gesturing at the two women. "I'll show you where you can change. Allison sent Brady to let me know she'd be here in just a bit to do your hair. By the way, Bess, Will's mother, couldn't make it. There wasn't enough time to make arrangements."

"That's too bad," Libby said. Secretly, Blythe was glad to put off meeting her new mother-in-law. She'd found out from Rachel that Will's father had died years before.

They followed Hattie through the foyer and up the curving staircase. The older woman opened a door on the right-hand side of the wide hallway and preceded them into a bedroom decorated in sunny yellow, creamy white and the palest of greens. Blythe thought it might be the happiest room she'd ever seen.

"Will sent word he'd be here by one thirty." The smile that crinkled Hattie's wrinkled face and twinkled in her eyes was as unexpected as it was sweet. "Said it would probably take him that long to scrape off his whiskers after not shaving for so long."

Recalling his untidy, rather rakish look, Blythe didn't doubt it. Her mental image of her husband-to-be made her head throb in sudden anxiety. Will was the exact opposite of Devon in every way, from physical attributes to mannerisms and speech. Will was all forceful, powerful male who didn't take any nonsense from anyone. He certainly wouldn't take any from her.

Another rush of panic swept through her. What on earth was she doing? Was there any way to get out of it without causing another scandal? The room began to spin and she pressed her fingertips to her temples.

"Oh, dear!" Hattie said. "Grab her arm, Mrs. Granville. She looks a little faint."

"Blythe! Blythe, sweetheart, are you all right?"

Blythe felt her two companions take her arms and guide her toward a small slipper chair sitting next to the fireplace. She sank into it and someone pushed her head down. Why? Oh, yes, she'd heard that helped restore blood flow to the brain or something.

"Take deep breaths, my dear," Hattie commanded. "You're going to be fine. This happens every now and again. It's just a bad case of megrims. The whole notion of marriage can be overpowering when two people are in love, much less when they're marrying for reasons of convenience the way you and Will are."

Good grief! Though her intentions were nothing but the best, Blythe couldn't believe that Hattie dared to put into words what everyone in town must be saying. It was *so* humiliating!

After a few moments the light-headedness passed and, with a last cleansing breath, Blythe sat up straight and rested her head against the back of the chair.

"Are you all right?"

When Blythe opened her eyes and saw her mother's concerned face near hers, she felt like crying. She'd never intended to cause her mother any worry. She'd never intended for any of this to happen. She gave a slow nod. "I think so."

"Here, my dear," Hattie said, holding out a clean, damp cloth. "Put this on your forehead. It will help."

"Thank you."

Blythe placed the cool cloth on her forehead and tried to will the hundred and one thoughts churning inside it to go away. She was committed to this marriage, wasn't she?

"You don't have to go through with it, Blythe," her mother said, even though Hattie was still in the room. "You know we'll stand behind you if you change your mind."

Blythe met her mother's troubled eyes. "I know you will, but I promised."

"People will understand. Even Will."

"I know it's none of my business," Hattie said, "but since I'm here listening to everything you say,

I'd like to tell you that even though you're worried, you don't have to be about Will." She smiled. "You probably don't know it, but he's my nephew. Bess and I are sisters."

Blythe wasn't the least surprised. No wonder Will had been able to talk Hattie into holding the ceremony here on such short notice.

"He was brought up right, but you know how young people are sometimes. They go off the rails once in a while and you can't talk a lick of sense into them."

Hattie might have been speaking about her, Blythe thought. "I'm guilty of that myself, Mrs. Carson," she said, knowing in her heart that no one could have said a word about Devon to make her believe he was anything but what he'd presented himself to be.

"At least you admit it. Eventually most see the error of their ways, and I truly believe Will has. Basically, he's a good, hardworking man, and he was hurt something awful by that wicked Martha. It's no wonder he took to drink for a while or that he's so distrustful of women. Not that I condone his actions, you understand."

"Of course I do," Blythe assured her.

Hattie blushed to the roots of her graying brown hair. "Like I said, it's none of my business, but if you ask me, the two of you have a good chance of making this marriage work. I see kindness and gentleness in you, and that's what he needs, and I see a lot of strength in him, and that's what you need. Someone to stand up for you. Take care of you. My advice is to be kind to each other, and see what happens. You both might be surprised."

* * *

The tall, broad-shouldered reflection staring back at Will from the cheval mirror in his aunt Hattie's downstairs bedroom showed a man divided. On the outside, he looked well-dressed. Some might even say he looked refined in his dark suit, carefully tied cravat and polished Sunday shoes. But anyone who looked closer would note the tightness around his mouth and the tenseness in his eyes.

His heart was racing and his palms were sweating. His legs felt as if they might buckle at any minute. He would rather be in the woods facing a nest of copperheads than the woman who would walk down the stairs in mere moments.

Once again, Martha had put him in a tight spot and, once again, he'd done something foolish. Marriage. Again. To a woman he barely knew. A woman whose brother wanted to put him out of business. What had he been thinking when he'd spouted off the comment about him and Blythe deciding to get married? *Had* he been thinking? He'd lost his mind, that's what he'd done. There was no other explanation.

He scrubbed a hand down his clean-shaved face. Martha's constant excuses for her behavior and persistent entreaties of forgiveness were like water drip-drip-dripping on a stone. At least this time he hadn't turned to the bottle. That was good, wasn't it?

Will began to pace the bedroom. Since his proposal, or whatever it had been, the previous day, he'd had several people tell him that despite the circumstances, he was getting a good woman. Allison had raved about how Blythe's dress-designing talent had helped her catch Colt's eye, and how Blythe had unselfishly volunteered to make the gown for her wedding on New Year's Eve.

He'd heard what a wonderful teacher she was, even though that wasn't her calling. He'd heard she was a good aunt to the Gentry children; she had a kind and tender heart, was a good Christian, daughter and sister.

If she was everything they claimed, all he could think was that she deserved someone better than he was. After all, she came from wealth and was destined for bigger and better things than marriage to a small-town sawmill owner. But thanks to that kind heart they said she had and the fury of Mother Nature, she would be stuck in a little house in the woods with no way to pursue her dreams, tied to a man who could give her little but a roof over her head and food to eat. He felt a sudden desire to march up the stairs and tell her that maybe they should think this through...

A knock sounded at the door and, without waiting for an answer, Colt stepped inside, a slight smile on his face. He'd been smiling a lot since he'd married Allison. "It's almost time. Are you ready?"

"No."

Colt's smile vanished. "What do you mean, no?"

"What do you think would happen if I backed out?"

Colt's hands curled into loose fists. "If you're serious, and I hope you aren't, I think that poor woman upstairs would crawl in a hole and never come out, and I think you'd qualify as the biggest good-for-nothing coward in Arkansas and that it would give me the greatest pleasure to knock you into next week."

Will actually flinched. "Ouch! You don't mince words, do you?"

"That's what friends do." Colt wasn't smiling. He walked over and put a hand on Will's shoulder. "Look, I know this is a really rotten situation, but here is where we are, and I truly believe that if you let this girl down, you'll be the one who loses standing in the community, not her."

"I know, I know," Will said, nodding. "It's just... scary, you know? Really scary. Evidently, I didn't do too well in the husband category before and it worries me to think I might let another woman down."

"Whoa! Whoa, Hoss!" Colt said, frowning. His grip tightened. "No one is perfect, and don't forget that Martha's the one who went looking for greener pastures. That had nothing to do with you and everything to do with her never-ending need for money and things and moving up in the world."

"What if I'm stepping out of the frying pan into the fire? I imagine Blythe Granville is used to having whatever her little heart desires."

"You're worried about Blythe doing what Martha did?" Colt actually laughed. "Set your mind to rest. I can assure you she's nothing like Martha, money or not."

Before Will could respond to that, someone knocked on the door and said, "It's time."

Will closed his eyes and murmured something that might have been a prayer...if he still remembered how to pray.

From where Will stood in the parlor, he could see his bride-to-be as she descended the last few steps of Hattie's wide staircase. He felt as if he were in suspended time or something. Aunt Hattie was playing the traditional wedding song, which was nothing but a backdrop for his thoughts. Though the room was filled with people, all he saw was the woman who would soon be his wife, the woman he would promise to love and honor and care for. How could he do those things when he hardly knew her?

He swallowed hard, realizing for the first time the importance of the words they were about to speak and what a truly monumental task lay ahead of him— ahead of both of them—if they made good on their promises to never dissolve the marriage. He drew in a deep breath and blew it out. He forced the troubling thoughts away and concentrated on the woman who would soon be his wife.

He watched as she took another step. Instead of a conventional wedding gown, she wore a dove-gray dress of some shimmery fabric that hugged the gentle swells and curves of her upper body and flared out gently from her slender waist. A deep vee edged with black-velvet ribbon and inlaid with delicate gray lace adorned the front and a black-velvet stand-up collar circled her neck. A pearl-and-silver brooch was pinned to the center. The long sleeves clung to her arms and ended with black-velvet cuffs closed with pearl buttons. More velvet edged the bottom of the simply styled dress. Black shoes peeked from beneath the hem.

Will's gaze moved from her toes back to her face. He sucked in a sharp breath. Why had he never noticed how pretty she was? Her mouth was perfectly shaped and her nose was what he'd always thought of as patrician. Dark eyebrows framed large brown eyes. She looked a lot like her mother, Will thought before he continued his examination.

Her dark hair was swept up into a loose knot atop her head. Pearl-and-ivory combs were her only adornment. A few unruly tendrils curled around her pale face. Her eyes were downcast, as if to make certain she didn't miss a step and take a tumble.

When she reached the bottom of the staircase where Edward Stone stood, she looked up at him. The man standing in for her father wore a charcoal-gray suit and was smiling as proudly as if he were giving away his own daughter.

She tried to smile back, but, even from where he stood, Will could tell it was an effort. Edward was using both his canes, so instead of crooking his arm for her to take, she looped her hand around his elbow and they proceeded toward the parlor. Once again, her gaze seemed glued to the floor. She hadn't once looked Will's way.

When she and Edward reached the spot where he, Colt and Brother McAdams waited, Hattie stopped playing and the preacher began the ceremony. Will hardly heard, he was too busy staring at Blythe, who looked scared to death.

"Who gives this woman in marriage?" the preacher asked.

"Her mother and I," Edward said, speaking the words Sam Granville would have, had he still been living. Leaning a cane against his body, he took Blythe's hand and placed it in Will's. Then Edward kissed her on the forehead and took a seat.

Her hand was ice-cold. Will's first instinct was to

chafe it between both of his, but instead he gave her fingers a squeeze. *That* sent her eyelashes flying upward. Even though just moments ago he'd wanted to call off the whole thing, the anxiety in her eyes left him feeling shamed. Shamed and strangely protective.

Yes, she was timid, but she had stamina and grit, or she couldn't have gotten him into the house. He couldn't imagine Martha having the forethought to do what Blythe had done. And timid or not, she was no shrinking violet. In his experience, most women were scared to death to speak their minds, but he'd seen her anger flare up when she'd come right back at him for being ungrateful for what she'd done for him. His wife-to-be was a walking contradiction.

"Do you, William Michael Slade, take Blythe Isabelle Granville to be your lawful wedded wife?"

The sound of the preacher's voice jerked Will's attention back to the present. Blythe was actually looking at him. Maybe she was trying to see something in his eyes that would give her encouragement. He was proud that his voice was strong and steady. "I do."

The remainder of the ceremony was pretty much a blur. A part of him was aware of them both repeating vows. He slipped a ring on her slender finger, something he'd run by Gabe's store and picked up on the way to the ceremony. It was nothing special, just a plain gold band. With a surge of guilt, he thought that someone like Blythe, accustomed to the best and finest life had to offer, probably expected precious stones of some sort, but it wasn't as if there was a lot to choose from at Gentry Mercantile. Will was just thankful that Gabe had had any kind of ring.

"I now pronounce you man and wife," the preacher

intoned, a note of satisfaction in his voice. "You may kiss the bride."

Will's sharp gaze snapped to the minister's. He was smiling, and why not? He'd had his way. Blythe's reputation had been reclaimed and Will, known scoundrel that he was, had been brought to heel, but surely the minister knew the statement would cause them both considerable embarrassment. Under the circumstances, couldn't he have omitted the traditional bride-and-groom kiss?

Will glanced at Blythe and saw her watching him with a wary expression. Deciding that the best option would be to just get it over with, he lowered his head and kissed her. He intended it to be a swift, impersonal brush of his mouth against hers, but the feel of her lips, warm and soft and pliable beneath his, sent such a tremor of awareness through him that the kiss lasted a second longer than he intended.

Feeling a bit disoriented, he lifted his head and looked at her again, trying to gauge her reaction. If possible, her creamy complexion held even less color and the expression in her eyes was as dazed as he felt.

Before he had time to think what it all meant, the preacher introduced them to the gathering as man and wife. In a matter of seconds he was surrounded by well-wishers who gave him slaps on the back, handshakes of congratulations and those awkward hugs men sometimes gave each other.

Blythe, too, was being hugged and kissed and smothered with well wishes. He noticed that even though she was responding to the goodwill, her smile was forced. He saw her lift a hand to her forehead.

"Please, everyone," Aunt Hattie said, "feel free to

enjoy the refreshments while Miss Priscilla Garrett entertains us with some of her lovely piano playing."

He might have been born in a country town, but his mama had taught him about courtesy. He was about to ask his bride if she would like a cup of punch when he felt a hand on his shoulder and turned to see Win Granville standing next to him.

"Thank you for stepping up, Slade," Blythe's brother said. "I was a bit concerned about your motivation, but she seems to find the crazy arrangement acceptable, so there's nothing for me to say."

"No, there isn't." Will said.

"Win, you aren't already harassing your new brother-in-law, are you?" Libby Granville said, a mock scowl on her attractive face. Without giving her son a chance to reply, she smiled at Will. "I'd give you a hug, but I don't know if you're a hugger or not," she said, extending her hand. "Welcome to the family, Will. It will be wonderful having another son."

As Will took her hand and attempted to return her smile, he couldn't help thinking that she was being much friendlier than he expected her to be. He also realized that Libby was a perfect picture of what Blythe would look like in twenty or thirty years.

Blythe. He caught sight of her from the corner of his eye. She was surrounded by her friends: Abby and Rachel Gentry, Allison Garrett, Ellie Carpenter, Meg Allen, Grace Mercer and Lydia North. Someone said something and everyone started laughing. He saw Blythe once again reach up to massage her right temple. Saw her eyelids flutter. Saw her sway... The next thing he knew she'd crumpled slowly to the floor.

Chapter Nine

Will felt as if the floor fell out from beneath him. Gasps of surprise swept through the room. Without thinking, without stopping to ask himself why, he pushed Win Granville aside and rushed to the group of women who were standing around Blythe's motionless body, varying degrees of shock on their faces. Rachel knelt beside her, her fingertips pressed against Blythe's wrist, checking her pulse. Will went down on one knee.

"Is she all right?"

Rachel smiled. "She just fainted."

"Fainted?"

"Yes. It happens sometimes when someone is in a state of constant worry or overstimulation. Not to mention that she's been sick this week." She smiled at him. "I'd say she's had her share of concerns the past few months, wouldn't you?"

For the first time Will fully understood how much Blythe had suffered since learning she'd been duped and discarded by the man she loved and then snubbed a second time simply for helping him.

"Here's the smelling salts," Hattie said, passing the jar to Rachel.

Rachel unscrewed the lid and passed the pungent stimulant in front of Blythe's face. She gasped and her eyes fluttered open.

"Thank goodness!" Libby said. Will saw the concern in her eyes. Though she'd been kind to him, he wondered what she really thought of her daughter's latest circumstances. And him.

"I want to get her outside into the fresh air," Rachel said, holding out a hand for Will to help her to her feet. Still holding on to him, she said, "We'll let her rest a bit and then you can take her home."

Take her home. His home. Their home. The thought that he wouldn't be returning to his place alone was hard to believe. He'd gotten used to being by himself, of not having to answer to anyone, and coming and going as he pleased. All that would change now. He had a wife.

"I'll take her for you," Win said, stepping between Will and Rachel.

That snapped Will out of his stupor. He reached out and gripped his new brother-in-law's shoulder. "I'll get her. She's my wife."

Granville stared into Will's eyes for long seconds. Weighing each other. Gauging. The room was so quiet you could hear the proverbial pin drop. Finally her brother gave a sharp nod of his head and stepped away.

Will bent and scooped Blythe into his arms. Hers automatically went around his neck and her head lolled against his shoulder. He doubted she weighed as much as Banjo. The scent of something sweet and floral drifted up from her shiny brown hair. If he turned his head the slightest bit, his lips would be touching her forehead...

His steps actually faltered. Where had that come from? he wondered as he carried her to the front porch. He knew exactly where it came from. Despite the fact that she was the kind of woman he'd vowed to stay away from *and* Win Granville's sister to boot, she was still a woman. A very warm and feminine woman, and, truth be told, he was as susceptible to her charms as any man.

Ruthlessly ridding his mind of the dangerous thoughts, he deposited Blythe on the swing and stepped back to make room for Rachel, who sat down next to her. Blythe's eyes were closed and her head leaned to the side, resting against the chain. Banjo sat near the steps, the eager thumping of his tail saying without words that he was happy to see familiar people, even if they weren't paying any attention to him.

"Will, will you fetch my bag? I need my stethoscope."

"Sure," he said. With a last look at Blythe, he went to do Rachel's bidding.

As soon as he left, Rachel took Blythe's wrist once more and glanced at the watch hanging around her neck to check her pulse. Blythe was glad Will was gone. His size and physical presence was intimidating, and the intensity radiating from him was exhausting. Would she ever learn to relax in his presence or was she so tense because his nearness reminded her of their kiss? It was all she could do to stop herself from pressing her fingertips to her lips that still throbbed from the touch of his.

What kind of woman did that make her? How could she believe she loved one man three short months ago and now feel a bewildering excitement at the touch of another? Even as she thought it, she realized the truth. Devon's kisses had never once made her feel the way one kiss with Will had.

"How are you doing?" Rachel asked.

Anxious. Frightened. Confused. As if he understood her need for comfort, Banjo moved to the swing and sat down in front of Blythe, placing his massive head in her lap.

"I'm fine." Her hand moved to caress his bony head in a gesture as automatic as breathing.

"Well, your pulse is still too fast," Rachel said. "You need to calm down. I know this is an unsettling situation, but it will be all right."

"How can you be so sure?"

"Because I know you and Will, and I trust that God will help you work things out. Now," she said, changing the subject, "do you still have any of the symptoms from your illness last week?"

"A bit of a cough. Nothing serious."

"Fever?"

"I don't think so."

Will stepped through the doorway carrying Rachel's medical bag, Gabe close on his heels. Edward followed more slowly.

"Can I do anything?" Will asked.

"Yes. You and Gabe can both bring the buggies around, please. Will, I suggest that you get Blythe to the farm so she can rest."

"Why do we need our buggy? Are you ready to leave already?" Gabe asked. "You haven't had any refreshments."

"And I won't be having any," Rachel said with a slight smile. "Your son or daughter is ready to make an appearance."

"What?" Gabe said as panic gathered on his face.

"Our child will probably be here before dinnertime," she said, smiling.

"I had a feeling today was the day," Edward told them.

"How could you tell?" Gabe asked.

"We doctors just see a lot of little changes toward the end of a term."

Without another word Gabe leaned over and picked up his wife. The dog skittered aside.

"Put me down, Gabriel Gentry!" Rachel demanded. "I'm as big as a house and you'll break your back."

"Hush, woman!"

"What's going on?" Caleb, who'd just stepped through the doorway, asked his brother.

"Rachel's in labor. I'm taking her home."

She glanced at Caleb, frowning crossly. "It'll most likely be hours before the baby comes. I don't know why he's in such a dither."

"Having the baby is your job. Dithering is mine," Gabe said as he carried her down the steps and headed toward the back of the house where the buggies were parked.

"I'll go let everyone know what's going on," Caleb offered.

Everyone but Will seemed to forget Blythe in the

excitement of baby Gentry's imminent arrival. "I'll bring the buggy around," he told her and then followed Gabe around the house.

At any other time, the antics of the three men might have been amusing, but not today. Blythe closed her eyes. She was tired to the bone, worried sick about her future and embarrassed beyond words that she'd fainted at her own wedding reception. What else could possibly go wrong?

"Well, if it isn't the blushing bride."

The sound of the mocking voice sent Blythe's eyelids flying upward. To her surprise, Martha Rafferty stood near the porch, her hateful gaze fixed on Blythe, who was speechless at the woman's audacity.

"What's the matter, Mrs. Slade? Is Will already too much for a little rich girl like you to handle?" A crafty smile curved her mouth. "He is a lot of man. I can attest to that."

Her implication was clear. Blythe felt hot color rush into her face. Her first inclination was to jump up and scratch out the other woman's eyes or to smack the gloating expression from her face, but she was a Granville, and ingrained years of learning to handle herself in these sorts of situations came to the fore. She would not sink to Martha Rafferty's level, would not even answer her question.

She was a Granville, and unlike her untidy appearance the day before, today she looked like the lady of polite society she was. The costly dress she wore and the fact that she was able to hold her own with the woman standing in front of her gave Blythe at least a measure of confidence.

"What are you doing here, Martha?" she asked,

adopting her mother's most imperious tone, even though her stomach was churning and her hands were clasped together to keep them from shaking. "I can't imagine that you came to wish me and Will your best, so I suggest you run along before he comes back."

As if saying the words made it happen, Will pulled the buggy around the corner of the house and came to a stop in front of the hitching post. The expression on his face was thunderous.

"What are you doing here?" he snapped as he jumped down from the carriage.

"Why, I came to wish you and your bride happiness," Martha said, her tone light and mocking.

"Forgive me if I doubt your sincerity. Now, if you'll excuse me, I'd like to take my wife home."

"I'll go for now," she said. "But you haven't heard the end of this."

"The end of what?" Will barked. "There is no 'this' to end. Anything between us ended long ago, so I suggest you take yourself back to the big city and find yourself another sucker."

Blythe was surprised at the sharpness of his voice, but as harsh as he was, she couldn't imagine anything but brutal truth deterring the determined Martha.

With a furious "Oh" from between clenched teeth, Will's former wife flounced off. He turned to Blythe. "What was that all about?"

"Just more of Martha being Martha."

Will looked at her for a few seconds, understanding without an explanation what Blythe meant. He gave a short nod. "Let's go home."

"We're here."

The two words woke Blythe from a troubled sleep.

She lifted her lashes and saw nothing but black fabric. Her cheek rested against something hard and scratchy that moved up and down in a calm rhythm. An iron-like band held her in place. She frowned. Groggy with sleep, she tilted her head back and saw a masculine jawline. For a moment she had no idea what was going on and then memory came rushing back like floodwaters in springtime.

Will's arms were holding her and her face rested against the jacket of his wedding suit. She sat up quickly, thankful that the world had stopped spinning around her. "I can't believe I fell asleep," she told him. "I'm so sorry."

"It's been a rough week for everyone," he told her, undraping his arm from around her shoulders. "Wait here while I tether the horse." He unfolded his tall length and hopped to the ground.

She watched him tie the horse to the hitching post in front of his house. *Their* house, she corrected, barely grasping the fact that the pretty little home she'd stumbled across a week ago was now hers, or that she had married the man moving toward her with so much vitality and confidence.

Suddenly nervous, she stood, still a little shaky on her feet, and waited for him to lift her down from the buggy. Instead he picked her up. With a little gasp of surprise, she slipped her arms around his neck.

"You shouldn't be carrying me," she told him. "You've been sick, too, remember?"

"Under the circumstances, that would be a little hard to forget," he said, but she heard no animosity or censure in his voice. "But it's no problem, since you're no bigger than a minute."

For some reason the offhand comment pleased her and a sudden longing for a more personal touch rose inside her. Though she barely knew this man, she felt safe in his arms, in his care. She knew the feeling stemmed at least in part from her weariness and emotional vulnerability and his obvious strength. It took every ounce of willpower she possessed to keep from burying her face in his neck and begging him to never let her go. Instead she clung to him until he set her to her feet just inside the door of her new home.

Her gaze traveled around the room, gathering impressions of it now that she knew it belonged to her. She was surprised to see that the room they'd left in such disarray a short week ago had been set to rights. The impromptu pallet she'd made on the floor was gone; the quilts were folded neatly and stacked on one end of the sofa. The woodchips from her fire stoking and the mud she'd brought in on her boots and skirt had been swept up. Even the knife she'd used on her cheese and bread had been put away. The cups had been washed and were turned upside down to drain on a clean towel.

"I wasn't expecting things to be straightened up," Will said. "I figured we'd walk in and find the mess we left it in." For once there was no derision or sarcasm in his voice.

"Probably Abby, Ellie and some of the others," Blythe offered, realizing what a kind gesture the simple act was.

"Probably." As if he'd realized that he'd let his guard drop, the stiffness returned. "Let me show you to your room. You can finish that nap you started on the way home and I'll bring in your things."

"I can help," she said, recalling the small cases she'd filled and the food Hattie and her mother had sent from their interrupted wedding reception.

"Not this time."

Instead of arguing, she followed him to the room at the opposite end of the kitchen. When he opened the door, she realized she was looking at his room, something that had escaped her when she was hunting for blankets.

Like Will, everything was oversize. The heavy Jacobean-style furniture was perfect for a man of his stature. Even the bed, with its massive posts, seemed longer than most.

Her startled gaze flew upward. "This is your room!"

"It was," he agreed. "I imagine you're used to something roomier than the other bedroom, so I'll take it. You'll be more comfortable in here."

"Absolutely not."

"What?" he said, surprised by her outburst.

"It's bad enough you're saddled with a wife you don't want. You work hard. You need a good bed, not one you'll have to draw up your knees to sleep in. I refuse to take your room, and that's final."

He started to protest, but she held up a warning hand. "No. This is not negotiable. I'll take the small room." Her lips twisted into a cynical smile. "I may have been spoiled, but I was taught respect."

Will stared down at her for a few seconds. What he saw in her eyes must have convinced him that she meant business. With a shrug, he turned and led the way through the large room that comprised kitchen, parlor and dining area to the smaller bedroom where she'd found the extra quilts. As with his room, she'd been so worried about Will when she was searching for blankets to warm him that she had paid no attention to the room's decor.

Weak afternoon sunshine poured through the windows that were draped with heavy, ruby-red taffeta and tied back with gold cord and tassels. A red velvet coverlet topped the bed. The wardrobe was heavily carved and the tops of the matching dresser and high-boy were covered with bric-a-brac and crystal. Good grief! It looked more like the bedroom of a demi-monde than a country wife.

She glanced up at her new husband.

"It's too gaudy for my taste," he said, understanding the question in her eyes, "but Martha had taken to sleeping in here a few months before she left."

The information, so freely offered, surprised Blythe. She wondered if Will knew just how much he was revealing with the admission.

"Money's a little tight right now," he told her stiltedly, "but feel free to do whatever you want to do to the place within reason. I have an account at the mercantile."

Seeing that he was self-conscious about his financial situation, Blythe felt even guiltier for adding to his burden. Of course, she couldn't say anything. Her mother had told her too many times about how the self-worth of any man was tied directly to his ability to provide for his family.

Without thinking, she reached out and placed her hand on his arm. "Thank you. I promise not to abuse your generosity."

Will jerked away as if her touch scalded him. He cleared his throat. "If you'll be okay for a while, I'm going to start a fire and then bring in your things. It's chilly in here."

"Yes, it is," she agreed. "Don't worry about me. I'm fine."

In less than half an hour Will had a small fire burning and had carried in her trunk and other bags. Blythe sat in front of the fire, letting its heat warm her, thinking that she should get up and do something, but unable to find the strength to do so. Will disappeared into his room, only to reappear a few moments later wearing his usual plaid shirt and denim pants.

"How are you feeling?" he asked as he buckled his belt.

She drew in a sharp breath. Though he'd done nothing wrong, the casual intimacy of his actions caught her off guard. "Much better, thank you."

"Have you changed your mind about telling me what Martha said?"

"Actually, you got there before she had a chance to say much of anything, thank goodness. I don't think I'd have been much good at a verbal sparring match today."

"I have no idea why she doesn't give up and go back to wherever she came from."

"She is nothing if not determined," Blythe agreed.

"Look," Will said, "if she ever implies that I care for her, you can go to sleep at night secure in the fact that I would never have her back."

Though she believed Will was smart enough not to be taken in by Martha again, the relief that flowed through Blythe was amazing. "I know that."

"You do?"

"I do. You already have a wife," she reminded him,

tongue in cheek. "I found out the hard way that you can't have two."

She saw the surprise on Will's face that she could make light of the very thing that had brought them to this point in their lives. She also saw that he was uncertain how to respond.

"Why don't you lie down?" he said at last. "I want to ride over to the mill and check on things."

Blythe couldn't help her disappointment. She wasn't sure what she'd expected her first afternoon of marriage to be like, but she certainly hadn't expected her new husband to leave her alone. But then, why shouldn't he? It wasn't as if they had much to talk about, or he wanted to spend time with her, and they were certainly *not* going to spend it the way she and Devon had.

Devon. She refused to think of him today of all days. To cover her sudden flustered feeling, she asked, "Does your crew work on Sundays?"

Once again he seemed surprised. "No, but I want to see how much they got done this week."

"Is whoever you left in charge someone you can trust?"

"My foreman is a hard worker and as honest as the day is long, but we have a pretty big order that needs to go out by rail on Wednesday, and I just want to see how things are coming along."

"I understand. Go."

"I'll be back by dark."

"All right," Blythe told him. "I'll work at putting my things away until I get tired and then I'll rest before supper. I think Mama and Hattie sent plenty for us to have for tonight."

The closest thing she'd seen to a smile made the briefest of appearances. "Knowing Aunt Hattie, I'm sure of it."

The first thing Blythe did when he left was strip the ugly comforter from the bed and replace it with one of the quilts from the parlor. Tomorrow, she'd find out where he usually stored his bedding so that she could put away the quilts. Then she could start doing what little things she could to turn Will's house into their home. She laughed aloud, certain few brides had spent their wedding day as she would hers.

Determined to sleep when bedtime came and not to lie there tossing and turning and worrying, she swept her room, dusted it and washed the windows. She even dragged the red, gold and navy rug next to the bed outside and flung it over the line. She took particular pleasure in beating it with the broom before letting it air awhile.

By the time she removed all the knickknacks from the room and replaced them with an exquisite Fabergé egg Philip had brought her from Paris, a Swarovski swan she'd received for her eighteenth birthday and an ivory-and-jade vanity set from her mother, she was exhausted and her back ached, but the room felt much more like her own.

She looked around, wondering what other changes she could make that would not strain her husband's funds. She wanted to feel as if she were in her own home, but she didn't want Will to think she was a spendthrift. She knew how to sew, which was a boon. As soon as possible, she would make some new, brighter curtains for the house and see if perhaps Meg

Allen and her mother-in-law, Nita, would help her
with a rag rug in some pretty colors.

That decided and weariness fast overtaking her,
she wandered back into the combined kitchen and
parlor and added another log to the fire. Even though
the days were warming, it was still chilly enough inside to warrant the heat. With nothing else to do for
the next hour or so, she decided to have a cup of tea.
Will had rebuilt a fire in the stove and the kettle simmered at the back.

Carrying her honey-spiked beverage to the rocker
near the fireplace, she sat down and stretched out
her feet to rest them on the hearth, finally allowing
herself to think about how on earth she would sur-
vive the rest of her life living with Will. He was so...
formidable and unbending.

Or was he? Though he hadn't wanted to marry, he
had. He had offered her his own room, when it was
obvious he would be uncomfortable in the one she'd
insisted on using. And though his finances were tight,
and Martha had tried to spend him into the poorhouse, he'd given Blythe carte blanche at the mercantile. Those were not the actions of a man who
would not bend.

She realized it was unfair to let the pain of Devon's
betrayal color her impressions of Will. The two men
were nothing alike. Devon had been sneaky and under-
handed. Will might be brash and bold, but there was
little doubt where he stood on matters.

She thought about her mother's past and how ter-
rible her first marriage to Lucas Gentry had been.
Even though he had kept her mother from her sons,
Libby had not grown bitter. Instead she had embarked

on a new marriage and a new life when she'd married Blythe's father. As her mother always told her, it all came down to choices. A person could choose to make the best of a bad situation or let it make you bitter.

So where did that leave her and Will? They'd married under less than optimal circumstances, turning sacred promises into a business proposition that benefited them both, and they had promised to stay together, despite their mutual disillusionment on the whole idea of marriage. That left little option but to try to make the best of things and hope that in time their civility would turn to friendship and perhaps even to love.

Love. She hadn't expected to feel any of the excitement for Will that she'd felt with Devon, but she had to admit that Will's end-of-the-ceremony kiss had been quite nice. She pushed the memory away. To go down that road was to invite disaster, and it certainly wasn't part of the bargain.

Actually, she thought she could be happy enough if she and Will built a marriage that was solid and dependable, based on mutual respect and kindnesses and the family they would one day have. Lord willing, they would.

The Lord. Where did He stand in all this? Blythe felt a sinking feeling in the pit of her stomach. She'd been so at peace about her situation and had such a positive outlook on things after she'd prayed. Was it only yesterday? And then she'd gone to see Will and he had come up with his marriage scheme, and then things had happened so fast after, there had been no time to consult the Lord about her decision.

You always have time for the Lord, Blythe. She

could almost hear her mother speaking the words, yet she'd been so busy trying to handle things herself—making decisions about how she would act, what she would do and the kind of wife she would be—that she'd neglected to ask God to help her. Wanting to handle things herself was something she'd always struggled with. She admitted to liking to feel as if she were in control, even though she knew she should pray more to let the Lord lead her where she needed to go.

She knew one thing. It was past time to stop whining about the past. Time to stop trying to place blame. God had given her free will and a brain, and she had made her choices, her mistakes. Now she had to live with them.

That sounded so cynical, and cynicism had never been her way. She was cautious, perhaps pragmatic even, but never one to see life at its worst. She might get down, but in the years before Devon an inherent optimism had always reasserted itself. Devon and that part of her life was in the past. She had to pick up the pieces and move on in a confident, even hopeful, way. Whatever choices she'd made, God was able to take the mess she'd made of her life and turn it into something good, if only she would step aside and let Him.

She was a wife, a decision she'd freely made, and that meant she had responsibilities not only to Will but also to his employees and his family. She'd been brought up with a wonderful example in her mother, who had been an asset to Sam Granville every day of his life. Blythe vowed that if she couldn't be a real wife, she could at least be a positive influence for Will in the community. And one day, who knew what might happen?

She lifted her chin and squared her shoulders, preparing to begin her new life in the best possible ways. One day, one step at a time. For now she would concentrate on making the best life she could with her new husband, whatever that might be, however she could.

Chapter Ten

William needed to get away for a while, not only to check on the mill but to really think about his new life with Blythe. Until he'd seen her fall to the floor, he hadn't really understood how much strain she'd been under. Just moving from a big city like Boston to a town the size of Wolf Creek was a huge adjustment, and when he added in everything else she'd been through, it was little wonder she was overwhelmed and anxious, or that her emotions ranged from meekness to irritation at the drop of a hat. So many things had happened to her that she probably didn't know how to react.

Now she was married to a man she barely knew. He wondered if she was as confused as he was about where they were headed with their new life. If she seemed uneasy and even standoffish, he really couldn't expect anything different after Devon Carmichael's betrayal.

It was perfectly natural for her to doubt his sincerity when he'd spoken his vows. She had no way of knowing that even though he'd sometimes been contrary, his heart was actually pretty soft. Or had been. She couldn't know that he'd been a fun-loving, easygoing kind of guy until Martha walked away from him and their marriage.

Two years ago.

Two years was plenty of time to pick up the pieces of his life and move on instead of wallowing in self-pity. Admitting that his actions had been less than exemplary since her infidelity was easier than he expected. He certainly wasn't proud of himself. In fact, he'd acted like a blamed fool. Drinking, carousing, behaving like the meanest cuss in town. He wondered why that was easier to own up to than to face the idea that he'd failed as a husband.

He had a chance to remedy that with Blythe. They'd said vows. Made promises. The moment he'd entered into marriage with her, he'd started a new phase in his life. It was high time he stopped dwelling on the ugliness of the past, and there was no better place to start than with his new wife and new life.

If this marriage stood the slightest chance of succeeding, he had to stop comparing Blythe's actions to what Martha had done or assuming Blythe would behave in the same way. It meant not expecting her to react in a certain manner just because she came from a wealthy family, and it meant relying on the Lord when he had nowhere to go and no one to turn to, something he hadn't done in far too long.

Like any newlywed couple, they would face ups and downs, as well as the adjustment of living together and the dozens of unexpected things that would crop up. Marriage was getting to know the other person and adapting to the differences between one another.

Just because they'd entered this new relationship in unusual circumstances didn't mean they couldn't have a satisfying life together. All his friends claimed she was a good person. A smart person. And while she'd had a lot of the advantages money could buy, she didn't seem to be the spoiled woman he'd expected her to be.

A memory of how she'd felt in his arms as he drove them home from town slipped into his thoughts. The slight weight of her resting against him and the floral scent that drifted up from her hair had been... unsettling in a way he wasn't prepared to deal with just yet.

To be truthful, she was very pretty and, under any other circumstance, he might have pursued her. She was lovely enough for any man to be proud to call his wife, and there was something about her that, despite their inauspicious beginning, made him want to protect her. He'd felt it from that day at the train station when he'd come between her and the pushy Boston reporter.

By the time he arrived at the mill, Will had reached a decision about his marriage. From now on out, he would do his best to rein in his impatience and at least try to build a friendship with his new wife. He knew that patience, kindness and civility could go a long way, and there was always the possibility that in time they would grow to care for each other. If there was any hope for them to make it through a lifetime together, it was the only course to take.

His decision made, Will checked the pile of logs that had been cut during his absence, as well as the boards that had been cut and stacked for the shipment.

Satisfied that everything at the mill was on track, he headed back to the house. It was getting along toward dark and he and Blythe were about to spend their first night as a married couple.

The first thing he noticed when the house came into view was light streaming through the windows. Even though it wasn't quite dark yet, the glow seemed to welcome him. It was far better than returning to a dark house.

Alternately curious about what would happen when he stepped through the door and dreading his next encounter with his wife, he unsaddled the horse, rubbed him down and gave him his nightly ration of oats and a small pile of hay. Then he headed to the house and pulled off his boots on the porch. Martha had been adamant that he not wear his dirty boots inside and he figured any woman would appreciate the gesture.

When he stepped through the doorway, his eyes went automatically to the table. He couldn't hide his surprise. A pretty globe lamp with flowers painted on the sides sat in the middle of a damask cloth topped with two pretty plates he'd never seen before and flanked by silver cutlery and elegant crystal stemware.

A plate of fancy-cut sandwiches surrounded by pickled okra, cheese slices and chunky sweet pickles his mother had given him sat near the plates, along with a selection of cookies, a crystal bowl holding some of the delicious Saratoga chips from Gentry Mercantile and two slices of Ellie's famous coconut pie.

Blythe had made the simple fare look like a formal

meal. Martha had been a pretty fair cook when the notion took her, but she'd made no attempts to make the food she prepared look appetizing unless they were entertaining someone she thought might help her move up the social ladder.

Will thought the formality might be a little much for the country life he lived, but he realized this was normal for Blythe. It *was* pretty and inviting, and he didn't think it would take much for him to get used to the change. His awed gaze moved from the table to his new wife, who was standing near the fire. He might have thought this was a real marriage and she was waiting for him to come in for supper, except for the wariness in her eyes and the fact that her hands were clenched together.

"Was everything all right at the mill?" she asked, breaking the silence stretching out between them.

This was the second time today she'd asked about his work. Will didn't recall Martha ever asking anything about the mill except in relation to whether or not someone had paid their lumber bill or if he'd collected any money to put in the bank.

"It looked like they did just fine while I was gone."

"That's good. Win says that sometimes it's troublesome to leave someone else in charge, but it has to be done from time to time."

"He's right."

She gestured toward the table. "I hope you're all right with what the ladies sent home with us. I haven't had time to check the larder and see what you have."

"Not much, I don't imagine," he told her truthfully. "The table looks very nice."

She tried to smile, but it was a feeble attempt. "I

know it may seem like a bit much…considering everything, but I brought my hope chest with me and, despite everything, I thought both of us might need at least one pleasant memory when we look back on our wedding day."

He hadn't thought of that, but she had a point. It would be nice to have one good memory of the day. "You're right," he said, attempting to reciprocate her smile. "Let me just wash up and I'll be right out."

He took off his coat and hung it on a peg by the door, then crossed into his room and closed the door behind him. He wasn't sure what to make of his welcome. Had Blythe, as he had, decided that they should go from here with as much courtesy as possible? He hoped so. If they both stuck to that, life would be much easier for them both.

When he emerged a few moments later, she was still standing next to the fire, waiting for him. Will might be a country boy, but he wasn't completely lacking in social graces.

He went to the table and pulled out a chair for her. She crossed the room and sank into it gracefully, even gratefully, it seemed. When he scooted her chair beneath the table, he caught a whiff of the same scent her mother wore, the same scent that had drifted up from her as he'd held her close against his chest on the way home. It was a fragrance he knew he would forever associate with her.

"What's that perfume you're wearing?" It never occurred to him that she might consider the question too personal.

She turned her head to look at him, surprise in her eyes. "Um…lilac."

"I like it," he told her, pulling out his own chair. "It's what your mother wears, isn't it?"

She placed her napkin in her lap. "Yes."

"I don't think I've ever smelled lilacs before," he told her, doing the same. "I don't think I've ever seen any."

"Probably because it's very hard to grow them in the South. They need some cold weather," she said, reaching for the plate of dainty sandwiches and passing it to him.

"Ladies first."

She did manage a small smile then. "Not if you're Libby Granville's daughter."

"She sounds like my mother," Will said. He grew serious all of a sudden and again spoke what was on his mind. "Look, Blythe, I realize you come from a very different lifestyle than mine, and I'm sure you're used to having people..." He paused, searching for the right words.

"Wait on me hand and foot?" she supplied.

He shrugged. "Something like that."

"I did grow up with a lot of advantages, but that doesn't mean that I'm worthless or helpless."

"I didn't mean to imply you are. I just wanted to let you know that I don't expect *you* to wait on *me* hand and foot."

"At the Granvilles', we consider waiting on our menfolk as more of a thank-you. Men are out working all day, making a living, and it only seems right that they should come in to a...pleasant place where they're treated with courtesy and respect. You'll soon learn that my mother is very big on common courtesy."

"Wonderful attributes to pass on to your children,"

he said truthfully. "But I've been taking care of myself for a couple of years now."

"Understood," she told him. "But as your wife, I want to make our house a home. It's what I've been taught to do. Now will you please take some sandwiches? This plate is getting heavy."

He took the other side of the plate. Flashed another half smile. "How about we take one at the same time?"

She sighed and did as he asked. He imagined he saw the corners of her mouth tip upward the slightest bit. Maybe it wouldn't be nearly as hard as he expected to build a life with this woman.

Blythe was surprised at how well their first meal together went. Like two people courting, perhaps, they talked about various things, just getting to know one another.

When Will had finished his pie and drained his second cup of coffee, he scooted his plate back, rested his forearms on the table and turned to look at her. The serious expression in his eyes set her heart to pounding in anxiety.

"Thank you."

"For what?"

"Making our first meal together special."

"It was leftover party food."

"Presented in a very nice way."

"It just seemed like the thing to do." The praise from him was as unexpected as it was puzzling.

"Do you feel like telling me about...what's his name? We can talk about it, and then if we never mention it again, that's fine with me."

Though she'd known they would have to discuss their pasts at some point, Blythe was a bit taken aback by the fact that Will was broaching the subject so soon and with such forthrightness.

"Of course," she said. "As long as you tell me about Martha." What was good for the goose was good for the gander.

"Fair enough."

Like Will, she pushed her plate aside. "When Devon arrived in town, he took Boston society by storm."

"How'd he get in?" Will asked, frowning. "I figured you'd have to be someone another person knew... or something."

"Oh, he said he was. He was very clever." Her voice held unmistakable sarcasm. "Devon knew just enough about a former friend of an elderly businessman in the city, convinced the gentleman that he was his friend's nephew. Devon was handsome and well-dressed and knew his way around society. The investigator Philip hired later discovered that his name was really Wilbur Delaney, that he had a wife stuck back in a tenement somewhere and that he'd been a valet to the real nephew."

"Clever. And he set his cap for you."

She could hardly believe she was talking about such personal matters with a virtual stranger, and a man, no less. But somehow it felt right, even natural. Of all the people she knew, Will probably understood her feelings better than anyone else ever could. After all, he'd been through a very similar situation. Besides, even though she hardly knew him, he was her husband, and if they were to make this marriage work, it was best to be honest from the start.

"I'd say he set his sights on me, but I didn't know the difference and I allowed myself to be swept off my feet and into a fantasy I'd always dreamed of."

"You loved him." It was a statement.

"I did. At least I thought that what I felt was love," she told him. "And you loved Martha."

"Yes." The scowl was back, bringing with it two little lines between his eyebrows that begged to be rubbed away. "Or, like you, I thought it was love. She was pretty and I was proud of her, and she made me think I was the best thing that ever happened to her. It took a long while for me to see that she wanted me because I was reasonably attractive and successful, and our marriage was a step up in the world for her.

"After a while I realized she didn't want to make a home or a life together. She wanted *things*. Now that I've had a couple of years to think about it, I'm not sure I understood what real love is."

"And you do now?"

"I think so."

"Well, I'm not sure I do," she told him, "but I know what it *isn't*. It isn't about being the perfect couple or having those 'things' you mentioned. Devon didn't want me. He wanted the money."

She brightened suddenly. "Perhaps he and Martha will cross paths one day. It sounds to me as if they'd be a perfect pair."

Will actually smiled at that. The quip was made in a mocking tone, but there was a certain truth in it.

"You know," she said, "I think the thing that both-ers me the most is that he made me look like a fool in front of everyone. I'm not sure my heart was hurt as much as my pride."

Will gave a thoughtful nod. "Exactly. I didn't like everyone talking about me not being man enough to hold her."

"Oh, surely people didn't say that." She couldn't imagine anyone saying such things about the man sitting across from her.

"Who knows? That's what I imagined them saying." He took another sip of his coffee. "Have you heard from him?"

"Hardly!" Blythe scoffed, the expression on her face reasonably close to a snarl. "The last thing Devon Carmichael wants to do is come anywhere near me. He knows that if my brothers had even the slightest inkling of where he'd gone off to, they'd have the Pinkertons after his sorry hide in a heartbeat."

Will's mouth curved into another wry smile.

Her eyebrows drew together. "Martha has come back, so it seems to me she still cares for you."

"She doesn't know the meaning of the word." Will got up and poured himself another cup of coffee. "Martha cares for Martha. I know how her mind works."

"Meaning?"

"The man she left me for was already married and had no plans to leave his wife."

"There seems to be a lot of that going around."

"So it seems," Will agreed. "Martha came back because she's exhausted all her other options and she thinks she can rope me in again. It's a good thing I've learned a few things the past couple of years."

"There's nothing like a few hard life lessons to teach you prudence."

"True. Besides, she's wasting her time."

Blythe looked at him questioningly.

"As I was reminded earlier, I already have a wife."

Blythe stared into his eyes, trying to gauge his feelings and failing. "Yes, you do."

"Regrets, Mrs. Slade?" he asked.

Hearing him call her by her new name caught her off guard, yet she couldn't help an unexpected and fleeting feeling that it sounded right. His tone was light, maybe even a little teasing, but the look in his eyes was dead serious. Was he as uncertain as she was about their new relationship?

Did she have regrets? Not a one. At least not yet.

"No regrets. What about you, Mr. Slade?"

"Nope." He lifted his coffee cup as if he were making a toast. "To marriage."

Blythe woke the next morning to the aromas of freshly brewed coffee and frying bacon. A quick glance at the clock at her bedside told her it was almost six. Evidently she'd overslept, but she'd been so weary the night before that she hadn't thought to ask Will what time she should get up.

After splashing water on her face to wash away the last cobwebs of sleep, she slipped her arms into a warm, woolen robe and padded into the kitchen in her bare feet.

Will, who was standing at the stove, turned when he heard her door opening. There was no welcoming smile from her new husband, not that she'd really expected one. For a moment he didn't say anything, just stood looking at her, letting his gaze roam from the braid hanging over her shoulder, past the robe knotted at her small waist and down to her bare feet. She curled her toes in embarrassment. Starting to feel uncomfortable, Blythe drew the edges of her robe together.

"Good morning." Her voice was husky with sleep.

"Mornin'," Will said. "Coffee's ready."

She cleared her throat. "That sounds wonderful."

"Have a seat. I'll get it for you."

"I thought we'd settled this last night."

"Settled what?"

"That I don't expect you to wait on me."

"Well, it won't hurt this once." He took a cup from a cabinet and poured her a healthy portion of the fragrant brew, then more for himself. "Cream and sugar?"

"Ugh. No," she said with a frown. "My daddy always said cream and sugar are for sissies. If you have to use them in your coffee, you like cream and sugar. Not coffee."

Will's heavy eyebrows lifted in query. "Is that so?" he said and proceeded to add two generous spoonsful of sugar to his own cup. His eyes never left hers.

Blythe couldn't help seeing the humor in the situation or stop the fleeting smile that claimed her lips. "I'm sorry. And I'm sorry I overslept. I'll do better tomorrow." *I hope.* "Do you come home for lunch or take something with you?" she asked before taking a sip of her coffee.

"I come in about noon."

"Oh."

"Is there a problem?" he asked, glancing at her over his shoulder.

"No, not at all. Just thinking."

"Eggs?"

"What?"

"Do you want bacon and eggs?"

"Oh, yes. One, please." There was something unnerving about Will cooking for her.

"Soft yolk?" he asked as he broke an egg into the hot bacon drippings.

"Please."

"I'm not usually in for the day until six or so. Is something wrong?"

"No," she assured him. "I was just trying to figure out how to juggle my day. Since the school board gave me a little time off, I'd planned to check the pantry and then go into town and pick up whatever we needed for the next week, but I'm not sure I can be back by noon."

How could she tell him that her experience ended with setting a pretty table? She had no idea how to cook anything…well, except for scrambled eggs and toast and maybe a couple of other equally uninspired items. The truth was that she'd planned on heading to town and spending the day with her mother for a few quick lessons on some easy meals. She could bake sugar cookies, though. Maybe Will would like them.

"That's not a problem. I'll just fry up a little more bacon and have a sandwich."

"Are you sure?"

"Positive. Do you know how to hitch up the horse?"

"I'm afraid not." She felt guilty for making the admission.

"I didn't think so. When we finish breakfast, I'll hitch Daisy up to the buggy and you can take all the time you need."

"Thank you."

Blythe felt all discombobulated. She'd had no idea how this marriage would unfold day by day, but this wasn't at all the way she'd expected marriage to the prickly lumberman to be. She was grateful that things between them were so *civilized*, and that he was being so understanding and so kind. But it was a good thing. Perhaps he'd decided to start out the way they meant to go on, just as she had.

When he'd finished making both breakfasts, he sat down across from her at the small table and picked up his fork.

"Would you like to say a prayer?" she asked, thinking once again that today should serve as a foundation for all their days together. Devon had made such a fuss over it that she'd taken to giving thanks silently.

Will stopped, blinked and stared at her for a couple of seconds. Then he gave a sharp nod and reached out for her hands.

"You ask the blessing," he said. "I'm not too sure my prayer would get any higher than the ceiling right now."

Blythe agreed, though she was accustomed to the man of the house leading the prayers if he was around. Later, she would have no recollection of what she said. The only thing she would recall was the warmth and strength of his calloused fingers holding hers. Tightly.

When she finished, their eyes met once more. Was she imagining the softness in those dark depths? She couldn't be sure.

"Thank you," he told her as he released his hold on her hands and picked up his fork again.

They ate their breakfast, their conversation more

hesitant and probing than spontaneous as it had been the night before. Hoping to surprise him with a home-cooked meal when he got in that evening, she asked Will what his favorite foods were.

Blythe listened to his reply with a sinking feeling. Chicken and dumplings, purple hull peas, corn bread and fried deer with gravy and potatoes. No one in her family cooked dumplings, though she'd had them at Ellie's. Blythe had no idea what purple hull peas were and found the notion of eating one of the beautiful deer she'd seen along the edges of the woods sad, even though Caleb and Colt had explained that deer were important staples in country life and that it was nec-essary to harvest them, since they multiplied quickly.

She drew in a determined breath. She could do this. She would do this.

When asked what his duties consisted of, he told her that he divided his time between overseeing the mill and going out into the woods with a crew that cut down trees, took off the branches and then snaked them back through the woods to the mill, where they sat until time to be cut into boards of varying lengths and widths.

In turn, he asked her how she usually spent her days in Boston. It was embarrassing to tell him that she often stayed out at balls or the theater until the wee hours and then slept until late the following day. Her afternoons were spent sketching or visit-ing friends and shopping and doing a little needle-work. Oh, there were days she did some work for the church, visiting shut-ins or taking food to sick people that one of the kitchen help cooked. She even visited the hospitals on occasion.

Looking at it now, it seemed a frivolous and worthless way to spend time. What had she really been accomplishing as she'd lived her privileged life? Unexpected shame filled her.

Deciding once more to be honest, she placed her napkin beside her plate and lifted her gaze to his. "I'm sure you won't be a bit surprised when I tell you that I did nothing much. At least nothing that made a difference."

Will leaned back in his chair and folded his arms across his wide chest, just listening as she told him about her days in Boston. As if he wanted to hear everything she had to say before he drew any conclusions.

"When I looked back at it just now, it all seems like a waste. I wasn't crazy about filling in for Allison, but I have to admit there's a certain satisfaction in seeing the children grasp something they didn't understand before and knowing that something I said or did helped them to get to that place."

"Would you like to keep teaching?"

"Oh, I don't think so. I'm not sure I'm really cut out for it. Besides, Homer will start looking for a single woman to take my place as soon as possible, but I doubt he'll find anyone before school takes up again in the fall."

"So what will you do here all day to occupy yourself?" he asked.

She blinked. What would she be doing? "Oh. Well. Whatever wifely things need doing, I suppose." She looked around. "The first thing I plan to do is give everything a good scrubbing. The windows in my room were in need of a good wash."

"You'll be bored silly in a couple of weeks."

"Nonsense," she scoffed. "I admit to not having a clue to living the kind of life you live here, so I expect that learning how to do everything will keep me occupied for a long while. It would help if you made a list of things I'm responsible for, besides cooking and cleaning."

"I'll be glad to make you a list," he said. "And you're right about things needing a good cleaning. I'm not much of a housekeeper. My mother cleans when she comes, but it's been several months since I've seen her."

His mother. Blythe's heart sank and a new feeling of inadequacy filled her. She'd forgotten about his mother. She hoped there would be time for her to learn how to take care of Will and his—*their*—home before his mother decided to pay a visit.

"When do you expect her?"

"Any day," Will said. "She didn't have time to make it for the wedding, but I imagine she's planning her trip as we speak."

"So soon? I hope I have time to get things straightened out before she comes. There's so much to do and I have all my things to put away and…and—"

"Blythe."

The sound of his voice stopped her in midsentence. "Yes?"

"Don't worry about it. She won't bite off your head. Like any mother, she'll want to make certain her baby boy has married someone who'll stand by him through thick and thin and be good to him. She pretty much wants for me what your family wants for you."

The words settled Blythe's nerves somewhat. Of

course, any mother wanted the best for her child. It was her job to make sure Will's mother understood her commitment to their strange union.

"Did she like Martha?" Blythe couldn't resist asking.

"No."

Leaving her with that short, succinct answer, Will pushed away from the table. "I need to get a move on. I'll go out and get the buggy ready and tie it up here in front of the house."

Blythe nodded. "I'll see you this evening, then."

"If the Good Lord's willing and the creek don't rise," he said, grabbing his jacket off the hook near the door.

"What?" she asked with a frown.

Will paused in the doorway. "Nothing. See you this evening."

Chapter Eleven

❧

Will left the house and headed to the barn, literally shaking his head in disbelief. His new bride had no idea what the common country saying meant. She didn't know how to cook. Probably had never cleaned a thing in her life or bought staples. He doubted she'd ever shopped for anything but fancy dresses and shoes and such. How on earth was she going to manage as a country wife?

Still, he thought with a reluctant admiration, she seemed game to take it all on. That should have been surprising, and in some ways it was, but he'd heard all about her mother's disastrous first marriage, how she'd worked hard to be a good wife to the fearsome Lucas Gentry, and how she'd picked up the pieces of her life and built a new one with the man Lucas had put in a wheelchair. At least some of Libby's toughness had to have been passed down to her daughter, didn't it?

From everything Will could gather, Sam Granville had sired a couple of scrappers, too. Win was proof that he'd raised at least one. Blythe came from fighting stock, and that had to be a good thing for their future.

One thing was certain. Even in the bulky robe she'd worn to breakfast and with her hair straggling around her face from her nighttime braid, there was no denying she was a beautiful woman. He grumbled beneath his breath, disgusted with himself for feeling anything for her. That was *not* in the deal, but he couldn't help it if he thought she looked real pretty all rumpled and sleepy.

Will sighed.

The next few weeks promised to be very interesting.

After Will left, Blythe headed to the pantry to see what was there and found several kinds of dried beans, an almost-full ten-gallon tin filled with flour and smaller ones containing sugar and coffee. Lard. Salt, pepper, dried fruit, a tin of crackers and canned items, both home-canned and from the mercantile. Tomatoes, corn, green beans and several cans of what looked like vegetable soup lined the shelves. Curious about Will's particular likes, she examined the cans from Gentry's. Peaches. Plums. Pears. Condensed milk. He must like fruit. She would ask her mother how to make pies.

With a good idea of what she had on hand, she wasted no time getting ready and heading to town. She didn't have to worry about Banjo following her; she'd seen him tagging along behind Will.

Blythe found her mother at the library. Libby, who was putting a book back on the shelf, glanced toward the door when she heard the bell ring. Unable to hide the surprise on her face, she shoved the book into place and hurried across the room.

"Blythe! What are you doing here?" she asked. "Is everything all right?"

"Everything is fine, Mama," she said, "but I need to see what other things I need from the mercantile, and you need to teach me how to fry deer, make dumplings and bake pies, and I have to clean the house and—"

"Blythe, slow down!" Libby said with a little laugh. "Why are you in such a tizzy?"

Blythe looked a bit surprised. Tizzy. It seemed her life had been in turmoil for months and now, when she'd hoped things would settle down and she could begin to live a quiet life in the country...

"Will's mother is coming," she blurted, getting to the heart of her panic.

"Oh. That's nice. When is she due to arrive?"

"He doesn't know, but soon, he thinks, and I have so much to do that I hardly know where to start, and I was hoping you could teach me to cook today, but here you are at the library and I don't know what I'm going to do."

"First of all, we're going to close the library for a while, and you and I are going to Ellie's for a cup of coffee and a talk. Bess Slade is only a woman. And if she's anything like Hattie, she's a sweetheart. But..." she added with a smile, "we have a stop to make first."

"Where are we going?"

"Rachel and Gabe's. I'm a grandma again," she said, a twinkle in her eyes.

Blythe's eyes widened. She'd been so worried about

her own situation that she'd completely forgotten Gabe had left the wedding celebration yesterday with his wife in his arms. "She had the baby! I'm an aunt! When did she have him? Or her?"

"It was another boy, born late yesterday evening," Libby said with a smile. "You should have seen your brother! For a minute I thought I was going to have to deliver the baby and Edward was going to have to take care of Gabe."

"What did they name him?" Blythe asked, heading toward the door.

Libby was right behind her. "Jude Thomas Gentry."

"I can't wait to see him."

Edward let them in when they reached the house, and Libby lifted her cheek for his kiss. Holding her mother's hand, he led them down the carpeted hallway to the bedroom where Rachel sat propped up in bed with a shawl thrown around her shoulders and her head resting on her husband's chest. Gabe's long legs were stretched out on top of the covers. Hellos were said all around, and one particular greeting sent Blythe's gaze winging to the person sitting near the bed, a small flannel bundle cradled in his arms.

"Will?"

Her husband of less than twenty-four hours looked at her, an expression on his face that resembled embarrassment.

"I thought you were at the mill," she said, trying to reconcile her impression of the stern man she'd married to the tender image of him holding a newborn.

"I was, but we broke a chain first thing and I had to come to town and get another one." He shot a look at his friend. "Imagine my surprise when I saw that the mercantile was closed for a 'few minutes.'" The words were drawled in a tone of false sarcasm.

"Hey," Gabe said. "I missed out on all this with Danny. I'm not about to with this one."

"I don't blame you," Libby said. She gave Blythe a gentle push toward the giant in the fragile-looking rocker. "Go take a peek at him, Blythe. He's so beautiful."

"Just as yours will be when you have one," Rachel said from the bed.

The chatter in the room stilled and Blythe's gaze once again found her husband's. The warmth she saw sent her heart racing double time. A dozen images flashed one by one through her mind, each evoking feelings she should not be having for a man who had married her without love. A man she had married without loving him. Breathtaking feelings, nonetheless.

"You're right," Will said at last, shattering the brittle silence but never breaking eye contact with Blythe. "It will be."

Was it her imagination or did his voice hold a husky, throaty note?

"Would you like to hold him?" Rachel asked.

"Oh! May I?"

"Well, of course, silly."

Blythe approached the rocking chair and leaned forward to take the baby from Will, who held the infant up in his two big hands and deposited him into her waiting arms. Their faces were so close she could see just how thick his ridiculously long eyelashes were. She caught a whiff of that tantalizing scent that seemed to be a part of him, something that smelled like pine needles and some sort of manly shaving soap that played havoc with her senses. She resisted the impulse to lean forward and take a deeper breath.

Madness.

Instead she cradled Jude against her shoulder and straightened, turning her back on her husband and hopefully on the feeling created by his nearness.

"Sit here," Will said from behind her. "I've got to get back to the mill, if I can tear Gabe away long enough to sell me some chain."

He stood and moved aside for Blythe, who sank into it gratefully. Her legs were feeling a little shaky. Gabe slid off the side of the bed and turned to give Rachel a brief kiss on the mouth. His smile was something to behold. "Have I told you today how much I love you?"

"Not more than ten or twelve times, but I don't mind hearing it again."

"I love you."

Rachel's smile was serene, content. "I know."

It was all Blythe could do to not look up and see how the tender exchange was affecting Will. Instead she kept her focus on the baby's sweet little scrunched-up face.

She felt something warm and heavy on her shoulder and turned to see Will's hand resting there. She looked up.

"I'll see you at home."

The intimacy of the act left her speechless. She could only nod. She watched him turn and follow Edward and Gabe from the room. Looking back at the two women in the room, she caught the glance that passed between her mother and Rachel.

"What's that look about?" Blythe asked.

"That's what I was about to ask you," Libby said.

Blythe ignored them and placed the baby on the bed, where she unwrapped him, marveling at his little feet and toes and brushing her lips ever-so-softly against his silky hair. After a few minutes of paying proper homage to the newborn, Libby announced that they should head on over to Ellie's and let Rachel rest. Blythe handed the baby over a bit reluctantly.

A smile resided in Rachel's eyes. "By this time next year, you may have one of these."

Blythe felt the heat of a blush rising up from her throat. "Oh, no. We're a very long way from that happening, *if* it ever happens."

"I've seen the look I saw on Will's face on Gabe's often enough."

"Stop it!" Blythe commanded.

Rachel laughed. "All right. I'll take pity on you. Now come and kiss this little sweetheart goodbye." She looked back down at the baby. "Grandma Pip and your auntie Blythe have to go now, sweet baby."

Both Libby and Blythe kissed the baby's forehead and Rachel's cheek before promising they'd be back soon. Blythe left wondering, like Rachel, what the look on Will's face meant.

As usual, Ellie was thrilled to see them. When she heard why Blythe was in town, she smiled. "Well, today is your day. I'm making chicken and dumplings for lunch. The first thing you need to do is boil your chicken, and when it's done, let it cool and pick the meat off the bone. I give the bones and skin to the dogs."

They arrived at the café during a slow time, so while Ellie's daughter, Bethany, who'd been born with a mental handicap, took care of the customers, Blythe and Libby followed Ellie to the kitchen and watched as she rolled out the dumpling dough. Blythe painstakingly wrote down the recipe and everything Ellie did. She decided she would make the delicious-smelling dish when Will's mother came.

"I usually have green beans with them, but you can do whatever vegetable you like. If you do green beans, they're much better if you cook them a long time with the seasoning you use. And I make fresh bread every day."

Homemade bread. The very thought struck terror in Blythe's heart. When she was a child and loved spending time in the kitchen with the cook, she'd often heard her complaining about "killing the yeast," which could happen if the water used to dissolve the yeast was too hot. Blythe voiced her concerns to Ellie.

"Well, if you're worried about that, you can always make a quick bread using saleratus," Ellie suggested. "It's denser than yeast bread, but still very good."

"Saleratus? What's that?" Blythe asked, wide-eyed.

"Bicarbonate of soda. You just mix everything up and put it in the oven."

"I have the recipe for Nita Allen's Irish soda bread, too," Libby said. "It's very good."

"Maybe I should start with that, then. Does Gabe carry the saleratus at the mercantile?"

Ellie smiled. "Of course. Here," she said, handing Blythe the knife. "You cut the dumplings."

Ellie watched while Blythe drew the knife through the rolled-out dough, making squares that would be dropped into the broth. "I have some news," she said.

"Something exciting, I hope," Libby said.

"Not all that exciting, I'm afraid, but it's something I should have done long ago." She looked from one curious face to the other. "I finally took everyone's advice and contacted a lawyer more than a year ago. I filed papers to have Jake declared legally dead."

Blythe looked up from the squares she was making with the knife. Jake was the husband who had abandoned Ellie and his daughter when Bethany was first born. "Why didn't you say something sooner?"

"It's been a lengthy process and I didn't want to say anything to anyone in case it all fell through. I was afraid to get my hopes up. My attorney had to post the notice in several papers around the country and jump through a lot of legal hoops, but I got my paperwork yesterday. I'm free of him at last."

"You deserve to find happiness," Libby said, taking Ellie into a warm embrace. "I couldn't be happier for you."

"Me, either," Blythe chimed in, putting the knife aside and following suit. The news would be very welcome among Ellie's friends who had long wished she could be free of the man who had deserted her. And whether or not he showed it, Win would be ecstatic.

"There's no way you can learn to cook in a day, honey," Libby told Blythe. "In the meantime, Ellie has today's lesson under control, so I think I'll get back to the library."

She pressed a kiss to Blythe's cheek. "Stop by before you go to Gabe's, and I'll have a list ready for you. I don't think you need much. Maybe a few spices and the baking soda."

Libby left and Ellie showed Blythe how to add a few of the dumplings at a time to the boiling broth. They were getting ready to make a thickening from flour and water when Bethany came through the swinging door to the kitchen.

The expression on her pretty face said without words that she was near tears.

"What is it, sweetie?" Ellie asked.

"That mean woman is out there."

Blythe frowned. "Mean woman? Who's she talking about?"

"Martha Rafferty," Ellie told her. "Whenever she comes in, which is daily, she complains about everything. Bethany gets so frustrated." Ellie huffed a huge sigh. "I'm telling you, it's all I can do to keep from telling her off."

"I can only imagine." Blythe took a peek out the pass-through window to take a look at the woman who seemed to be everyone's nemesis. "I don't believe it! Some people have no sense whatsoever!"

"What?"

"Guess who she's with."

Ellie took a quick look and her face drained of color.

"Ooh!" Blythe fumed, whirling away from the window. "If I didn't know how smart he really is, I'd think my brother lacked basic intelligence."

"When it comes to women like Martha, the thought processes of most men become a bit cloudy." Ellie's tone was light enough, but the haunted expression in her eyes told the real story of how she was feeling.

What perfectly rotten timing! Blythe thought. Win had been playing a subtle game of flirtation with the sweet café owner since the first time he'd set eyes on her, and everyone, including his family, thought that eventually, if Ellie ever rid herself of her no-account husband, the two of them would become a couple. What was he thinking? Surely he was smarter than to fall for someone like Martha Rafferty!

Blythe would love to go out there and give him what for, but she was a Granville, and Granvilles didn't cause scenes. The first time she got her brother by himself, though, she'd let him have it. In the meantime she could be an unofficial chaperone. As much as she disliked the woman, she would march out there, sit herself down at their table and insinuate herself smack-dab in the middle of their little tête-à-tête.

Whipping off her apron, she proceeded to do just that.

"Where are you going?" Ellie asked.

"Out there to break up this unholy alliance!"

"Oh, Blythe! If you're worried that he's hurting me, don't be. I already know I could never be the right woman for someone like your brother."

"Well, neither is that hussy!"

Blythe pushed through the swinging door, a wide, false smile on her face. There was no denying that her brother was a handsome man or that Martha was a beautiful woman, or that, together, they made a stunning couple.

"Hello, Win! What are you doing here in the middle of the morning?" Without waiting to be asked, she sat down in the chair between her brother and Will's former wife.

"Hello, Blythe. Won't you please join us?" Though his voice dripped sarcasm, he was nothing if not courteous. Win never got ruffled about anything.

Blythe knew she'd caught him off guard, since being so pushy was definitely not her style. He had that wary look in his eyes that said he knew she was up to something but he wasn't sure what that might be at the moment.

Little did he know that she'd learned some hard lessons from Devon. One of them was to not lie down and let someone walk all over her.

"Hello, Martha. I must say that I'm surprised to see you're still here."

Both Martha and Win sucked in sharp breaths at her ill-mannered behavior. To her surprise, Win kept silent. Martha was regarding her in a calculating manner, as if she were trying to figure out what had happened to the diffident, spineless woman she'd encountered the day before.

"I thought I'd stay around for a few days. There's nothing pressing at home, and I thought I might find some entertainment here for a while." She cast a playful glance at Win.

Blythe could well imagine the kind of entertainment the other woman had in mind. "Well, the old guys at the store are having a checkers tournament this Friday, and Win is a whiz at chess if you're up to taking him on," she said, pretending to deliberately misunderstand.

The glint in Win's eyes told her that he'd caught on to what she was up to, and that he didn't know whether to laugh or cry. Instead of doing either, he looked Blythe straight in the eye, cleared his throat and said, "If you ladies will excuse me, I saw Caleb go by. I need to talk to him for a moment."

Without waiting for a go-ahead from either of them, he stood and began to weave his way around the tables to the door. Knowing she was now facing her enemy one-on-one, Blythe felt her bravado slip.

Sensing her sudden vulnerability, Martha relaxed against the ladder-back of the chair. "My, my, the little kitten has grown claws overnight. I wonder what brought that about. I told you Will—"

Her meaning was obvious. "Don't say a word about my husband," Blythe interrupted, suddenly finding her voice and her backbone.

All pretense aside, Martha leaned closer, her attractive features twisted in an ugly sneer. "I wouldn't get too full of myself if I were you, missy. Will Slade may have married you to save your precious reputation, but maybe you should ask him if your brother's offer had anything to do with his willingness to go to the altar."

Win's offer? What was Martha talking about? Blythe felt her confidence ebb once more. "I have no idea what you're talking about. What offer? What does my brother have to do with Will agreeing to marry me?"

"Plenty," Martha said bluntly. "I heard him talking to Will the other day."

"Oh," she said with a lift of her eyebrows. "Eavesdropping. Why doesn't that surprise me?" Blythe felt compelled to make the accusation in an effort to delay whatever it was Martha was determined to tell her.

Martha gave a throaty trill of laughter. "When I can, Mrs. Slade," she confessed boldly. "Eavesdropping is one of the best possible ways to learn little tidbits that might come in handy at a later date."

"And what did you learn when you listened in on their conversation?" Blythe asked, her heart in her throat.

"That Will is only marrying you because of your money."

After what she'd been through with Devon, the accusation cut to the bone. It was one thing to marry someone to save her reputation, but for them to want her for her money was something else altogether. It was Devon's modus operandi all over again.

Blythe refused to give the horrid woman sitting next to her the satisfaction of knowing how much her words hurt. Instead she laughed. "Then the joke is on him. I have no money. My first husband saw to that."

Martha smiled. "Your brother has plenty."

"Meaning?"

"Meaning your brother offered Will money to marry you."

"You should take your lies somewhere else, Martha," she said, even though the assertion robbed her of a portion of the peace and security she had begun to feel with Will. "Win would never do something like that, just as he would never let me influence him on anything to do with his business decisions."

Martha gave a delicate shrug. "All I know is that he told Will that marrying you could be very good for his business. I'll let you ask him what he meant by that. I thought it was important that you know the offer just might have had the *teeniest* bit of influence on Will's decision." With a smirk, she measured a scant half inch of space between her fingers. Chin high, she pushed away from the table, picked up her reticule and headed toward the front door.

Blythe sat where she was, her self-esteem once more trampled and bleeding in the dust of betrayal. Intellectually she knew Martha was no good and certainly not above lying to cause trouble. Blythe also knew Win was hard-nosed when it came to his business dealings, but she could not fathom him paying someone to take his sister off his hands. He might be ruthless, but he was scrupulously honest. A hard negotiator, but a fair one. And he loved his family dearly. Even her, his bratty little sister.

Still, the joy had gone from her day and she left the café with a heavy heart.

Chapter Twelve

Will thought about Blythe all the way from town back to the mill. He admitted to being surprised at how easily they'd talked about their pasts the evening before. The qualities he saw in her were not what he'd expected and he'd been impressed with the things she'd said.

Martha had never asked what he liked to eat, never asked when he would be home, how things were going at the mill or anything to show she had an interest in him and who he was as a person. Blythe might have been brought up with money, but she seemed to have her priorities in order.

Even though he'd known she was headed to town, he hadn't expected to run into her at Rachel's. Seeing her with baby Jude in her arms had been a revelation. They'd both said they wanted a child at some time in the future, but seeing her with the Gentry baby made the possibility more real. Real and very desirable.

He knew it took time to get to know someone, but he felt that he'd gained a fair amount of knowledge about his new wife in a relatively short time, and despite feeling that he would never love anyone again, he believed the two of them could deal with each other with respect and friendliness.

As he worked through the day he found his thoughts wandering to Blythe again and again. How had her day gone? Had she spent all day in town or come back to work on putting her stamp on the house? She'd said she didn't know much about cooking, so, naturally, he was curious about what she would have for supper. He recalled the welcoming light shining from the windows the evening before. At least he wouldn't be going home to an empty house. For the first time in a long time he wasn't dreading walking through the front door. Whatever she fixed would be fine.

When he reached the house, he pulled his boots off on the porch and went inside, Banjo trailing behind him. The first thing that greeted him was a cloud of smoke. His gaze flew to where Blythe stood, stirring something on the stove. It was hard to tell what it was with the acrid odor of burned…something filling his nostrils.

She looked at him and he thought he saw her chin quiver before she pressed her lips together and turned away.

"Everything okay?" he asked, hoping the question was neutral enough. He'd learned a few things during his marriage to Martha. One of them was to leave a cranky woman alone. When she was ready to talk, she'd talk.

"Fine."

"How are you feeling?"

"Fine."

Unfazed by the tension, Banjo went over and plopped down in front of the fireplace. Will sighed and glanced at the table, which was once again set with the pretty china. A plate holding what he suspected was corn bread sat in the center of the table, but it was charred so badly it was hard to say. It had been baked in a skillet, so there was a chance it was cake of some sort, but he was pretty sure it was corn bread. No wonder Blythe looked as if she was about to burst into tears.

"Is there anything I can do to help?"

"No."

His mellow mood and tentative hopes for the future vanished. If he didn't know better, he'd think he'd done something to make her mad, but that was impossible, since he hadn't even seen her since that morning. Hoping to air out some of the smoke and maybe clear a little of the tension, Will left the door ajar and took off his jacket. Without saying anything else, he went to his bedroom to wash up for supper.

When he returned a few minutes later, she was ladling whatever was in the kettle into a tureen. Soup, maybe. Not his favorite, but he didn't mind it every now and again. She finished and placed the ladle in the tureen. She was about to pick it up when he saw the cloth wrapped around her palm.

"What happened to your hand?"

"Just a little burn."

"How'd you do that?" He crossed to her and took the soup or whatever it was out of her hands.

She glanced up at him, irritation clouding her brown eyes. Mockery laced her voice. "Perhaps you noticed that I burned the corn bread."

Smoke still hovered over the room and he was pretty sure the stench had burned all the hair from inside his nostrils. He set the covered bowl on the table, placed his hands on his hips and nodded. "I did notice that."

"I burned my hand taking it out of the oven."

"Let me see."

"It's fine," she said, tucking the hand behind her.

"Okay," he said as if her attitude was of no consequence. "So what's for supper?" *Besides burned corn bread.*

"Beans and corn bread," she said.

"They smell good," Will said, trying once more to establish a better footing. It wasn't a fib. Now that the room had cleared somewhat of smoke, he could actually smell the beans. He sat down next to her, and when she held out her hand for him to take so they could give thanks for the food, his questioning gaze met hers. It seemed she was going to pray, even though she was barely speaking to him. He refrained from heaving a deep breath. Lord knew they needed prayer. He took her hand in his.

"Why don't you say it tonight?" she suggested, and he thought he saw a hint of challenge in her eyes.

Will shook his head. "No."

Blythe looked taken aback, but, without a word, she began to pray. When she finished, he cut them each a pie-shaped wedge of the corn bread and proceeded to cut off the burned crust. Then he slathered it with butter as if it was something he did every day.

"Shall I do a piece for you?"

"I can do my own."

"You need to keep that bandage clean."

Answering him with a glower, she began to emulate his action, awkwardly using the tips of the fingers of her left hand to hold the bread.

Will pretended not to notice what a time she was having. His pride had kicked in. He'd bent over backward to try to help her and it was clear she didn't want anything from him. She might need it, but it didn't look like she was willing to admit it. So much for his earlier notion that they might be headed for a better place in this blasted marriage.

More than a little put out at her attitude, he ladled some beans onto his corn bread. He was starving, and even though they didn't look exactly like others he'd eaten, there were plenty of them. Martha had never understood how hard he worked and how big an appetite he had. It looked like Blythe had cooked a fair amount of salt pork in them, which always made good beans.

With his mouth watering, he took a big bite and began to chew. Stopped. Blythe glanced over at him, the expression on her face almost daring him to find fault. The beans were still hard. Not hard enough to break a tooth, but far from done. Determined not to add to the tension that was as thick as the smoke now clearing from the room, Will swallowed the mouthful and took another.

Blythe took a bite. Her eyes grew wide and filled with tears. Without a word, she swallowed, washed down the food with some of the milk sitting at her place, stood and went to her room.

With a heavy sigh, Will pushed back his plate. Even though he'd known it would take months, if not years, for them to reach a place of easy coexistence, he didn't know why he was so surprised that tonight was such a disaster.

He took a big swallow of his milk and then crumbled another big slab of corn bread that had been decrusted into it. It wouldn't be the first time he'd had corn bread and milk for supper, and it wouldn't be the last. When the glass was empty, he stood and gathered up their dishes, scraping the remains into the chicken scrap bowl. Then he took the big enamelware kettle from the back of the stove and poured hot water into two dishpans. It wouldn't be the first or last time he did dishes, either.

Inside the gathering shadows of her bedroom, Blythe lay across her bed and cried. She'd so wanted the first meal she cooked for Will to be good, and she'd tried so hard to make it so. Instead it was a total disaster.

She was so tired. Tired of fighting the world and for every crumb of respect. Weary of worrying about being enough. Good enough. Kind enough. Helpful enough. She was tired of people like Devon and Martha thinking she would believe everything they said. She was tired of trying and failing, and tired of being so tired all the time.

She wished she were more accomplished. Oh, she had plenty of education and was smart enough to have done quite well in school. She had drawing and sewing talents, but what good were they when she couldn't even prepare a decent meal for the man she'd married?

Why *had* Will changed his mind about marrying her? She knew she was crazy for believing anything that came from Martha Rafferty's lips, but Blythe couldn't help the niggling doubt Martha had planted in her mind.

It was that doubt that had made her so short with him when he came in, even though she'd known she was behaving like the spoiled brat he thought she was. But what else was a woman to do when they heard that kind of accusation against their husband? Was there a certain way they were supposed to react? How could she find out the truth? Could she trust that Will would be honest if she asked him? Of course, she could always ask Win.

Never!

It was simple. Either she believed Will was committed to their marriage bargain or she didn't, and even though she'd been proved wrong before, something said she could trust him. By the time she finally fell into a restless sleep, she was no wiser about mankind or marriage and no closer to an answer than she'd ever been. She was pretty sure, though, that she owed her husband an apology and maybe an explanation for her behavior.

Blythe tossed and turned most of the night, and when she finally did fall asleep toward dawn, she slept like the dead. The sound of the front door closing woke her. Another morning and she hadn't sent her husband off with a good breakfast. She rolled to her back and stared at the ceiling, awash in a sea of failure.

But daylight had brought back some of her determination. She had no time for disappointment or feeling sorry for herself. There was so much to do that she wasn't sure where to start. Washing the dishes from the night before would probably be a good place. Knowing Bess Slade would be arriving soon only added more pressure to her "settling in" process.

Determined to make today more productive than the previous one, she went through her morning toilette, dressed in the oldest skirt and shirtwaist she owned, and left her room.

When she stepped through the door into the combined parlor and kitchen, she was surprised at how neat things were. Will had washed their supper dishes, which only made her feel small and selfish and more inadequate. A piece of paper lay on the table and, as she approached, she saw that it was filled with a bold scrawl.

Coffee's on the stove. There are some biscuits left. Not the best, but not as hard as your beans, and pretty good split and fried in a little bacon grease in a skillet.

Blythe frowned and then read what he'd added.

The part about the beans was intended to make you smile. I put them in the crock with the lid in the springhouse. You can cook them some more this afternoon and we'll have them for supper. Cooking on a woodstove takes time to learn. See you later. Will.

Blythe followed his instructions about the biscuits, topped them with some jam she found in the pantry and opened a can of the store-bought peaches. She didn't know if they were as good as they tasted, or if they tasted so delicious because she was so hungry.

When she finished her breakfast, she swept all the floors and then found a bucket, some lye soap and some rags. Starting in the bedrooms, she mopped the floors on her hands and knees, which was a chore, since she could use only one hand in the mop water, and leaning on the burned palm was definitely uncomfortable.

When she finished those rooms, she felt as if her back were breaking, and she was worn-out. She wanted nothing more than to sit with her feet propped up for a while, but there was no time. The mantel clock showed that Will would be home for lunch in less than an hour.

She'd heard her mother say that potato soup was quick and she had watched her make it a time or two, so she stoked up the stove, put some water on to boil, peeled some potatoes and an onion and chopped them into the water. She salted and peppered the mixture and dropped in a generous spoonful of butter. It might not be a three-course meal, but it would be hot and filling, and this time, she'd be sure that she didn't burn anything and she would taste it to see the potatoes were done.

In a matter of minutes the mouthwatering aroma of cooking onions filled the room. Once again, she set the table and put the butter in the center. Rummaging around in the pantry, she unearthed a tin of saltines, which she arranged on a plate. She added more of the sweet pickles he'd seemed to like that first night, and sliced more of the cheese, and set the bowl of leftover peaches on the table.

Finally she tasted the soup and found that the vegetables were done, but it was a bit too salty for her taste. She sighed and set it to the back of the stove to stay warm.

It would have to do.

At least this time the food was edible.

By the time she heard Will step onto the porch, she'd tidied her hair, changed her apron and was pouring some of the deliciously cold water from the springhouse into two glasses.

She heard the thud of his boots as he went through his ritual of taking them off before he came inside. It was a small thing to do, but thoughtful. It must be cold for him to take off his boots outside in the wintertime, and what if a spider—or, God forbid, a snake—crawled inside one during the summer! She'd have to figure something out that would make things better. Maybe a rag rug just inside the door.

When he stepped inside, he paused just for a moment. It was impossible not to realize just what a big man he was, since he filled the opening. It was also impossible not to realize just what an attractive man he was with his broad shoulders, tousled hair and a light stubble of whiskers already making an appearance on his lean cheeks. Whatever else her husband might or might not be, there was no denying that she would be the envy of several of the single ladies in town. Womanlike, she admitted that she was not at all opposed to the notion of having a handsome husband.

His eyes met hers across the room. "Smells good."

"It's just potato soup, but I got so busy mopping the floors that I lost track of the time."

"Potato soup is fine," he said. Will closed the door,

shrugged out of his jacket and hung it up. He crossed the room to stand in front of her. "I know you want things to be just so for my mother, but if it doesn't all get done, it's no problem, I promise you."

"It is a problem. She'll have heard all the gossip, and I don't want her thinking that you have a lazy wife on top of a silly one. We made a bargain and I want to do my part."

Her part. Will's heart took a little misstep. It seemed that, like him, she was taking their marriage bargain and her new marital duties seriously. He knew she'd cleaned in his room; he could smell the soap. His windows also sparkled and his furniture gleamed with a fresh rubbing of beeswax and lemon balm. The fact that she wanted to put her best foot forward for his mother was thoughtful of her. Martha had never cared one way or the other what Bess Slade thought.

"Look, you've had a rough couple of days." He offered her a sardonic smile. "Actually, you've had a rough few months. You passed out a couple of days ago, and you burned your hand yesterday. You don't have to do everything today. You really shouldn't be putting that hand in dirty water."

"I haven't been. I've only been using my right hand in the water," she told him, trying to state her case. "I do think maybe the blister popped, though."

Without stopping to think, he placed both his hands on her shoulders. To his surprise, she didn't try to pull away. "Blythe." His voice was soft but firm. "Burns can get infected if they aren't taken care of properly. I need to take a look at it."

Seeing the seriousness in his eyes, she gave a reluctant nod.

"Sit," he commanded, turning the chair next to hers so that they would be face-to-face. She did as he commanded and held out her hand. Will untied the ends of the cloth she'd used to bind it and began to unwrap the injury. When he pulled the last bit away, she hissed in pain.

He grimaced. "Sorry." When he saw the angry wound that stretched from the area between her thumb and fingers across her hand, he whistled. "It looks like you had a doozy of a blister. And you're right. It broke. What did you do for it when it happened?"

"Put it in a bowl of cold water and then put butter on it."

"The cold water probably helped as much as anything." He went to a small cabinet and took out a strip of clean cloth and some ointment. Her expression seemed to ask why he had medicines so readily available. "My mother sees to it I have what I need to treat wounds, since accidents happen pretty often in the woods."

He sat down, took her hand and began to apply the salve.

"What kind of accidents?"

"Someone may get caught in a chain or the tree falls the wrong way if the wind gets it just right. The occasional snake bite, and then the mill has these big saws…"

"Stop!" The gaze that met his was filled with panic. "You're careful, aren't you?"

Will looked up from his task. Her alarm was indisputable and surprising. All the resentment he'd sensed in her when he'd arrived home the previous day was gone. So was her unwillingness to engage with him in any way but a dutiful, superficial manner.

"I try to be." He scooped some ointment onto his finger and began to smooth it over the burn. She drew in a little breath.

"Sorry." He glanced up from his task. "Would it matter to you if something happened to me?"

The shock in her eyes was genuine and she sounded a little breathless. "Well, that's a silly question. Of course it would matter. It would be horrible if anyone was hurt, but you…you're my husband." Her voice trailed away at the end.

And what did that mean? Would she care because they were legally bound to one another, or would she be truly distressed at the thought of him being injured? Maybe a bit of both, he thought as he wrapped the clean bandage around her palm.

He was beginning to see that there was much more to his bride than frills, feathers and fluff. In the short time he'd known her, he'd seen that, despite the silver spoon in her mouth, she'd been brought up with good morals and taught the worth of a hard day's work. He was also realizing that his aunt and others in town were right. Blythe was a decent person with a tender heart.

He tied the bandage. "All done. Once you get the cleaning done, it would probably be a good idea to take off the bandage and let some air get to it."

Will was afraid he sounded more abrupt than he intended, but knowing that Blythe would care if something happened to him and holding her small, soft hand in his were doing strange things to the heart he thought was so badly broken it would never love again. Battered and bruised though it was, he felt a stirring of something that he thought, but was almost afraid to believe, might be hope. To cover the bewildering reaction, he smiled at her and said, "There you go. Almost as good as new."

She gave him a tentative smile back. "Thank you."

"And you should know that my mother is not an ogre. Like any mother, she's protective of me, but she's reasonably nonjudgmental and fair to a fault."

She gave him that look that women through the ages had perfected. The one that said, "You just don't understand."

"I'm sure she's very nice, but it's your mother," she said. And that said it all. She stood abruptly. "I'll get the soup."

End of conversation.

Thirty minutes later, when they'd finished their meal, Blythe set her water glass onto the table and said, "I'm sorry about last night. I behaved badly and immaturely, but I...had a bad day in town and took it out on you, and I was so upset about the beans. I wanted you to have a good supper when you got home."

The apology came out in a rush, but at least it was a beginning. "And I appreciate the effort," Will told her, "but cooking on a wood-burning stove is tricky if you've never done it before. It will take you a while to learn how to make your fire just right and where it's hottest. I can help you, but Mother can show you more when she gets here."

"Well, I've already put the beans at the very back

of the stove, so they should be done by suppertime. Maybe I won't burn them."

"I'm sure you won't. Look, Blythe, we've said we'll be honest with each other, and I'd like to ask you something, but I don't want to upset you."

What could he possibly have to say? she wondered, feeling nervous suddenly. "All right."

"Why *were* you so angry with me yesterday? Was it just that you'd had a bad day? If I've done something, I need to know what it is so that I can fix it."

Should she tell him what had happened in town? It seemed he was intent on doing his best to maintain the even keel of their marriage. Could she do any less? Was there any hope of them succeeding as a couple if she didn't? Instead of answering, she replied with a question of her own. "Did my brother offer you money to marry me?"

"What!"

Will's explosive reply was almost denial enough. Almost.

"Where on earth did you get an idea like that? We both know exactly why we went into this marriage."

"I saw Martha—"

Will got to his feet. "I should have known she had something to do with it."

Blythe waited until he finished his tirade before she continued. "When I was in town yesterday, she told me she'd overheard my brother offer you a deal to marry me."

"It's a lie. Win did not offer me money to marry you. I'll be the first one to admit that I have more than my share of faults, but I haven't sunk to the depths of taking bribes or payoffs yet."

"But she said…"

"Look," he told her, resting his palms on the table-top and leaning toward her. "Everyone in town knows she's trouble looking for a place to happen, and you and I both know she'd like nothing more than to drive a wedge between us. The old line 'hell hath no fury like a woman scorned' could have been written with Martha in mind."

Blythe looked into his dark eyes and saw nothing but sincerity. She knew that what he said was true and she believed him. At least as far as it went. A part of her longed to be more specific and ask him if Win had suggested that marrying his sister would have certain benefits, but the other part of her, the part that wanted her life to be strife-free and stable, was afraid to press the issue.

Will had been everything a bride could ask for in a husband. Kind. Helpful. Caring. Why would she take a chance of toppling this shaky foundation of their marriage? She couldn't. She vowed to at least try to be more mature in her response to whatever else came her way.

Chapter Thirteen

The beans were done that night and, to Will's surprise, Blythe had opened a jar of the pickled beets from the pantry and made more corn bread. This batch wasn't burned, but it had a dip in the middle, and when he cut into it, he found that the center wasn't completely cooked. Still, it was progress.

While they were eating, she'd made the light, offhand comment that her knees were sore and her back hurt. Will had given her a look that said without words that he wondered why. In his opinion she was doing too much all at once. She looked so exhausted, he insisted on helping with the supper dishes.

When they were done and put away, he sat down at the table with his ledgers while Blythe, who had changed into her nightgown and the ugly flannel robe, sat on the sofa in front of the fire with her feet propped on a footstool, doodling on a pad of some sort. Banjo, who'd abandoned Will for Blythe, lay near her feet, snoring softly. Will couldn't help but smile at the picture they made.

The light from a nearby lamp and the fireplace

cast the feminine curves of her face into provocative patterns of light and shadow; the graceful arch of an eyebrow, the tantalizing shape of her lips, the sweet line of her chin. Not for the first time, it struck him that his wife was a very pretty woman, but he'd been too angry at the whole female sex to see anything beyond the fact that she was Win Granville's sister.

As he cast surreptitious looks at her, he realized again that things between them were better than he'd expected them to be. She'd had her share of disasters the past couple of days, but she hadn't given up on making his place—their home—something he could be proud to show his mother. He admired her for her grit and determination.

For the first time since they'd spoken their vows, he felt pretty good about their future. Blythe Granville Slade wasn't a quitter, and regardless of what had happened in her past, he knew she was a decent person, a woman any man would be proud to call wife. Including him.

He wondered what it was she was drawing but didn't want to interrupt and ask. Instead he turned a page and started tallying up column after column of numbers, hoping to find money for replacement equipment where there seemed to be none, praying he would somehow be able to hang on to the mill. After all, he had a wife to provide for, and regardless of Martha's claims, he had no plan to sell to Granville, if there was any possible way to keep from it.

Thinking about his duty to provide for Blythe brought another responsibility to mind. He'd been brought up with the belief that not only was the man to provide for his family, he was to be the spiritual leader of the home. He'd fallen down on that job during his marriage to Martha, but he'd had no aspirations to lead a godly life, and he'd been too busy trying to make her happy to do what he knew was right. Then, when she'd walked out, he'd allowed his misery to take control of his life and lead him into paths he knew better than to travel.

His heart told him it was time to make things right with God. Following Jesus was not a magic elixir, did not guarantee a life free of trials or disasters or fix life's every problem, but he knew it did guarantee that there would be someone on his side who was able to help carry the load, and it would go a long way toward smoothing out the trouble spots in his marriage and his life.

He sighed.

"Is everything all right?" Blythe asked, looking up from whatever she was doing in the book.

"Fine. How's your back feeling?"

"Better, now that I'm resting."

"Good."

"What's on your mind, Will?"

He looked at her in amazement. Once again she'd sensed something was amiss with him. "I was wondering if you'd like to go to church Sunday."

"Church?"

She looked as surprised by the suggestion as he was for making it.

"Yeah. I was thinking it might be a good thing to do if we really mean to start out as we intend to go."

"You have a point," she said, "but I haven't been but once since I came back. I felt like I had a target on my back."

"Not much understanding, huh?"

"It's hard to say," she told him, pushing a lock of hair out of her eyes. "I know that some people realize that what happened wasn't wrong, although eloping is a bit of a scandal," she added, almost as an afterthought. "The people who matter to me have been very forgiving and caring. But there are others…"

"I can only imagine," Will said.

"I'm afraid I've been too busy being miserable to have much time for God." She looked at him curiously. "What about you?"

"I haven't stepped through the church doors since Martha walked out. Considering everything that's happened, I think it's time to change that." He smiled at her. "Maybe if we show up together, we can prove to everyone that we've both moved on, that we're done with the past. What do you say?"

He watched as she seemed to digest his suggestion. Then she looked up with a smile that took his breath away.

"Yes," she said. "Let's go to church."

Will went back to his numbers, more content than he had been in months, years, maybe. He was re-adding a column of numbers when a soft thud broke his concentration.

Will glanced over at Blythe. Banjo looked up at her as if to ask what was going on. She'd fallen asleep. Her head drooped to the side and her notebook had dropped to the floor. Besides the emotional strain she was under, he knew she was worn-out from the work she'd done around the house.

She was a tiny thing, and sitting there with a quilt over her legs and the thick braid hanging over her shoulder, she looked more like a little girl than a woman. Will covered a yawn and glanced at his pocket watch. Time for bed.

He closed the ledger and went to the sofa, intending to give her a little shake and send her to her room. Instead he picked up her drawing tablet. She'd been sketching a ladies' dress, something that looked suitable for church. There was a list of fabric amounts, lace and notions to adorn the creation. He didn't know anything about ladies' fashion, but he thought the design was pretty.

Curious, he flipped through the other pages, finding more of the same. One page held the drawing of a wedding gown, stunning in its simplicity. He wondered if she'd sewn the dress and worn it for her sham wedding to Devon or whatever his name was. He was shocked by the intensity of emotion that swept through him at the thought of her as another man's wife, brief though the time had been.

Reminding himself that he couldn't change the past, Will placed the sketchbook on the sofa and stood staring down at her, wondering if he should say something to wake her or give her shoulder a little shake. Before he realized he'd made a decision, he was bending over to pick her up.

Blythe made a soft murmur of objection but curled an arm around his neck and snuggled her face against his throat. The simple act of trust filled his heart with a rush of emotion. What that feeling was, he couldn't have said, but it was far different from anything he'd experienced before. It was something good and warm that pushed away all the coldness and doubt that had taken up residence in his heart.

His senses were awash in the sweetness of the lilac scent she favored. It occurred to him that if he dipped his head the slightest bit, his lips would be touching hers. Instead of giving over to the allure of her lips, he carried her to her room and shouldered open the door. Somehow he managed to pull the covers aside and place her onto the bed. Blythe's eyelashes fluttered upward a fraction of an inch and once again she made sounds of objection. The arm around his neck tightened.

He froze, afraid to move, afraid to even breathe. Her eyes might have opened for a few seconds, but she was asleep and unaware of her actions. Wanting closeness. Craving touch. As any man in his situation would, he wondered if she even realized who was carrying her. Whom she was holding close. To let that thought bear any significance was to invite disaster. He banished it the only way he knew how.

He kissed her.

Her eyelashes fluttered upward, and recognition flickered in her eyes. Instead of pushing him away as he expected, he felt the arm around his neck loosen and her bandaged hand slip to his cheek, the unwrapped fingers skimming over his face and down his jaw. It was all the acceptance he needed to deepen the kiss, which lasted longer than he intended. He drew away reluctantly, while he still had enough wits about him to think straight.

As he straightened, her eyes opened again. Briefly. A soft sigh soughed from her lips and she whispered a soft, "Please…" Then, without another word, she rolled onto her side and slipped her hand beneath her cheek. Will stood there for a moment, just staring at her and wondering what on earth had just happened. Then, with his heart and mind reeling, he pulled the blankets over her shoulders and left the room.

He was afraid that, despite his anger, resentment and disillusionment, he was falling hard and fast for his bargain bride.

Chapter Fourteen

It wasn't quite daylight when Blythe woke the following morning. Her arm was a bit sore from all her scrubbing, but her back felt better and she felt more fully rested than she had in days. She was also becoming accustomed to her new bed and had slept soundly, in part because she and Will seemed to have reached a certain level of comfort in their dealings with each other. She stretched in contentment until a sudden thought sent her bolting upright.

The last thing she remembered was sketching a new walking dress. She had no memory of coming to bed. How had she gotten here? An elusive recollection of clinging to something warm, strong and safe teased the edges of her memory. The only thing she knew with those qualities was Will.

She pressed her fingertips against her lips that had begun to throb. She closed her eyes, trying to recall something she couldn't quite put her finger on. Something…nebulous. Momentous. The memory surfaced bit by bit. A face near hers. Dark eyes. Intent. Intense. Wondering. Whatever had happened had to do with

Will. Her heart took a sudden tumble and her breath hung in her throat. Will. Had. Kissed. Her.

And she'd let him.

Close on the heels of that startling realization came the need to justify the incident. She'd allowed him to take advantage of her simply because she'd been asleep. It wasn't as if she'd wanted him to.

You held on to him. You didn't stop him.

An undeniable truth.

But why had he kissed her when he said he would never fall for another woman after Martha's betrayal?

Finding no answers, she rose, took care of her morning toilette and removed the bandage from her hand to let the air get to it as Will had suggested. Deciding that it looked better, she dressed in more of her old clothes, put on a clean bibbed apron, lit a couple of lamps and went to stoke the fire in the stove. By the time the blue-speckled coffeepot had been filled and set to boil, the sun was making its first tentative appearance above the treetops.

Will's ledger still lay on the table. She started to open it but realized that would be intruding on his personal business. A business that was hers now. She bit her lower lip, debating whether or not she should take a look. Like her brothers, she was good with numbers, and it appeared that dealing with them was frustrating to her new husband. No, she wouldn't look, but she would offer to give him a hand when the timing seemed right.

Egg basket in hand, she stepped onto the porch and stood for a moment, watching the sunlight inch upward to mingle and merge with the clouds, creating a panorama of orange-reds and gold and various tints of lavender while the sounds of the waking world filled her senses. There was a chill in the air, but she knew the day would be a glorious one. She heard the twitter and chirp of half a dozen songbirds welcoming the morning. They, too, sensed that springtime was fast approaching.

How long had it been since she'd awakened early enough to greet the day? How long since she'd really listened and looked at the world around her or enjoyed the many riches God had blessed the earth with? Too long. Smiling, and drawing in a deep breath of the clean, fresh air, she whispered a soft, "Good morning, God," and felt her heart soar.

Banjo, too, seemed to enjoy the scents around him. He stood silently beside her, his nose lifted, sniffing out the various smells mingling in the chill morning air. If she didn't know better, Blythe would vow he was smiling. She laughed aloud at the notion and her companion looked at her questioningly. She reached down and scratched him behind one of his floppy ears.

Filled with a sense of well-being for the first time in months, she drew in another deep breath of the clean country air and made her way to the smokehouse for a slab of bacon, adding it to the basket she carried. Opening the gate to the chicken pen, she unlatched the door to the house and stepped inside. She was feeling happy and confident as she gathered the eggs for breakfast.

She was reaching beneath one of the birds when, for no apparent reason, the hen on the nest flew at her with a loud squawking. Blythe dropped the basket of eggs and let loose an ear-piercing scream. Her panic seemed to incite the other fowl and soon the chicken house was filled with flapping wings and loud cackling that sent Blythe into a screeching and arm waving of her own.

Only when Banjo barked and bolted for the door did she realize what she'd done. She'd left the gate open and the dog had followed her inside. Still yelling and waving her arms to deter a hen that seemed intent on settling atop her head, she ran behind the dog, tripping over him in her haste and landing hard on her hands and knees.

With her palms and knees smarting, her ears still ringing with the sounds of a dozen birds screeching, and very near tears, Blythe heard the front door slam against the house and the sound of someone running down the steps and across the yard.

In seconds she felt strong hands circle her upper arms and draw her to her feet. Still unnerved, she looked up at her husband. His calloused hands rested on either side of her face. Seeing the genuine concern in his dark eyes, she lost control over her tears and felt their wetness begin to slip down her cheeks.

"What happened? Are you all right?"

Was she all right? She really hadn't been all right for months. And now, despite the disastrous results at her inept attempts at making a home for her and Will, she'd begun to think that maybe they could make a success of their strange marriage, after all. They'd made huge strides the past few days, but now she'd managed to undo everything with one silly city-girl mistake.

Instead of answering, she gave a great gulping sob and wrapped her arms around his lean middle. She heard him draw in a surprised breath and then felt his arms circle her shoulders while that same breath trickled slowly from him.

She didn't know how long she cried, only that as miserable as she was, there was comfort in his arms. So much comfort she wished she never had to move away. His chest was broad and warm and…bare. She jerked away from him as if he were hot to the touch.

"What's wrong?"

She blurted the first thing that came to mind. "You're not dressed."

The scowl was back. "Actually, I am dressed. I was putting on my shirt when I heard all the commotion."

He *did* have on a shirt, but it was unbuttoned.

"No sense going into a flap," he growled in a low, irritated voice, even as he began to do up the buttons. "We are married, and I'm sure there will be a lot more of these moments through the years."

The thought was very disturbing. She released him and whirled away.

"What? What did I say now?" he asked, catching her hand to turn her to face him once more.

She hissed in pain.

"I'm sorry. I forgot about your hand," he said, lifting and turning it palm up to gauge how badly the fall had affected it.

"I'm sorry I'm such an incompetent wife," she said through clenched teeth while he picked pieces of dead grass and grit from the raw wound.

"This needs a good washing out and a good dousing with Mercurochrome or iodine so it won't get infected," he told her.

Blythe gave a slight shudder. She wasn't a fan of either.

"And you're not incompetent," he told her, finishing his assessment and letting go of her hand. "You've lived a completely different kind of life. You're not used to country life or wifely duties. It will take you a while to get the hang of things," he told her in a clumsy attempt to soothe her misgivings. "I'm sorry I can't afford some help. If I can get the mill turned around, maybe we can hire someone to come a day or two a week."

Hire someone! Her chin began to quiver again. He must think she was so inept that he wanted to hire someone to do what she couldn't. Well, she would not have it.

"I don't want someone to help me. I want to do it myself. I want to be the best wife I can to you. In every way."

The provocative statement hung in the air between them, charged with unspoken meaning and unstated possibilities. Meaning and possibilities they both chose to ignore for the time being.

"Why?" he asked, planting his hands on his hips. "To uphold your side of the bargain?"

She was surprised by the bluntness of the question. *Honesty, Blythe.* "Partly." She lowered her gaze, fearful of what she might see in his eyes. "And partly because you're an important person, someone whose business is vital to the welfare of a lot of families in Wolf Creek. I…I want everyone to know that I want to help you in whatever you endeavor, and I want you to be proud to walk down the street with me on your arm and call me your wife. And later…

when we have children, I want you to be proud to have me as their mother."

Will stood there, dumbfounded by the passion in her voice. If there had been any lingering doubts about her commitment to their marriage, they vanished. She considered her role one of worth and usefulness. In that moment he knew beyond a doubt that she was the kind of wife any man would be proud to call his own.

And children? The thought of having children with Blythe was both frightening and heady. For a moment thoughts of what kind of husband he would be scattered before a new notion. Would he... Could he be a good father?

"You don't have on any shoes."

The inane comment in the midst of such a meaningful exchange caught him off guard. "What?"

"You aren't wearing your boots."

Will looked down at his sock-clad feet and back to her face. "When I heard the ruckus, I didn't take time to put them on."

He looked at the fowl now contentedly scratching at the warming soil. "What did happen?"

Will could see her gathering her thoughts and her courage. One thing about it: his wife was no coward.

"I got the bacon from the smokehouse and went to gather the eggs." She raised her chin a fraction. "I forgot to close the gate to the chicken yard and Banjo followed me inside the coop."

Hearing his name, Banjo, who was lying peacefully a few feet from them, began to beat his tail against the ground.

"Did he attack one of them?"

"No," she corrected. "He was just there beside me, and I guess when the hens saw him, they assumed he would come after them and they got all flustered and started flying at me."

Will could picture the whole thing. He couldn't help the smile that claimed his mouth. "And *you* got all flustered."

"I did, yes," she said, pushing straggles of hair out of her eyes. "And it isn't funny," she tacked on.

"It is to me."

He wasn't expecting her playful jab at his midsection. If the startled expression on her face was any indication, she hadn't expected it, either. His sharp reflexes enabled him to catch her wrist in a loose grasp. He hadn't seen this lighthearted side of her. He thought he liked it.

"I'm sorry," she said, that fearful expression back. "I did that without thinking. I suppose it's a spontaneous reaction from all the teasing Win and Philip dealt me while I was growing up."

Will was still smiling. "No offense taken. I figured as much." His hold on her tightened and he drew her a step closer. "Blythe, you don't have to be so afraid that I'll be angry over every little thing you do. I've been surly the past couple of years, but I've never laid a hand on a woman in my life, and I never will. I was brought up better than that."

"I'm sure you were."

"And for the record, Banjo has been taught to leave the chickens alone. If they panicked when they saw him, it was a basic, instinctive reaction."

"Oh."

"We do have a problem, though."

"What's that?"

He glanced at the fenced pen and then around the yard. "We have chickens to put back in the pen. The coyotes and foxes aren't nearly as tolerant of them roaming around as Banjo is. We'd better catch them and put them up."

Fifteen minutes later, with much running and shooing, arm waving and shrieks of dismay, all the chicken were once again captured and put back in the yard. Will had salvaged their breakfast makings and gathered the other eggs from the nests. Fortunately, the bacon was still in the basket. Only one egg had broken.

He carried the basket as they headed back to the house. Out of habit at the door, he started to toe off his boots and realized he wasn't wearing any. His socks were dirt-covered and twigs and pieces of dead grass clung to the soles. He and Blythe stared at each other with rueful expressions.

They both looked a bit worse for their effort. Their faces were flushed; Blythe's hair had suffered both from her mad dashing around the yard and from flailing around trying to fight off the fowl.

Will reached out and plucked a white feather from her tangled hair.

"Your socks are filthy."

Blast the woman! She had the most uncanny way of saying something nonsensical during the most meaningful moments. Which might be the best thing, since Will was still having trouble with the knowledge that he was liking his new wife far too much.

"I have a wife who'll make them look brand-new," he quipped in a light tone.

To his surprise, she responded in kind. "That's a tremendous amount of pressure to put on a city girl whose only experience is washing out her stockings in the basin on the rare occasion."

"I'm confident she can handle it."

"Are you?" The seriousness was back.

"I am." He saw the question in her eyes fade away and the tension ebb from her small frame.

"I'd better get cleaned up and start breakfast. I don't want you to be late to the mill. There's no telling what your workers would be saying."

Will could make a calculated guess but thought it best to keep it to himself.

"I'll clean up and help you." He smiled. "'Many hands make light work,'" he quoted. "I can't tell you how many times I've heard my mother say that when she wanted to get me and my brother up off our backsides."

"You have a brother?"

"Jase. And two sisters, Lorna and Liz," he told her, standing on one foot to peel off a dirty sock. "They're scattered all over Arkansas. Did you think I was an only child?" he asked, shedding the other one.

"Things have been so hectic, I don't think I gave it any thought. What about your father?"

"He died when I was fifteen. Mom was never the same after that. They were crazy about each other. That's what she wants for all of her kids, so don't be put off if she comes across a little chilly in the beginning."

"I didn't really need to know that," Blythe told

him. She pulled the pins from her hair and it tumbled across her shoulders like a swathe of sable.

She gave her head a little shake and whatever he'd meant to say to ease her misgivings fled before an image of him threading his fingers through her hair and kissing her again. Will's heart, the one he thought was damaged beyond redemption, took a tumble. He might have gotten in over his head with this marriage of convenience. With the way and speed his feelings for Blythe were changing, he wasn't sure how long he could keep up the pretense of civility without at least trying to take things further.

Fifteen minutes later Blythe found Will slicing the bacon. He wore clean Levi's and another from his seemingly endless supply of plaid shirts. His hair was damp, as if he'd given it a quick wash. She knew that if she got close enough she would smell the tangy scent of the pine soap he favored.

She couldn't help comparing him to Devon, who was always perfectly turned out. She could not imagine him dressed as Will was. How had she ever thought that Will's brand of attractiveness was not the type she was drawn to? With his wide shoulders and narrow hips, he looked every inch wonderful male.

And he's yours.

She stopped in her tracks, shocked at the inappropriate thought that flashed into her mind. But was it unseemly, really? Will was her husband, after all, and handsome to boot. It made sense and was perhaps even inevitable that the more time they spent together, the closer they would become. Learning to love each other could only be a good thing.

Love! Despite everything she'd suffered because of Devon, was it possible she *was* learning to love Will bit by bit?

"Everything all right?" he asked, turning toward her. A lock of damp hair fell over his furrowed brow. He looked like a little boy...how their little boy might look.

She drew in a shaky breath. "Fine."

"Did you get that hand cleaned up?"

"Yes." She held up her hand so that he could see the rust-hued stain on her palm. "It hurt like the very dickens."

Another of those fleeting grins made an appearance.

"I'm going to try to finish the house today," she said, going to take the knife from him. As she did, their fingers brushed and Blythe felt a little tingle shoot up her arm. The expression in his eyes was disturbing in ways she couldn't begin to describe.

Wordlessly, Will handed her the knife and moved aside to fetch a couple of cups. He poured them both some coffee and sat down at the table. "Everything looks fine," he told her again.

"I know I won't be able to do everything I'd like to before your mother comes, but I want to finish up a few little things and get my belongings put into their proper places." She glanced at him over her shoulder. "Have you heard from your mother?"

"No, and I probably won't." Will pushed back the ledger that still lay on the table and cocked back in the chair. "Bess Slade is notorious for just showing up when the mood strikes, but I'd look for her any day. She'll want to check you out as soon as possible."

"You're scaring me," she said.

He took a hearty swig of the fresh-brewed coffee. Blythe saw him swallow and grimace.

"Is it okay?"

"Uh, yeah. Fine. Wouldn't you want to check out the woman your son married, especially knowing how he came to marry that particular woman?"

Another picture of the little boy she'd imagined earlier slipped into Blythe's mind. She sighed. "I suppose I would," she said grudgingly. "But I'm not one to look for something to criticize."

"Neither is my mother, but she will do a lot of looking and weighing."

Blythe laid the bacon strips in the skillet and turned to look at him. "Like I said. A little scary."

"That's the way I feel every time I'm in the room with your brother, and I definitely come up short in Win's book."

"Win is really a good man," she told him in all seriousness. "He can be a trifle stuffy and more than a little bossy at times, but at the end of the day he has a wicked, sort of sarcastic sense of humor, and he loves his family dearly."

"He was certainly protective of you."

"Well, I'm the baby of the family, so that's to be expected. I've always thought that part of his problem is that he's never recovered from losing Felicia."

"His wife?" Will asked, taking another sip of coffee.

"His fiancée. She was killed in a carriage accident on her way to the church. Unfortunately, instead of dealing with his grief, he blamed God for taking her away from him. It's been almost ten years, and he's done everything imaginable to try to fill the void losing her left in his life. I think one reason he moved here is that he's still running away."

"I get the impression he's quite the ladies' man."

"Oh, he is. It's all a defense thing."

"I'm not following you."

"If he has several girls on the string, there's little chance of him falling for any of them."

"What about Ellie? Everyone seems to think there's some spark between them."

"Wee-ell," she said, drawing out the word. "Ellie is different, and it's awfully complicated. I do think there's an attraction, but they come from two vastly different ways of living, and she's afraid the differences in their upbringing will be too much to overcome. You know—rich city boy, poor country girl."

"Like us, only in reverse."

"Yes," she said, her eyes troubled. "Exactly like us. And then there's Bethany. Taking on the parenting of a child with the mental shortcomings she has is a huge responsibility. I think Ellie worries about any husband being able to deal with it. And then there's Jake."

"The husband," Will said. "I have a vague recollection of him. Never did care for him much."

"I don't think anyone else does, either. Until recently, Ellie has used Jake's existence as a way to hold potential suitors at arm's length so that she can't fall for someone and run the risk of being hurt again."

"What happened recently?"

"She told me on Monday that she finally took everyone's advice and had him declared legally dead."

"So something could develop between her and your brother."

Blythe shrugged. "Who knows?"

Will's eyes widened at the precise moment the scent of something burning registered in her mind. "The bacon!"

Will watched as she whirled to see the ruins of their breakfast. He was beside her in a second. The bacon was charred on the bottom and blisters of raw fat had bubbled up on the top.

"I'm a total disaster as a wife!" she cried while he brushed her aside and moved the skillet.

"It's my fault," Will said, guiding her toward the chair he'd just vacated. "I kept you talking."

"Any woman worth her salt could talk and cook at the same time," she snapped.

At least she was reacting with irritation and not tears. It felt as if someone was stabbing his heart with a hunting knife whenever she cried. Anger meant she was getting a little starch in her spine. When she was seated, he picked up his cup of coffee and pressed it into her hands. "Drink."

She hesitated for just a moment and then did as he said. Once again, their gazes met. There was an implied intimacy seeing her place her mouth where his had been just seconds before. He could almost imagine she was placing her lips against his, an exciting image.

"This coffee is dreadful!" she cried after forcing a swallow down her throat. "Why didn't you tell me how bad it was when I asked if it was all right?"

"Settle down," he said in a gentle voice.

"How can I settle down? If a man has to marry a

pig in a poke, the least he should get out of it is a decent cup of coffee."

"It's just a little strong, is all."

"A *little* strong?" she retorted. "I daresay it would take the varnish off the table if it sat there long enough."

Will didn't know whether to laugh or cry. She was taking this far too seriously. "I'll add some more water to the coffee and finish breakfast," he offered, hoping the gesture would ease her consternation.

"No, you will not," she said, leaping to her feet. The fire of determination blazed in her eyes. "I'll not have you doing your work and mine. I'll cook your breakfast if it kills me. And you'll eat it if it kills you!"

"Yes, ma'am." Surprised by this new side of her—a spunky side he sort of liked—Will backed away from the stove, his hands raised in a gesture of surrender, though it was all he could do to keep from laughing.

A little later they were sharing bacon, eggs and biscuits. There was little conversation. Blythe was already regretting her outburst, but she noticed that Will ate every bite she'd cooked, even though she'd once more overcooked the bacon slices and the yolks of the eggs were as hard as the crunchy crust around the edges. The biscuits were a little hard on top, but they were as light as a feather inside. Unfortunately they tasted like baking soda. It had not escaped her attention that Will had poured at least a third of a quart of blackstrap molasses over everything and washed it down with more of the bitter coffee.

When he'd finished and placed his napkin on the table, he rose and said, "Thank you, Blythe."

"For what?"

"The delicious breakfast."

Blythe saw the twinkle of amusement in his dark eyes. It only served to irritate her more. "Don't add lying to your sins, Will Slade," she said in a low, measured voice. "It was all I could do to choke it down."

"I'm not the best of cooks, either," he told her. "A year from now we'll be laughing about this."

A year from now. Even though they'd vowed to stay together, Blythe couldn't help wondering if there would even be a marriage a year from now. She had a lot to learn during the next twelve months.

"Will we?

"Of course we will. Neither of us is a quitter."

"You're right," she said, lifting her chin to a determined angle.

"That's my girl!" he said, turning and heading for the door. Blythe's gasp of surprise halted him and he turned. "Sorry."

"Nothing to be sorry for," she told him in a voice that sounded slightly breathless even to her own ears. "I guess I am your girl…for better or worse."

"I guess you are." The smile made another brief appearance before he reached for the doorknob.

"See you at dinner," she called as the door closed behind him.

The room felt empty without him, but her heart felt full. Full of hope for the future they would build together despite the circumstances of their marriage. Full of confidence that they could weather any storm. They had made mistakes. They'd left God out of their lives while wallowing in their misery and heartbreak, but they'd turned a new page. They had decided as a couple that they would make the Lord the center of their lives. If they did that, how could they fail?

Chapter Fifteen

When Will came in at noon and opened the door, he was greeted with the scent of something that did not smell burned. There was no smoke in the house. No woman hiding a burned hand behind her back. In fact, Blythe was nowhere to be seen.

She'd been busy while he was at the mill. The windows, which had developed a film over the winter from the wood smoke, gleamed in the noonday sun. There wasn't a speck of dust anywhere.

He paused in the doorway, trying to figure out what smelled so good. Bread? Apples? Both? He padded across the floor to the stove and lifted the lid of the cast-iron Dutch oven, where some of the vegetable soup his mother had canned simmered. An apple pie sat on a folded towel on the worktable and a peek into the oven revealed browning bread.

As Will closed the oven and straightened, he heard a sharp intake of breath from the entrance of the spare bedroom. He turned to see his wife coming through the doorway, smoothing a lock of hair behind her ear.

"I went to tidy up and didn't hear you," she explained, regarding him with a frown. "Is everything all right, Will? You look a little…strange."

"I'm fine," he said with a nod. "Please don't take offense," he said, waving his hand toward the stove, "but how did you do all…this? I mean, this is a far cry from breakfast."

To his surprise, she laughed. It was the first time he'd ever heard her laugh; in fact, her smiles were rare. The happy sound echoed throughout the room, mingling with the delicious aromas of their meal and filling him with an indefinable something that wrapped itself around his heart and settled there like a cat looking for the perfect place to curl up for a long rest. If he weren't too afraid to believe in the feeling, he might say it felt like home.

"Did you think my fairy godmother had come while you were gone and granted me a wish?"

"I don't know what to think," he confessed.

"Nothing so miraculous," she said, crossing to the kitchen and reaching for the apron that hung on a peg next to his jacket. "It was Nita."

"Nita Allen?"

"Yes. She stopped by with some things that she called a little wedding gift, and she brought her famous basket filled with all sorts of wonderful goodies. Like the pie."

"You didn't make the pie?"

She gave him an impish smile. "Technically, I did bake it, but Nita brought it ready to go into the oven. I'm not brave enough to try pie just yet. She did show me some things about the stove, and I did make the bread."

"You made bread from scratch?" He heard the disbelief in his voice.

"'Oh, ye of little faith,'" she quoted. "Actually, it's the soda bread her late husband, Yancy, brought over from Ireland. Nita gave the recipe to my mother and she passed it on to me. There's no yeast, so I thought I'd give it a try. If I don't burn it, maybe I'll have my first culinary success."

"It looked almost perfectly brown to me," he told her.

"Will you fill the glasses, or would you rather have coffee? Nita showed me how to make that, as well."

"Water is fine, but coffee would be great when I come in this evening."

Will stood there, bemused by the change in Blythe. All because she felt she'd finally done something right. It wasn't so surprising, really. He knew how good he felt when he accomplished something at the mill he'd never done before.

He watched as she grabbed a couple of towels and opened the oven door. A rush of fragrant, hot air filled the room. Careful of not burning herself, she lifted the pan from the oven and set it next to the pie. Then she placed her hands at the small of her back and arched against them.

"You okay?" he asked. He hadn't forgotten how her back had been hurting or that she'd fainted at their wedding. He thought she was doing too much, but he suspected there was nothing he could say to stop her. Hadn't he already tried?

"My back's just tired," she told him offhandedly. "Nita said to let the bread sit a couple of minutes and then turn it out. It will get soggy on the bottom if you leave it in the pan."

Will had always liked Ace Allen's mother and never more so than at that moment. "How are Ace and Meg doing?" The couple had married on Valentine's Day.

Blythe took a ladle off the hook and began to dish up the soup. "Nita said, and I quote, 'They're as happy as two fat hogs in the sunshine.'"

"Good." Will took the bowl she'd filled and handed her the empty one. If ever there were two people who'd suffered during their lives and needed happily-ever-afters, it was Meg Thomerson and Ace Allen.

"Go ahead and sit," Blythe said, going to the bread and turning the skillet upside down on a plate.

"A gentleman doesn't sit until the ladies do."

"I appreciate the sentiment, but please. Indulge me."

She lifted the cast-iron skillet and it came right up, leaving a perfectly browned round loaf of bread. Will wasn't aware he was holding his breath until he heard it whoosh from him in relief.

She whirled toward him, exultation on her face. "Look, Will!"

"It looks delicious," he told her truthfully.

A glimmer of worry crept into her eyes. "I hope it is."

"'Oh, ye of little faith,'" he quoted back to her.

"You're right. I followed the instructions to the letter. It will be wonderful."

To their mutual surprise, the meal was everything they'd hoped for, though Blythe was too tired to fully enjoy it.

"Great meal," he said, cutting himself a second slice of pie.

"Thank you, but I can't take credit for much of it." Blythe pressed the tines of her fork into the crumbs of crust on her plate. "Will?"

He glanced up from his task, a quizzical look on his face.

"I couldn't help noticing that you left the mill's ledger on the table last night. I know you were looking over some figures, and you seemed…frustrated about something." She drew in a breath, as if she were trying to gather the courage to continue. "I was wondering if you'd like me to take a look. I'm a much better mathematician than I am a cook."

"You haven't already taken a peek?" he asked.

Blythe was horrified at the suggestion. "Of course not! Whatever is between those covers is none of my business."

"Actually, it is," he told her. "You're my wife, remember?" He stared at her thoughtfully for a moment in the quiet of the room, and then he nodded. "Since our future depends on the mill, yes, I'd be happy for you to have a look. In fact, if you don't mind, I'll get you the records for the last couple of years. Things started going wrong and money started getting tight before Martha left."

"Who kept the books?"

"Until she left, Martha did."

Martha. Recalling the way Will's first wife dressed, Blythe had a pretty good idea where some of the money had gone without ever opening the ledgers. Of course, her theory might be prejudiced because of her intense dislike of the other woman.

"All I know is that, with so many of my machines needing to be replaced, I haven't been able to catch up since she left."

"I almost have the house in order. I may have a chance to get to them this afternoon."

A look of relief spread across Will's features. "Thanks, Blythe. That would be great."

After he returned to the mill, Blythe set to work getting a head start on their evening meal. Nita Allen had left some deer meat in the springhouse and told Blythe how to fry it and use the drippings for gravy. She knew how to mash potatoes and she'd seen a jar of corn in the pantry that she would open up and warm to go with the meal. There was enough bread and pie left over to go with it. With one decent meal behind her, she was confident she could pull off another.

She finished waxing the parlor furniture and dusted and washed the globes of the lamps and the glass on the pictures on the wall. Though she was chomping at the bit to get to Will's books, she wrestled the parlor rug outside and somehow managed to get it flung over the clothesline. She spent the next several minutes beating it and then lugged it back inside.

Hands on her hips, she arched her back against the nagging ache and surveyed her handiwork. Floors and furniture glistened and gleamed. The scent of lemon balm and beeswax left a clean scent in the air. Finished! Or at least as finished as she could be until she and Will could financially manage to change out some things. Bring on Bess Slade. Blythe was ready for her.

Free to examine the mill's books, she poured herself

a cup of the coffee left warming on the back of the stove and sliced herself a small sliver of the pie.

Three hours later she had at least part of the answers Will was seeking.

Will was stacking some freshly cut boards to air-dry when he saw the approaching buggy. His jaw tightened as the well-dressed man jumped from the carriage and headed his direction. Win Granville, no doubt coming to check on his sister.

Will slapped one of his workers on the shoulder and asked him to finish while he went to greet the newcomer, who was looking at the operation with definite interest.

"Slade," Win said, extending a hand in greeting.

"Granville."

The adversaries shook hands and Will decided to take the initiative. "I suppose you came to check on Blythe."

"If I'd wanted to check on her, I'd have gone to the house," he said, then ruined it by asking, "How is she?"

"Working hard to put her own stamp on the house before my mother arrives," Will said. "After the way she fainted at the wedding, I think she's doing too much, but I'm not there to stop her."

"She can be hardheaded."

"I'm finding that out. So…to what do I owe the honor of your visit?"

"I thought I'd try one more time to make you see reason."

"Which means you want me to sell you the mill."

"I'd settle for part of it. It would solve your current financial problems and make going forward a lot easier."

"There's only one problem with that."

"Which is?"

"That Slade Mills was started by my father and has always been operated by Slades."

"I have no problem with you running things if that's what's holding you back," Win said.

"What's holding me back is that I know this business inside and out and I'm perfectly capable of getting it back on track on my own."

Win's temper was on the rise. "What's holding you back is your stubborn pride."

"Maybe it is," Will agreed. "Look, Granville, I'm thinking pretty clearly these days, and I think I've come up with a plan to have the mill back in the black in a year or so."

"You're a fool, Will Slade. Instead of clinging to your pride and the way things used to be, maybe you should think about my sister. She's grown accustomed to a certain lifestyle, and I hardly think your little cabin in the woods will be enough for her in the long run."

Will thought he'd choke on his fury. Attacking a man's ability to provide for his family was a shocking breach of conduct. "That was a low blow even for you, Granville."

Win knew he'd stepped over the line. Regret lingered in his eyes and he had the grace to blush. "You're right. It was uncalled-for. My apologies. It's just that I want the best for her, especially after all she's been through."

As much as Will disliked Granville, he knew that

most of that sentiment was rooted in the fact that the blasted man would not take no for an answer when it came to buying the mill. Will also knew his concern about Blythe was genuine. He felt the same way about his sisters.

"Apology accepted. It might come as a surprise to you, but I want the same thing for Blythe that you do. We're going to be forced to spend a considerable amount of time with each other, and I think we both know that she would feel a lot better about things if she knew we'd buried the hatchet. Preferably not in each other's backs."

"You're right," Win agreed.

"Another thing."

Granville regarded him with a lift of his sandy eyebrows.

"You might not know your sister as well as you think you do."

"Meaning?"

"Meaning Blythe and I both know we started out with a couple of strikes against us. It was an insane idea, but we both agreed to it, and despite what we've both been through, we believe in the sanctity of marriage. We made promises before God, saying we were in it for better and for worse. So far, I haven't heard her complaining."

Win nodded. "Point taken. Now, can we go inside and talk about this plan of yours?"

Will's conversation with Win stayed in his mind the rest of the afternoon. When his brother-in-law left the mill, things were better between them, though Granville still maintained Will was a stubborn fool. Will didn't deny it. Maybe Win would stop hounding him about the mill now that they'd reached a tentative truce and he'd given his plan the stamp of approval.

When Will stepped through the door, he was once again greeted with an abundance of delicious smells. Blythe was standing at the stove, her hair drawn back with a ribbon at the nape of her neck, the long, dark tresses falling down her back in gentle waves. She was stirring something in the cast-iron skillet and turned with a shy smile of welcome when she heard him come in.

"How was your afternoon?"

"Good," he said, marveling again that she was interested in his work. "We shipped the big order out and got another one from a place in Little Rock."

"That's good news."

"What's for supper?"

"Deer steaks, mashed potatoes and gravy, corn and the bread and pie from lunch."

Will couldn't help smiling at the satisfaction on her face. She might have been raised with a silver spoon in her mouth, but clearly Libby Granville had passed on the grit she'd developed from her days as Lucas Gentry's hardworking wife. Blythe seemed determined to do her part to make their marriage a success.

Will walked over to the stove and peeked over her shoulder at the bubbling gravy. He was so close he could smell her sweet lilac scent. He closed his eyes and drew in a deep breath, filling his senses with the floral aroma.

"Smells delicious."

She turned to look over her shoulder and their faces were mere inches apart. The memory of the sweetness of her lips against his the previous evening flashed into his mind. It was all he could do to keep from repeating the act.

Her eyes were wide and filled with a combination of expectancy and curiosity. He forced himself to say something in an attempt to break the mood. "Looks good."

As he'd hoped, the inane words shattered the intimacy binding them. With a quick, mischievous smile, he reached around her and snatched a piece of the fried steak from the platter.

"William Slade!" she said, smacking the back of his hand before he could pull it away. "Stay out of my food. You remind me of Win."

Heaven forbid! Instead of answering, Will popped the meat into his mouth. It needed a little more salt, had a bit too much pepper, and it could have been tenderer, but definitely would be no hardship to eat.

"Pretty tasty, wife."

"Why, thank you, husband," she said. "What about the gravy?" She let a spoonful drip back into the skillet. It was more like a plop than a steady stream. "I think it's too thick, but Nita said to err on the side of too much flour instead of too little."

The milky sauce looked thick enough to stand a spoon in, but Will didn't want to be the one to burst her bubble. "Um…maybe a bit. Nita's right, though. It's easier to thin it than thicken. Why don't you add some water?"

Blythe did as he suggested, but there wasn't room enough in the skillet to thin it as much as was needed. In the end, the gravy was almost the same consistency as the mashed potatoes, but after they'd given thanks for their food, Will dived into the meal with his usual enthusiasm. Once again, he had few complaints. It wasn't perfect by a long shot, but it was tasty enough, and if Blythe continued to improve, she'd be a great cook in no time.

He was finishing his pie when Blythe said, "I had time to look over the mill's finances. I haven't finished, but I can already tell you a couple of things with certainty."

His appetite fled. "And?"

"First, there's no rhyme or reason to the money you took from the mill for your personal use."

That wasn't much of a surprise. He shrugged. "I don't doubt it. Whenever Martha started harping on wanting new curtains, clothes or a trip to Little Rock or St. Louis, I just took the funds from the mill's profits. I figured it was mine, and I wanted to give her whatever she wanted." A look of chagrin flashed across his face. "It was easier than hearing her nag about it for months on end."

"Well, if it makes you feel any better about her leaving, I can tell you that if she *hadn't* left, she'd have spent you into the poorhouse in less than a year."

As bad as things were, he'd had no idea that he'd been so near ruin. Probably still was.

"I can also tell you that only a portion of the money you were giving her to deposit actually made it into your account."

Will just stared at her, trying to reconcile what she was saying with what his ears were hearing. "Are you saying she was stealing money?"

"Technically, yes, though I doubt she looked at it

that way. I imagine she felt that it was as much her money as yours and that she was entitled to it."

"She could have just asked me and—"

Blythe reached out and covered his hand with hers. "It wouldn't have mattered, Will," she said. "It would never have been enough."

Without thinking, he curled his fingers around hers. "What do I need to do to get out of this mess?"

A sudden memory of his kiss the night before slipped into her mind, causing her heart to skip a beat. She struggled to make her voice and her gaze steady. "The best advice I can give you is to take Win up on his offer."

Will pushed away from the table and got to his feet. "Win actually came out to the mill this afternoon and tried to talk me into at least a partnership. I turned him down."

"I know you say you don't want to, but taking him up on his offer would help you get back on your feet."

"No. The mill is mine. Ours. That's the way it's going to stay. We may have to tighten our belts for a while, but I think I can have us in the black in a year."

Blythe shook her head, but there was a slight smile on her lips. "I just realized that the reason you two butt heads all the time is because you're as alike as two peas in a pod."

"God forbid."

She laughed. "All right," she said. "If you're dead set on doing this your way, you have to have a plan. First of all, there can be no more drawing out money on a whim."

"What do I do?"

"Give yourself a weekly salary, and don't take another penny for your personal use. After I wash the dishes, we'll sit down and make a list of all your expenditures. If I go back the past eighteen months and average your gross income, I'll have an idea of what you bring in monthly. We'll allocate money appropriately from there—employee wages, your salary, my household budget from your salary and so on. That way, we'll know where every penny is spent."

"Blythe Granville, belle of the Boston elite, is going to live on a budget?" he asked, recalling what Win had said about her being accustomed to a certain lifestyle.

"Since she is penniless, Blythe *Slade* will be glad to help her husband so that she does not have to be dependent on her brothers for every penny." She grew serious suddenly. "In return, I'll do my best, however I can, to be the kind of wife to help you and our business reach the next level. That help includes handling the accounting, if you like."

The relief that swept through Will was palpable. Her willingness to live within his means was a surprise, but even though he was relieved that she wanted to take over the bookkeeping, he held back. Hadn't she just told him that Martha was partly responsible for the mess he was in?

As if she sensed his turmoil, and knew what was behind his uncertainty, she said, "I'm not Martha, Will."

Will reached out, took her hands and pulled her to her feet. She looked up at him, confusion on her pretty face. "Believe me, I know that."

And then, because he was so grateful that she was willing to do whatever it took to carve out a place in his life, because she was a confusing mass of contradictions that kept him guessing how she would respond to any given situation, because she'd suffered for things that were not her fault and still maintained a quiet dignity, but mostly because he couldn't help himself, he kissed her.

Chapter Sixteen

Blythe's first reaction to Will's kiss was shock, quickly followed by wonder. How could a simple kiss convey so many things? It was masterful; he was no novice. His lips were firm yet incredibly tender. Coaxing, yet at the same time she was aware of the tension, passion kept carefully on leash, so unlike Devon's kisses that had demanded a response. Responding to Will took no effort at all. She gave a little whimper of denial and at the same time grabbed the front of his shirt to steady herself.

She knew she should stop him, pull away, but she couldn't find the strength or the will to do so. As crazy as she knew it was, she felt so…safe in his arms, even though she also knew that to trust her feelings was not always a good thing.

Finally, Will raised his head and drew in a shaky breath, but he didn't release her. Embarrassed and dismayed by her reaction to the kiss and unable to look him in the eye, Blythe rested her forehead against his chest. Why had he kissed her and why had she responded as she had? What must he think of her?

Quite possibly that you are a loose woman.

Was she? Anger at herself for her reckless behavior began to push aside her discomfiture. How could she have believed she'd loved a man just over three months ago and then respond to another man's kisses with such unconstrained eagerness?

"I'm sorry. I didn't mean for that to happen."

The softly spoken apology penetrated Blythe's self-castigation. What did he mean? That he hadn't intended to kiss her or that he hadn't intended for it to get so…so…

"What did happen?" she asked, finally lifting her head to look up at him. His midnight dark eyes were as troubled as her heart.

"I'm not sure." He released her and crossed the room, his long legs eating up the space. "I think it could be a good thing."

Oh, it could be a very good thing, she thought and immediately sought to justify her reasoning. Yes, he was a virtual stranger who was also her husband. The kiss proved they were attracted to each other. Any fool could see that that would be a plus for them both when it came time to think of adding children to their family.

Blythe reached out as he passed, grabbing his shirt. "The kiss was…lovely, Will. As ashamed as I am to say it, I don't deny that."

"Ashamed? Why on earth would you be ashamed to admit that the kiss was…very nice?"

To her chagrin, she felt the tears return. "Because I've always thought I was a decent person. But how can I be if I loved someone enough to run away and marry him and less than four months later—" her voice broke, but she forged ahead "—find another man's kisses pleasing? I'm not sure what kind of woman that makes me."

Will took her shoulders in his hands and gave her a single, gentle shake. "It was a kiss, Blythe. A kiss between a married couple. Does liking it make you a terrible person? Hardly. It makes you human. I certainly don't think less of you." He released her and raked a hand through his hair. "I liked it, too. Far too much, considering what Martha put me through."

She pressed her lips together to still their trembling.

"When we first met, I'd formed an opinion of you by assuming you were a spoiled city girl. I figured that your name and social position were the only things that mattered to you, and I disliked your brother. Do you know what changed my opinion?"

She shook her head.

"Seeing you tackle things you have no knowledge of with hardheaded determination and a desire to be a good wife in spite of everything, even though I'm not the husband you wanted."

"I'm not the wife you wanted, either."

He offered her a wry smile. "Well, despite what we wanted, we're stuck with each other, and I'm not dissatisfied." He reached out and trailed a finger along the curve of her jaw. "I don't know about you, but I think we're doing okay so far. Let's just take things slow and easy and see where it leads."

The warring emotions racing through her battled for supremacy. Lingering shame. Hope. Confidence and a growing certainty that she had done the unthinkable. She had fallen in love with her husband.

What could she do but nod in agreement?

* * *

Blythe hardly slept that night. She relived the kiss and the conversation over and over and called herself ten kinds of fool, but by the time the sun peeked over the horizon, she was more certain than ever that she loved her husband, no matter what kind of woman that made her. It remained to be seen what she would do with that knowledge. Arching her back, she stretched, knowing that she couldn't hide from him forever.

She levered herself into a sitting position and the room began to spin, as it had several times lately. When things settled, she rose and began to dress. As she brushed her hair and twisted it up into a no-nonsense knot atop her head, she regarded her reflection carefully. Her skin looked pale; there were dark circles beneath her eyes and hollows in her cheeks.

She wondered if she should see what Rachel had to say about the recurring dizzy spells but figured she would just blame it on the stress she'd been through and hard work, just as she had before.

Even though she was moving slowly, she had breakfast almost finished when Will stepped out of his room. Unlike her, he looked refreshed and energetic.

He stopped dead in his tracks when he saw her. "Are you okay?"

"Fine." She whirled to reach for the coffeepot and the kitchen took a dip. She reached for something to grab hold of, but there was nothing. As she crumpled to the floor, she heard Will's voice calling her name. She thought she heard a note of panic in it.

When she awoke, she realized she was in the back of the wagon, which bounced along the road. She wanted to ask where they were going, but it seemed like far too much effort to talk. Instead she closed her eyes and let the darkness take her once more.

The next time she woke, Will was carrying her.

"Where are we going?"

"To see the doctor."

"I'm fine. Just tired."

"You're not fine."

Edward must have seen them barreling across the railroad tracks, because he was opening the surgery door by the time Will gathered Blythe into his arms.

"What's going on?" Edward asked, gesturing toward one of the empty rooms.

"She fainted again. Is Rachel up?"

"She's up, but she's not taking patients for a while yet."

"Oh, the baby…" Blythe murmured, surfacing from the darkness for a moment. She'd forgotten that Rachel's baby was only a few days old.

"Yes, the baby," Edward said as Will deposited Blythe onto the narrow bed. "But don't you worry your pretty little head. I think I can handle things for a while." He gave her a mischievous smile and gave her hand a pat. "I taught Rachel everything she knows, you know."

He took Blythe's wrist between his fingers and looked at his watch. "What happened?"

"You know she fainted Sunday at the wedding, and Rachel seemed to think it was strain and anxiety, but ever since the wedding, she's been cleaning like a madwoman, trying to get ready for my mother's visit." He offered a wry smile. "I don't think the marriage has eased her worry any."

Edward nodded and turned his intelligent gaze to Blythe. "Anything else?"

"Some dizzy spells that come on without warning," she told him truthfully. "They usually pass in a few seconds. And my back has been hurting, but as Will said, I've been doing a lot of cleaning."

"Nausea, sleepiness?"

"A little, but nothing that doesn't go away when I eat something. I have been really tired, but all the cleaning…"

"Did you have any of these symptoms before the wedding?"

Blythe's forehead wrinkled in a frown of concentration. "Yes, now that you mention it, I did. Nothing serious, though."

"Okay, then," Edward said. "Since this has been going on awhile, I'll need to give you a full examination. Will, why don't you go into the kitchen and have a cup of coffee with Gabe? And please send Danny to get Libby. I'm sure my lovely fiancée will want to know Blythe's under the weather."

"Is she going to be all right?" Will asked. Blythe wondered if she imagined the concern in his eyes. "I'd have made her come sooner if I thought there was something wrong."

"You did fine, Will. Neither of you would have any way of knowing if there's something more at play here. That's why you have me."

"What's going on?" Rachel stepped through the doorway wearing a robe that looked as if it belonged to her husband.

"You need to go back to bed," her father told her. "I know you hardly slept a wink last night."

"I need to be right here. I'll just sit and observe."

Edward regarded his daughter with dismay but nodded his acceptance. It was clear he and Rachel had butted heads before, and that he knew when further argument was futile. He pointed to the chair next to the bed. "Sit." He pointed to Will. "Go."

Will lost no time heading for the door. As soon as he'd left the room, Rachel went to stand by the bed. Her expression was solemn as she took Blythe's hand in both of hers and looked at her father.

"Sit down, Rachel," he commanded, indicating the needlepoint chair again. When Rachel complied, he continued. "Blythe fainted again," Edward said. "Some extreme tiredness, a bit of nausea. Backaches."

"What are you thinking, Pops?"

Blythe looked from one concerned face to the other. Clearly, they suspected something more than constant worry was causing her fainting spells. "You're scaring me," she whispered, her eyes wide and her face devoid of color.

Rachel tried to smile, but it was a poor attempt. Giving Blythe's hand another comforting pat, Edward said, "There's no need to be scared, and I won't be sure until I do an exam, but I'm inclined to think you're with child."

"B-But I can't be."

Both Edward and Rachel looked at her with raised eyebrows. "Surely you and Devon—" Rachel said.

"Yes! Yes!" Blythe exclaimed, waving her hand to silence Rachel before she could put her question into words. She drew in a deep breath and tried to find calm. "Yes, our marriage was…consummated, but since then, I… Everything has been…normal."

"That can happen," Edward told her.

"Dad's right. It can," Rachel added. "But when you put everything together...the dizzy spells, the backaches, the sleepiness and occasional queasiness. It's time to look a little deeper, don't you agree?"

"No!" Blythe cried, her wild-eyed gaze moving from one doctor to the other. Every part of her being rejected what she was hearing. She couldn't be expecting a baby! Surely God wouldn't do this to her, not when it looked as if she and Will might be able to make their marriage work.

"If you are expecting, it's not something you can ignore," Rachel said in a gentle voice.

The door opened and everyone looked in that direction. Libby stood there, more disheveled than Blythe had ever seen her, the concern in her eyes undeniable.

"Edward?" she questioned in a quavering voice. "What is it? What's wrong?"

Edward held out an arm and Libby rushed to his side. "It's okay, sweetheart," he told her as he slipped an arm around her shoulders.

"Did I hear something about a baby?" she asked, glancing at her daughter, whose face was wet with tears. "Blythe?"

"They think I may be with child," she said and lost all control of her crying.

"We won't know until she's examined," Edward said. His words were spoken to his fiancée, but he was looking at Blythe. "There's no sense upsetting yourself until we find out the truth. Then you can figure out how you're going to...go forward."

His meaning was impossible to miss. If she was

carrying Devon's child, she would have to tell Will. Blythe felt more tears slide down her cheeks. She brushed them away with an angry gesture. "I'm not sure I can...deal with one more thing! It's too much. Will...Will...he'll think I only married him to try to trap him and get a father for...for Devon's—" her voice broke on a sob "—baby!"

"Shush," Libby soothed, leaving the comfort of Edward's side and rushing to the bed. "Everything will be fine."

"It *won't* be fine, Mama. Will didn't really want a wife. How do you think he's going to take to the idea of a baby?"

"Blythe, listen to me," Libby said, laying a hand on Blythe's clenched fist.

"I'll just tell him we can have the marriage annulled."

"Blythe, calm down!" Libby said in the tone that told her daughter she wasn't in any mood to be trifled with.

Blythe nodded, sniffed and knuckled the tears from her eyes.

"Let's don't get the cart before the horse. Let Edward have a look at you, and we'll go from there."

Moments later, Edward drew the blanket up over Blythe and announced, "You are definitely having a baby. Judging from the time you and Devon eloped, I'd say you're just over three months along."

The words fell into Blythe's consciousness with all the weight of stones sinking to the bottom of a well. For the second time in less than half a year, her dreams had been dashed, her tentative hope for a better future shattered.

* * *

Will wasn't sure how long he wandered around the Gentry kitchen, his mind whirling with concern for his new bride. Gabe had left him with instructions to help himself to any of the leftover breakfast items sitting at the back of the stove, but for the first time in a long time, Will found he had no appetite.

He was trying to drink yet another cup of coffee when he heard steps in the hallway. Rachel stood there, looking drawn and concerned.

"You can come in now."

He set the cup onto the table so hard the liquid sloshed over the side. When he stepped out into the hallway that led to the surgery, Rachel was already at the door. She stepped aside for him and closed it behind them.

The tension in the room reached out and grabbed him by the throat. Will's troubled gaze moved from one woman to the other. Blythe's eyes were red from crying and she was looking at him with actual fear. Libby stood straight and tall next to the bed, her usually pleasant face firm with resolve, as if she were readying herself to go into battle. Only Edward seemed his usual professional self.

"Sit down, Will," Rachel said.

Hearing her tone of voice, Will felt as if the bottom fell out of his stomach. What was it? Was there something seriously wrong with Blythe, some terrible condition? He stood with his legs slightly apart, bracing himself for whatever it was coming his way as he looked from her to Edward. "I'm fine. What's going on?"

"We thought we should break the news to you

before everyone in town finds out about it, and they will."

He frowned. "Finds out what?"

Rachel glanced at her father, who got straight to the point.

"Blythe is expecting a baby."

Will felt as if Big Dan Mercer had given him a punch in the gut. For the first time in longer than he could remember, he was speechless. His new wife, the woman he had promised to love and cherish and honor just days ago, was expecting a child. *A baby.* Another man's baby.

He looked at Blythe, but she was staring at the hands twisting together in her lap. Without a word, he spun on his heel and left the room.

The last things he heard before slamming the door shut behind him were Libby's horrified gasp, Blythe's wail of sorrow and Rachel's sharp voice calling out, "Stop being so holier-than-thou, Will Slade."

The command gave him only momentary pause. He stormed through the house out onto the front porch, where he found Banjo waiting. Without acknowledging the dog's presence, Will began to pace. He plowed both hands through his hair and clutched his head, trying to make some sort of sense of what he'd just heard.

Had she known about the baby when she'd agreed to marry him? Surely a woman knew these things. Had she planned the night she'd stayed at his cabin all along, knowing everyone would expect him to do the right thing?

As soon as the thought entered his mind, he dismissed it. She didn't even know where he lived, and even if she had, she'd had no idea she'd find him passed out in the woods or that it would storm or—

"According to the ladies, it happened during the few short days she was married...or thought she was."

The comment, something Will had already figured out for himself, was delivered by the man coming around the side of the house. Caleb Gentry, another of Blythe's brothers, the wealthiest farmer in the county.

"Where did you come from?" Will asked.

"Gabe told me a little of what was going on, so I thought I'd come and check on things. Rachel told me about the baby and sent me to look for you. Are you okay?"

Will stared at the porch boards. Was he okay? He was still trying to reconcile the things he'd just heard with the future he'd begun to envision with Blythe. A future that had been hazy at best, but one he felt had become a little clearer the night before. Now all that was changed because there would be a baby.

Unaware of the torment in his eyes, he looked at Caleb. "I'm barely used to the idea of having a wife, and now I'm supposed to become a father, too. What do I do, Caleb? I didn't sign on for that. Is this one of those 'for worse' things that happen in a marriage?"

Sensing his owner's distress, Banjo whined.

Caleb smiled and gave Will a brotherly slap on the shoulder. "It's not a 'worse,'" he said. "It's a baby."

"What on earth will I do with a baby?"

"Love it."

If the idea of a baby was foreign, the idea of loving another man's child was doubly so. "How do I do that?"

Caleb smiled his rare smile. "Believe me, it's easier

than you may think. I do understand how you feel, Will. More so than most. I didn't sign up for marriage to a widow with three kids when I asked Abby to come be a wet nurse for my Betsy after Emily died, but here we are."

"But you love Abby."

"Of course I do now. But the day we said our vows I was angry and resentful and scared to death. My first marriage wasn't all that good. Abby's had been the best, and I was afraid of failing. I was so different from her first husband, and didn't know how to be what she wanted or how to be a father, but the first time Laura smiled at me, I was a goner. And here I am. Father of five."

Will had been aware of the scandal when Abby Carter had moved into Caleb's house to care for his baby daughter after his wife's death during the delivery. He recalled how the gossip had more or less forced them into marriage, too.

"We had a rocky start," Caleb added, "and at one point I even told her to leave, but she wouldn't go because she said her Ben told her that the two of us had made a promise to God." He offered a wry smile. "Out of the mouth of babes…"

He gave a shake of his perpetually shaggy head. "I can't tell you what to do, my friend. I guess it all boils down to whether or not you meant the words when you said them and if you're willing to let God help guide the two of you through the rough patches."

Will knew his reason for marrying Blythe was less than honorable. How many men married one woman to rid himself of the nuisance of another? Talk about needing to rid himself of the beam in his eye before condemning Blythe for the mote in hers!

"Look, bud, I need to get back to the farm, but I'll be praying for the two of you."

"Thanks, Caleb," Will said as his friend went back around the house. Something told him they'd need all the help they could get.

After a long while Blythe regained control of her crying. She'd managed to tamp back her shame, at least for the moment. Her mother and Rachel hadn't spoken in several minutes, either because they didn't know what to say or because they were giving her a chance to gather herself. All her thoughts centered around her future with Will...or what was left of it.

Where did she go from here? Should she go back to the farm or just cut her losses and forge ahead as she had when she'd left Boston? Would Will even come back? What would he say if he did? Was he done with the marriage before it even got started? If so, did it really matter to her beyond the shame and embarrassment of yet another debacle?

Oh, yes. It mattered.

"It's going to be okay," Rachel said. "Will can act the fool sometimes, but he'll come to his senses and do the right thing. He's always taken his obligations seriously."

Blythe felt like bursting into tears again. In a matter of minutes she had gone from a bride Will didn't want to a woman he would stay with out of a sense of duty.

"Well, that sounds just grand," she said in a bitter tone.

Rachel didn't bother replying.

As she had once before, Blythe pushed her misery aside as best she could and gathered her dwindling courage. Lord knew she'd need it in the coming weeks. The first thing she needed to do was think the situation through and then talk to Will. She needed to gather herself before she saw him. She needed to be calm. Collected. Sure of herself. She'd seen the ravages of her prolonged crying often enough to know that her complexion was red and splotchy and her eyes were swollen and irritated. She brushed back a straggling wisp of hair that clung to her wet cheek and began to prepare mentally for the upcoming battle.

"Mama, can you hand me a wet washcloth?"

Without a word, Libby rose to do her bidding.

Rachel watched the emotions chase across her young sister-in-law's face. *Young.* That was maybe the best word to describe Blythe. Most women of her age might have held up better through all the travails she'd been through, but then most women, at least those Rachel knew, had grown up in situations that forced them to mature much faster than Blythe had. Many already had two or more children by the time they were her age.

But despite the way Blythe had been raised, Rachel knew her sister-in-law was very adult in other ways and possessed knowledge and skills in other areas. Her problem was that she'd been caught up in two very volatile situations in a very short time, both of which were forcing her to grow up much faster than she might have otherwise.

Though Rachel knew that this unexpected baby

was a bitter pill for both Will and Blythe to swallow, deep in her heart, she felt that they were a good match. Blythe was as far removed from Martha as night from day, and Will, cantankerous though he may be, was at heart a good and honest man.

Rachel prayed that they could both find a way to ease the pain that gripped them and find peace and happiness. Though she had no idea what that might be, she knew from her own experience that the Lord had things under control and that He had already set some sort of plan into place.

Chapter Seventeen

Blythe lay against the pillows, bathing her face with the cool cloth and wishing she were anywhere but where she was. Now that the initial panic had passed and she'd settled down somewhat from the pain Will's storming off had inflicted, there was no way to keep from thinking of the changes that having a baby would make in her life. She placed her palm on her tummy to see if that would make it seem any more real. It didn't, but just because it didn't seem real, didn't mean it wasn't. She was terrified, and she was scared and very angry.

Why, God?

Wasn't it enough that she'd been dealt such misery through Devon's other wickedness? Wasn't it enough that she'd been forced to marry a stranger for performing an act of kindness? Why did the Lord continue to punish her? What had she done to deserve *this*? Even as she thought it, she knew blaming Him wasn't fair.

My grace is sufficient unto you.

The words slipped into her mind with the ease of

her foot into a comfortable slipper. Deserving had nothing to do with it. Choices did. Sometimes the choices were the wrong ones and bad things happened. God could straighten things out, but often there was pain along the way before a good place was reached.

Because he had been so very good at deception, she had chosen to listen to Devon's pleas, even though she'd known full well she would be the subject of gossip. But believing he and his vows of love and marriage were on the up-and-up, she'd behaved accordingly. There was no fault in that. She'd had no control over his actions.

Stumbling onto Will in the woods had been an accident, pure and simple, and she would go to her grave believing she had done the right thing by staying through the night with him, no matter the consequences.

And now this. A baby. A baby fathered by a man who had done her tremendous wrong. It wasn't fair.

My grace is sufficient unto you.

The words echoed through her mind once more. As a Christian, she had no doubt that the Lord wanted the best for His children. She'd always believed that even when things happened, good or bad, God was in control. His thoughts and His ways often looked like tribulations to His children.

Like Ace and Meg. Meg had made choices that had put her squarely into a life and a marriage that had been almost unbearable to endure, but the hardships she'd overcome had made her the woman Ace needed after suffering through his own trials.

Blythe was dabbing at her eyes with the cloth when

the door burst open. Will stood in the aperture. He didn't look a lot better than she figured she did. His hair stood on end and there was a grim tightness to his mouth that reminded her of his anger when he'd said he wasn't marrying anyone.

Especially not her.

Whatever he had to say, she couldn't imagine it was going to be pleasant. His gaze darted from Rachel, who sat at her side, to her mother on the opposite side of the bed.

"Would you mind giving us a minute?" he asked.

Rachel, who seemed to have lost all patience with her longtime friend and was already furious at the way he'd bolted from the room, looked as if she'd like to give him a piece of her mind. Both women looked at Blythe, trying to gauge her reaction to his demand. She gave an almost imperceptible nod of her head. "It's all right."

The moment the door closed behind them, some of the tension seemed to drain from the room. And Will.

"Please. Sit." Blythe gestured toward the chair sitting next to the bed.

"I'd rather stand."

Ah. It was going to be that way, was it? She'd expected it, of course, but somehow she'd treasured a tiny bit of hope that things would be different. Yet even as she'd hoped he wouldn't walk away from her, she wondered why she wished it.

Years of watching her mother wield the iron fist in the velvet glove stood her in good stead. Always take the initiative. "There's no reason to be so defensive. I have no intention of holding you to the marriage," she told him in a crisp, businesslike tone. "I've already told mother to contact Philip to see what it will take to have it annulled."

Will regarded her with narrowed eyes. "What?"

"The marriage," Blythe said. "I'm sure you think I only accepted your preposterous proposal so that I'd have a father for my baby."

He nodded, wary of her taking the lead in such a confident manner. One thing about it, she had a way of keeping him on his toes. He was never certain how she'd react to any given situation. Her take-charge attitude changed everything he'd been thinking.

"It crossed my mind," he said, "but it doesn't wash. There's no way you could have planned on stumbling across me in the woods and you were pretty adamant about not wanting to marry me even if I did ask. What I can't understand is that when I made the suggestion that we marry to help us both out of sticky situations, you changed your mind pretty quick. Why?"

"What are you implying?"

Will raised his hands in a gesture of surrender. "I don't know what to think, Blythe. I don't know who you are or what's going on in that pretty head of yours."

"I don't understand."

"Well, that makes two of us. Half an hour ago you were a mess. Now you're sitting here as calm and unruffled as can be, talking about hiring a lawyer to put an end to our marriage. You actually sound a lot like your brother, and I'm starting to think that maybe you're more like him than people think."

"Meaning?"

"Meaning the workings of the female mind are way beyond me. Maybe your refusal was some sort of convoluted plan to catch me off guard. How should I know? I'm just a simple country boy who works hard for a living, who married a woman who did me wrong, even though I did everything I could to make her happy. And for that, she walked out on me. Now this."

Blythe pressed her lips together tightly to keep from saying something she knew she'd regret and blinked hard and fast so she wouldn't appear to be a "mess" again.

"Let me make sure I understand," she said when she had her emotions more or less under control. "You think that I knew I was pregnant, refused to marry you at first, just to what? Make you less wary? And then when you did suggest we marry—just to keep your ex-wife at arm's length, I would remind you—I agreed to so that I'd have a father for the baby I didn't know I was carrying?"

She gave a sarcastic laugh. "If that's how your mind works, it's no wonder your business is a shambles."

As soon as the words left her lips, shame swept through her. It wasn't like her to be so spiteful, but she was tired of being taken in by words and her emotions were as raw as the hand she'd burned on the skillet.

Coldness crept into Will's dark eyes, something she'd seen often in the gaze of her brother. It was a deliberate distancing. A way of separating themselves from anything that might hurt them. Protection.

She realized with a sinking heart that their relationship was doomed. Since there were far too many obstacles for them to overcome, she decided to get everything off her chest.

"While we're on the subject of ulterior motives, what about you agreeing to marry me for my money?"

"You said you were broke," he reminded her, "and I thought we already had this conversation."

"I am broke, so I'd say that the laugh was on you, except that Martha told me that she'd heard Win offer to recompense you to marry me."

Will felt like punching someone. Was there no end to Martha Rafferty's deviousness? He tried his best to recall the conversation he'd had with Win the day he came to talk to him in this very room. "I thought we'd settled this."

"We did discuss it," she said, "but it's a long way from settled. I chose not to pursue it so that I could keep fooling myself that everything would be okay between us. Didn't Win say something along the lines of there being advantages to your marrying into the family?"

Will stared at her, feeling his life slip away for the second time. He was many things, but he wasn't a liar, so he might as well tell her everything.

"He did say something like that. You'd have to ask him what he meant. Either way, I told him I didn't want to marry anyone." Will began to pace. "When we talked at the mill, and I turned him down on the partnership again, I told him about a plan I had to get back on my feet. Since he's a successful business-man, I asked him if he thought it would work and, if so, if the bank would be willing to give me some financing."

"Ah. Those advantages," she said in a smug tone.

"No. When I explained that you'd looked at the books and found out what Martha was doing, Win realized I could pay the money back, no problem. So even if we weren't married, I'd have gotten the loan. A loan, Blythe. Not a sellout or a handout from my brother-in-law so that I'd marry you."

His announcement robbed her of the last remnants of her anger. She didn't think she'd been so miserable since the day she'd found out the truth about Devon.

"So now I guess we know exactly where we stand," he said.

As ashamed as she was, she refused to give him the satisfaction of an apology. The hurt went both ways. "It appears so."

She heard the barest hint of a quaver in her voice and wanted nothing more than to get rid of him before she broke down again. "If you'll send my mother in, I'll tell her to have Win start the process to end our marriage as soon as possible."

"No."

"No?"

"We made a promise to God. We said that we believe in the sanctity of marriage and we agreed there would be no divorce, no matter what."

"B-but that was before either of us knew about the baby, before there was so much…anger and distrust between us."

He ignored her comment and continued. "We took vows," he stated firmly. "And whatever else you may think I am, I don't go back on my word."

Blythe stared at him, her mouth parted in surprise. After everything that had just passed between them, she could hardly believe what she was hearing.

"But you don't like the idea of a baby."

He didn't say anything.

"Will. Be reasonable. We both know that we were going into this marriage as a way out of our problems." She gave a weary shake of her head. "I'm not sure how we fooled ourselves into thinking we could get through a lifetime together, but after today I can't see anything but disaster ahead."

"Maybe," he said again. "My mother has always said that nothing worth having comes easy, and this sure won't be. I guess this is where the commitment comes in. Are you feeling well enough to travel?"

"Why?" she asked.

"I'm going to go have a talk with Edward. If he says it's okay, we're going home."

"I'm sorry, Will. There's no way she can ride that far in the back of a wagon at this point," Edward said. "Rachel and I both think she's in danger of losing the baby."

For the second time in a matter of hours Will felt the world fall out from under him. Alarm sent his heart to racing. Just minutes ago he'd been furious with his wife for her lack of trust in him and upset because she was having another man's child. Now all he could think about was how small she'd looked lying in the big bed. How young. How defiant she'd been, refusing to give an inch, even though he could see in her brown eyes that her heart was as broken and bleeding as his. He couldn't bear the thought of her going through the emotional shock of losing a child, even if she'd known of its existence only a short time. She'd been through enough.

"What's the matter with her?"

"I'm sorry, Will," Edward told him. "I can't say with any certainty. Women sometimes have a hard time carrying babies to birth for any number of reasons. The anxiety she's been through could very well be part of the problem. She's run-down and doesn't look as if she's been eating well."

Edward sighed. "It's just hard to say. On the other hand, if she gets a few days' bed rest, puts on a little weight and has nothing to worry about but getting better, things could turn around."

Will nodded, weary though the morning wasn't half over yet. "Will she need to stay here for a while?"

"No, I sent Libby home to fix a room for her there. She has a downstairs bedroom, and if Blythe needs something, I can be there in a matter of minutes. I think she'll be more satisfied with her mother nearby."

Will nodded. "I'm sure she will. Let me know when she's ready to go and I'll drive her over."

"Will."

The feminine voice came from behind him. He turned to see Rachel, a look on her face that hovered somewhere between determination and sorrow.

"Blythe doesn't want you to drive her over. She doesn't want to see you at all."

"What are you talking about?"

"She said she changed her mind," Rachel told him. "That even though she told you she'd stay no matter what, she just can't do it, considering how things are."

"What does that mean?"

Rachel shook her head. "Oh, Will. You know what happened in there. I don't. I'm just relaying her message."

Will felt all the fight go out of him. Something

powerful squeezed his heart. He gave a single nod of acceptance. If this was what she really wanted, who was he to deny her?

Like Blythe, he'd been running on emotion for days, fighting against doing things he didn't want to do, fighting for things he wasn't even sure he wanted because it was the right thing to do. Fighting.

"I'll get her things together and bring them in as soon as possible." He pivoted on his boot heel and headed for the door.

As he passed Rachel, she said, "Will!"

"What?" he growled, pausing.

"Don't be in too big of a hurry bringing her things back."

He lifted his heavy eyebrows in question.

"She's in a lot of mental turmoil right now. I think that when she has time to think things through, she may change her mind."

Will's lips twisted into an ironic smile. Knowing his bride as he was beginning to, that was certainly a possibility, but this time he doubted it. Without a reply, he turned and walked out of the room.

Chapter Eighteen

Blythe was settled in her mother's downstairs guest room by lunchtime.

"Is everything okay?" Libby asked. "Do you feel all right?"

Blythe longed to say something to erase the concern in her mother's eyes, but nothing came to mind and she was too weary to care overly much.

"Everything is fine, Mama. Stop fussing over me."

"Worrying and fussing are what a mother does best," she said. "What sounds good for lunch?"

"I'm not really hungry, but I think I can sleep."

"Of course," Libby said. "I'll check in on you in a bit. I put Gramma's little brass bell there on the table. If you need something before I get back, just ring."

"I will."

When her mother left the room, Blythe turned on her side and placed her hands beneath her cheek. The ache in her heart was almost unbearable, but she wasn't even sure why she was so heartbroken. Was it because her life was a shamble? Was she angry because life as she'd known it was gone forever?

Because seeing Devon's child would be a daily re-
minder of him and all the harm he'd done her? Or
was it because the life she'd hoped to forge with Will
was doomed before they'd had a chance to make it
work?

*It's your fault, Blythe Slade. If you weren't so stub-
born and hadn't sent him away, Will would be sitting
here beside you right now, like the dutiful husband
he would be.*

That was the problem. He would be at her side
because it was his duty. She didn't want dutiful. She
hadn't sent him away because she believed that he'd
taken money to marry her or used their marriage as
leverage to get a loan from Win. She wanted him to
stay because he couldn't bear to not be in the same
room as she was.

She loved him, plain and simple. Loved a man who
was the total opposite of the men who had claimed
her interest in the past. When compared to Will, all
those men, including Devon, seemed…less in every
way. Will was simply…what he was. He had no
need to pretend to be upstanding. He was. He didn't
need to put on airs, since anyone could see that even
though he was a little rough in his appearance, he
was a man of his word. Besides, he could look as
well-groomed as the next man, as he'd proved on
their wedding day.

Will Slade was a giant of a man who ran his business with fairness and caring for his employees. He
was a man who felt more at home in the woods or
a noisy sawmill than behind a desk dealing with in-
voices and numbers. He was terrible with mathemat-
ics. He was all that and much more. He was the man

she loved and lost. She wondered how he'd responded when he'd been told she didn't want to see him.

A sharp rap sounded at the door and her brother poked his head into the room. "Asleep?"

"No," she said, pushing herself into a sitting position.

Win strolled into the room and sank into the wingback chair next to the bed. "I hear congratulations are in order." There was no joy in his tone or his eyes.

"So it seems."

"And how do you feel about that?" he asked, reaching out and taking her cold hand in his.

She shrugged. "How do I feel?" she asked. "Blindsided. Sad. Overwhelmed."

"Everything will be fine once you have time to get used to the thought."

"Will it, Win?" she asked with a wan smile. "Knowing that I'll have a child by a man who used me in the most hateful of ways is very…troubling. Having a baby shouldn't cause a woman to feel as if a millstone were hanging around her neck. It should be the source of anticipation and joy, the result of love and an intimacy sanctioned by God, all the things I believed while I was with Devon. You're right. I was a fool."

"No, Blythe. I was the fool. You had the courage to follow your heart, which is more than I've done." One corner of his mouth lifted in a wry smile.

"I'm ashamed to say that when all the brouhaha broke with Devon, Philip and I were more concerned about the Granville name and our position in society than what you were going through and how you were feeling. We were wrong, and I'm incredibly sorry."

"It's all right."

Neither spoke for several seconds. Finally, Win said, "I understand you told Slade you didn't want to see him anymore and that you planned to have the marriage annulled."

"Yes."

"Why? Because you believe Martha's claim about what she heard that day? I can tell you she misconstrued everything."

"So you didn't say there were advantages to marrying me."

"As a matter of fact, I did," Win confessed. "But I meant that the family knows a lot of folks back east that we can introduce him to. Men who are potential buyers of his lumber, which could be great for expanding his business and making more money. That's all."

Blythe believed him. She'd believed Will over Martha, but hearing Win explain reinforced her certainty.

"He took your wedding vows seriously, little sister. With that kind of commitment, there's a good chance the two of you can make this marriage a success."

"I know that."

"Then why end it? Why send him away?"

"I know I've been difficult since the *fiasco* with Devon." She tried to smile as she used the same word to describe her marriage that he had. "I've been hard to get along with, angry, and my moods have swung from one side of the pendulum to the other. One minute I'm acting like a child, the next like our mother."

Win smiled then. She was right.

"I've learned a few things since November, and

now, with this, I think I can say that I'm really growing up. I know exactly what I want, and it's a lot different from what I wanted at Thanksgiving."

"And what do you want?"

"Maybe I know what I don't want," she told him. "I don't want Will just because we took vows. I don't want to settle for second best in a husband, or to have a marriage that's little more than a civil arrangement.

"Not only that, but if I'm having trouble accepting this baby, how can I expect him to? He didn't ask to become father to another man's child when we agreed to marry. I don't want Will to take on the raising of this child just because it's suddenly become part of the deal and he's a man who always keeps his end of the bargain."

For the first time in a very long time, Blythe allowed the things in her heart to be revealed in her eyes.

Win searched her gaze. "Oh, dear, little sister," he said at last. "You're in love with him."

After her brother left, Blythe and her mother shared some chicken soup together in the bedroom. Then, while Libby worked on some embroidery, Blythe told her mother about her conversation with Win and how she'd never seen him so penitent for his actions.

"I agree," Libby said. "Even though he got his way, he's truly sorry for pushing you and Will so hard. He may have finally realized you've grown up and are perfectly capable of making your own decisions."

"I don't feel very grown up," Blythe told her. "And the choices I've made haven't been very good ones."

"I think your decision to marry Will was a good one."

"I was starting to think the same thing, and then I found out about the baby. He didn't agree to that, Mama," she said, repeating what she'd told Win. "And I…" She paused. "I care for him too much to force him into staying."

"You love him." It was a statement.

Blythe nodded. "Yes."

There was so much anguish in the admission that Libby felt as if her own heart might break. "Then trust that love, Blythe. And trust God to work this out in His own way, His own time."

They talked until Blythe grew sleepy, and Libby went upstairs so that they could both get some much-needed rest. Libby slept restlessly, listening in the special way understood only by mothers, when she heard a terrified scream from the bedroom below. She bolted upright in bed, flung back the covers and raced down the stairs, praying as she went.

After a night of tossing and turning, Will woke around daylight and put the coffee on. Even though she'd been there only a matter of days, the house seemed empty without Blythe scurrying around trying to fix him breakfast.

A reluctant smile claimed his lips. She was a disaster in the kitchen, but she was a determined disaster and, because of that, she'd made some pretty impressive strides in a short length of time.

Any doubts he might have had about whether or not she was a good person had been laid to rest. She was still young, still untried in many ways, but smart, adaptable, willing to learn and a hard worker. She was principled and God-fearing.

Will laughed out loud. Who was he trying to convince?

Across the room, Banjo woke, gave a huge yawn and stretched.

And his dog liked her, which was a major plus.

Slicing a couple slabs of the bread she'd made, he buttered it on both sides and laid it in a skillet to brown, his favorite version of toast. By the time it was crispy on both sides, the coffee was ready and he sat down with his makeshift breakfast.

He was finishing his second cup of coffee and wondering what he could do to convince Blythe to come home when he heard hoofbeats thundering down the lane. He got to his feet and opened the front door.

Win Granville, hatless and wearing denim and chambray, sat astride a big roan gelding. It looked like the city boy knew his way around a horse, Will thought grudgingly. Close on the heels of that came the question. Why in blazes was Granville coming to the house at this hour of the morning?

"Mornin', Granville. Do you want a cup of coffee?"

"Good morning, Slade," the banker said, slipping his foot from the stirrup and slinging his leg over the rear of the horse. "There's no time for coffee. You need to saddle up."

Will didn't miss the intensity in his brother-in-law's tawny-hued eyes. Every nerve in his body responded. "Why? What's wrong? Blythe?"

Win nodded. "She lost the baby a couple of hours ago. Mother said I should come and get you."

"No!" Will said, grabbing the door frame so hard his knuckles turned white. His knees felt week and he fought the urge to bawl like a baby himself. Though he'd been warned that this was a possibility, he hadn't really expected it to happen. Blythe was young and strong...and that tiny little baby had done nothing but try to live...

"She said she didn't want to see me." Will heard the way his voice had grown thick with unshed tears.

"She needs to see you."

Will's head came up like an animal sensing danger. "Why would you say that?"

"She loves you."

For a moment the statement lifted the weight on his heart. Then reality set in. He laughed, a sound without any joy. "Then why did she tell me to leave, that she wanted to end the marriage?"

"Because everything was so messed up between the two of you from the beginning, and then when she found out about the baby, it was sort of the last straw. She was having a hard time dealing with it herself, and she didn't want you staying in the marriage out of obligation and duty. My sister wants to be loved. And she has a lot of love to give in return."

Will was overwhelmed by the overture of understanding and kindness from his brother-in-law. "I do love her. I didn't think I'd ever love anyone after Martha, but Blythe...she's...she's the face I want to see next to me when I wake up every morning."

Win slapped him on the shoulder. "Don't tell me, Slade. Go tell her."

Less than an hour later Will reined his horse in at the front of Libby Granville's house and Win went home. Libby must have been watching for him because she flung open the door before his feet ever hit the step.

"Will!" she exclaimed, greeting him with a welcoming hug. "Thank God you're here."

The warmth of her welcome took him by surprise. "What happened, Mrs. Granville?" he asked as they walked side by side into the wide foyer.

"Only God knows, Will," she told him, pausing at the foot of the stairs. "Edward said that from everything Blythe's told him, there have been signs of something being awry from the beginning. We can only speculate that everything that's happened contributed to the problem. But then again, sometimes these things happen for no apparent reason."

"How's she taking it?"

"She's cried a lot, but it's hard for me to say. Sometimes my Blythe closes herself off from everyone and everything, even her own feelings. Maybe you can help her open up."

Once again Will felt his throat tighten. He understood completely. He'd done the same thing. His voice was husky as he said, "I doubt it. I imagine she'll be furious that I came."

Libby smiled. "Did Win tell you how she feels about you?"

"He did," Will said, nodding, "but I'm not sure he knows what he's talking about."

"They had a long talk, and he knows. Now go on up and see her, and if she gets contrary, don't listen to anything she says," Libby told him. "I'm going to fix some breakfast and I'll bring you both some when it's ready." She turned toward the kitchen.

"Mrs. Granville."

"Pip," she corrected, turning back to face him.

"I want you to know that even though you may think I've lost my mind, and I can't possibly know how I feel about her after such a short time, I love her. I love her determination, her strength, her little bursts of irritation. Just being in the same room with her makes me happy. And even though hearing about the baby knocked me for a loop, I'm truly sorry she lost it."

"I don't find that hard to believe at all, Will. Now go."

"Yes, ma'am."

Blythe lay in the big four-poster, her forearm over her face. All the tears were gone. She placed her other hand over her tummy that felt strangely empty, even though she'd known of the existence of the baby only a short time and had not had time to get over the shock of its existence before it was gone...just like that. Just like so many things in her life. There one moment, gone the next.

As she had so many times before, she blamed herself. If she hadn't allowed herself to be filled with so much sorrow and emotion... If she hadn't worked so hard at getting things ready for Will's mother...

Both Edward and her mother had insisted that she was wrong. Sometimes these things just happened. Sorrow, an emotion she was on close terms with, filled her heart.

Where had she gone wrong? Always the cautious

one, she had thrown that caution to the wind and trusted her heart when she'd run away with Devon. A disastrous choice.

And then she'd literally stumbled across Will and her life had spiraled out of control for the second time. Feeling as if her heart had died, lacking any hope of happiness, she'd listened to his cockamamie notion of a marriage of convenience and decided that it was as good a plan as any.

She'd been happy at the farm. Always one who liked to learn, to be of help, she'd relished the challenges of living in the country and felt a keen sense of accomplishment for every little success. She'd been looking forward to making changes to the house that would do away with all reminders of Martha and make the house a reflection of her and Will's personalities.

Now that dream was gone, too.

A knock sounded at the door and before she could answer, someone pushed it open. She turned her head and lowered her arm.

Will stood there, his thumbs hooked into the belt loops of his Levi's, looking big and healthy and strong, his dark hair windblown and messy, as usual. There was an emotion in his midnight-hued eyes that she couldn't define. Just the sight of him filled her empty heart with a sudden surge of happiness. She wanted him to grab her up and kiss her senseless and, at the same time, she wanted to pull the covers up over her head and hide from the intensity radiating from him.

Why was he here when she'd told him things were over? What on earth could he possibly want?

He closed the door and approached the bed. "Hi."

The simplicity of the greeting was not what she expected.

"Hi."

"How are you?"

She tried to smile. Failed. "I've been better."

He nodded. "I know you said you didn't want to see me, but I heard about the baby and I had to come. I'm sorry."

"Are you?"

The color drained from his face. "Hearing that you were having a baby was a shock, but surely you know me better than to think I'd want anything bad to happen to it."

Blythe saw the sheen of tears in his eyes, heard the break in his voice and was filled with shame for even suggesting such a thing.

"I do know," she said, her own voice quivering. "I'm sorry. I'm just a disaster right now." Even knowing she was inviting more heartbreak, hoping against hope she would hear the words she so longed for him to say, she asked, "Is that why you came, Will? Because of the baby?"

He drew in a breath as if to fortify himself for some upcoming battle. "No. I came because you're my wife."

Responsibility. An invisible, giant hand squeezed her aching heart.

"We took vows, Blythe Slade. We promised each other and God that we would be together for better and worse, in sickness and health, till death parts us. No annulment."

Blythe closed her eyes in defeat. There it was again, that sense of duty he was so proud of. Anger—at him and herself—pushed aside her sadness. She glared at him and gave a shake of her head.

"Well, the death part can certainly be arranged," she snapped.

Will frowned. "What are you talking about? What do you want me to say, Blythe?"

"For a man about town, you're incredibly dense, Will Slade. I want you to say that you want me to come back because you can't live without my bread, or my potato soup, or because you need a bookkeeper. Some reason you want *me*. Blythe Slade. Any reason but because I'm your obligation!"

She watched the emotions play across his face, saw understanding replace his confusion. Saw a look creep into his eyes she'd longed to see at the same instance he smiled that wonderful Will Slade smile and burst into laughter.

The next thing she knew he was lying next to her on the bed, gathering her into a tight, protective embrace.

Shocked, she said, "I can't breathe, Will. Let me go."

Lying facing each other, Will rested his forehead against hers and whispered, "Never."

Her heart took a little leap.

"I want you to come back to the farm with me because I love you, Blythe, and I'll love you for the rest of my life, and when you're ready and want another baby, I'll be more than happy to help out."

Seeing the mischievous look in his eyes, she actually giggled. "William Slade, you are impossible."

"But you love me anyway."

"I do."

Epilogue

"I do." Blythe beamed at her husband, who smiled back and gave her hand a squeeze.

"I now pronounce you husband and wife," Brother McAdams intoned. Again. "You may kiss your bride."

This time around, Will didn't hesitate.

The quiet in Hattie's parlor erupted into cheers while friends and family gathered around, offering hugs and well wishes as Cilla Garrett's nimble fingers danced across the keys of the pianoforte.

It was just over a month since Blythe and Will had declared their love to each other. Wanting to do everything right, she had insisted that they have a second ceremony before truly becoming man and wife.

In that short month she, Abby and Rachel, all her new friends, had put together the details of the wedding she'd always dreamed of; with Meg Allen's skilled needlework, that included the lace-covered gown Blythe had designed for the special occasion.

This time, Will's brother, two sisters and mother had come with their families. Though she'd been leery of meeting Bess Slade, the older woman had literally welcomed her with open arms after confessing that she'd asked everyone in town about her son's wife-to-be and received good reports from those who mattered. The Wolf Creek grapevine at work.

Once again, Hattie's parlor was decorated for the occasion, only this time there was more food, and more spring flowers scattered around the room. And there were smiles on the faces of their guests this time.

Blythe looked up at the man next to her, so handsome in his new suit. She slipped her arm around him and he smiled down at her.

This time everything was perfect, exactly as she'd dreamed it would be…especially the groom. The happiness she'd wanted was in her future at last, standing next to her.

* * * * *

A young woman desperately needs a husband to avoid a life of drudgery. Will the handsome stranger in town be her Prince Charming?

Read on for a sneak preview of
TEXAS CINDERELLA,
the next book in Winnie Griggs's miniseries
TEXAS GROOMS.

"Are you talking to the horses?"

Cassie Lynn turned her head to see a freckle-faced boy of six eyeing her curiously.

"Of course. They're friends of mine." Then she smiled. "I don't think we've met before?"

The boy shook his head. "We just got to town a little while ago. I'm Noah."

"Glad to meet you, Noah. I'm Cassie Lynn."

"My uncle Riley likes to talk to horses, too."

"Sounds like a smart man." She held out her apple slices and nodded toward the two mares. "Would you like to feed them?"

The boy smiled and took the slices. He stepped up on the fence so he could lean over the top rail.

She smiled as the boy stroked the mare's muzzle. "I see you've done this before."

The boy nodded. "Uncle Riley has a real fine horse."

Well, at least she knew the boy wasn't alone. "Are you visiting someone here or do you and your folks plan to settle down in Turnabout?"

The boy shook his head. "We don't know anyone here.

And I don't have folks anymore. It's just me, Pru and Uncle Riley."

Before she could form a response, they were interrupted.

"Noah, what are you doing out here?"

Noah quickly turned and lost his footing. Cassie Lynn moved to stop his fall and ended up landing in the dirt on her backside with Noah on her lap.

"Are you all right?"

She looked up to see a man she didn't know helping Noah stand up. But the concerned frown on his face was focused on her.

"I'm a bit dusty, but otherwise fine," she said with a rueful smile.

He stooped down, studying her as if he didn't quite believe her.

She met his gaze and found herself looking into the deepest, greenest eyes she'd ever seen.

Cassie Lynn found herself entranced by the genuine concern and intelligence reflected in the newcomer's expression. It made her temporarily forget that she was sitting in the dirty livery yard.

"Can I help you up?"

She quickly nodded. "Yes, thank you." Hoping there was no visible sign of the warmth she felt in her cheeks, Cassie Lynn held out her hand.

He took it in his, and she had the strangest feeling that she could hold on to that hand forever.

Don't miss
TEXAS CINDERELLA by Winnie Griggs,
available September 2016 wherever
Love Inspired® Historical books and ebooks are sold.

www.LoveInspired.com